WHY YOU SHOULD NEVER KISS YOUR BEST FRIEND

WHY YOU SHOULD NEVER...

ERIN NICHOLAS

THE SERIES

Why You Should Never…

ABOUT THE BOOK...

Cody Madsen has stayed away from Olivia Dixon for almost two years—technically. Even though he talks to her every day and sees her every weekend. But there's no kissing, touching, or telling her how he really feels.

Olivia wants what her three sisters have—true love. She could almost believe she's found it with Cody, if it weren't for the fact that he's her older brother's best friend and her brother won't have it.

She needs to move on. Fall in love with someone else once and for all.

Her solution? The "Perfect Pick" dating site where they can each finally find love.

But how will she handle someone else being his soul mate? Or someone else being hers?

CODY MADSEN HAD NEVER SEEN Olivia Dixon naked.
Until today.

And there was a very good reason for that.

Two, in fact.

She was his best friend. And her brother would kill him.

But damn, the sight was breathtaking.

Breathtaking enough that his entire system short-circuited and all he could think was *Every day for the rest of my life.*

"Cody! Oh my God! What are you doing here?"

She'd obviously just stepped from the bathroom. Her hair was wrapped in a towel, the scent of her favorite shower gel and lotion were strong in the air and, most significantly, she was as naked as the day she was born.

Which had to be why his brain and mouth would not connect.

Olivia crossed an arm over her breasts—her glorious, perky, perfect breasts—and put a hand over her even-more-private part —the mouthwatering, holy crap, light blond hair that was trimmed into a perfect *V* pointing the way home—and said louder, "What are you *doing*?"

But it wasn't until another voice hit his ears that Cody was able to pull himself out of the Olivia-is-even-hotter-than-I-thought daze.

"Cody! I'm heading to the fuse box!"

Olivia's eyebrows arched. "Is that Conner?"

It was. And Cody's first spoken word on the matter was, "Fuck."

He grabbed her upper arms, backed her into the bathroom and kicked the door shut.

That proved to be the biggest mistake of all. Her skin was silky and warm and he should *never* have touched her.

"What's Conner doing here?"

Cody was an idiot. When he'd first seen that she was naked, he should have turned around and gotten the hell out of here. Instead, what had he done? He'd touched her. Then he'd put himself in a closed room with her.

A tiny closed room.

"There's a good reason we instituted the conservative-clothing-at-all-times rule," he said gruffly.

She still had her arm and hand covering the most important parts, but that didn't matter one iota. He was never going to be able to forget what he'd seen.

"That rule is for when we're together," she said.

"We're together now." Wow, were they. Her scent was imprinted on his brain. Now, standing submerged in a cloud of it between her and the bottles on the shelf behind her, he found himself taking deeper and deeper breaths—and growing harder and harder.

The naked-breasts-and-other-parts thing wasn't helping.

"I didn't know we were going to be together now," she returned. "What are you—and *Conner*—doing here?"

"Fixing the outlet in the kitchen that's not working." He

breathed deeply and concentrated on keeping his eyes on hers. "I texted you."

"My battery died."

"Why are you naked?"

"I took a shower."

"You're not in the shower *now*. Do I need to buy you a robe?"

"I don't need a robe when I'm in my house, presumably alone."

"You always walk around the house naked when you're alone?"

"Yes."

He had nothing after that. He pressed his lips together and resolutely continued to focus on things *above* her shoulders. Like the two empty towel racks. "Where are your other towels?"

"In the dryer."

He pulled the towel from her head, handing it to her. "God. Cover up."

She wrapped the towel around her body, her wet hair falling past her shoulders, big blue eyes staring at him. "You okay?"

"Yeah, why?"

"You look…weird."

"This is, apparently, how I look when I'm trying with every fiber of my being not to kiss you."

She made a soft choking noise and her hand grasped the towel tighter against her breasts.

"I've never seen that look before."

"Yeah, I saw a few things for the first time today too."

And she grinned.

That was one of the things he loved most about his "friend" Olivia. She had a fantastic sense of humor.

"What I mean is," she said, "I thought there have been times in the past when you've had to try not to kiss me. And I've never seen *that* face before."

There sure as hell had been times he'd had to resist grabbing her and pushing her up against the nearest wall. Or the nearest desk. Or the nearest copy machine, car door, refrigerator…

He cleared his throat. "Those times I was trying to resist kissing your *lips*."

"But wh—"

She broke off as understanding dawned. And her cheeks got pink.

"God," she finally breathed. "The not-talking-about-sex rule we have is a good one too."

So were the other three rules they'd established nineteen months, two weeks and three days ago.

First and foremost was no kissing.

Second was conservative clothing only when they were together. He didn't go shirtless, even when he was cleaning out her rain gutters in ninety-eight-degree weather. She didn't wear fitted tank tops or short skirts. He didn't wear fitted tank tops either—she'd added that to the list after the last time they'd gone to a baseball game together. If swimsuits were required, he wore baggy trunks that reached almost to his knees, and she had a two-piece with bottoms that looked like shorts and a top that covered her stomach and chest completely.

Third was no talking about sex—with anyone specifically or the overall topic in general. No innuendos either.

Fourth was no getting drunk together—they'd made that mistake once and would have made all kinds of horrible choices if Olivia's sisters hadn't come home early.

Fifth was no avoiding each other. That wasn't acceptable. They were friends. They enjoyed being together. They had an entire group of friends in common.

It didn't matter that they were more attracted to each other than they ever had been to anyone else. They weren't going to let it keep them from being friends, and they weren't going to let it make things awkward between them.

In fact, their friendship was one of the barriers they'd put up in hopes of fighting their attraction. They'd become even *better* friends, entirely on purpose, after the one and only time they'd kissed.

Nineteen months, two weeks and three days ago.

The thing was, the friends-only deal worked. It had started off as "let's go to a movie" or "want to grab a burger" here and there, but once they'd started talking and laughing together, it had grown. When they'd discovered a mutual love for baking and had started baking together—even when he sometimes wished *baking together* was a euphemism for other things—their friendship had evolved into something real. There was something very innocent and fun and, of course, sweet about baking together. And in the process of mixing up cookies, muffins, brownies and new inventions here and there, they'd talked and shared and bonded.

Now they both protected the friendship staunchly. He'd never survive if he lost having Olivia in his life, and if that meant never kissing her again, so be it.

Or so he typically thought.

When she wasn't naked in front of him.

"You're still making that face," Olivia said, her voice soft and a little breathless.

He was sure that he was. "You're still standing here in a towel."

"I can't fix that until you move out of the way of the door," she said with a smile.

He nodded. "It would make sense for me to move then."

She swallowed. "If you want me to get dressed, anyway."

"Right."

He didn't move out of the way.

Instead, he put a hand on the side of her neck, then slowly slid it to cup the back of her head. Even more slowly, he pulled her forward. She took a reluctant step. Reluctant, maybe, but she definitely took the step.

"Kind of wish your phone hadn't died," he said.

"That would definitely have made this easier," she agreed.

"I swear, even shut in the bathroom with you, if you had a T-shirt on, I'd be good," he said.

She grasped his wrist, not to resist, but seemingly to hold him where he was. "I was wearing jeans and a baggy sweatshirt the last time this almost happened."

It had been February. Six months ago. He'd gone six months without almost kissing her. Not without *thinking about* kissing her, of course, but without any of this—the looking into her eyes, the touching her face, the voice that sounded like he was a three-pack-a-day smoker.

He looked at her now. This was Olivia. He could tell her anything. And they were very upfront about the attraction between them and the reasons to avoid it.

Especially the main reason. Not that they were friends. Not that he knew he'd never recover.

The main reason was Conner.

Olivia's older brother. Cody's best male friend.

The man they would both do anything for.

The man who had specifically asked them *not* to get involved.

The man who was outside the bathroom door right now checking out a bad outlet.

Fuck.

Cody dropped his hand. "I can't."

Olivia's hand fell away from his. She was clearly torn between disappointment and relief.

Cody knew how she felt. That combination of emotions was a near-constant in his life where she was concerned.

"I should get dressed."

He shoved his hands into his pockets. "Yeah. Probably."

He shifted to the side, so she could open the door. She still had to brush against him to get by—there simply wasn't room to avoid touching.

Cody held his breath.

When her foot was on the threshold, she looked back. "We're in trouble now, huh?"

He took a deep breath and nodded. "Now that I know your breasts are the best I've ever seen…yeah, we're in trouble."

He was a better man—person, whatever—than she was.

He'd pulled back. Or dropped his hand. Or whatever.

She, on the other hand, had been all in.

She knew the rules as well as he did. She knew the reasons for the rules as well as he did.

The main reason for those rules was in her kitchen fixing the outlet that wasn't working—Conner. Her brother. Cody's best friend.

But they could make four hundred more rules and it wouldn't change the fact that Cody Madsen made her hot.

Her eyes slid closed and she thought about Cody. His dark hair, his dark eyes, his big hands… He was a running back for the Hawks, the popular and successful local amateur football team, so he was solid but trim. He was, quite simply, gorgeous.

She could—and did—ignore it.

She could—and did—acknowledge that there were more important things than sex and that having a friendship with Cody was worth resisting her baser urges.

Cody was…special. He let her be herself. Fully, completely, unabashedly herself. And he seemed to really like the things that made her different from her sisters.

Olivia loved her sisters and her big brother. She admired them, enjoyed spending time with them, would do anything for them. But she was different from them. She liked quieter things, simpler things—staying home curled up on the couch, baking, movies, reading. She was great at her job, but she wasn't driven to advance or move up any career ladders. She liked to have fun, but she preferred a small dinner party to hanging out at Trudy's. She cared about her family and friends, but didn't feel the need to insert herself into the midst of any and all happenings in their lives.

Growing up as the youngest of the Dixons, Olivia had found that getting a share of the spotlight could be difficult. It was hard to get a word in edgewise, rarely did anyone ask her what she wanted to do, and any conversation that had to do with her favorite topics—baking and movies—was met with barely concealed yawns and glazed looks.

Cody, on the other hand, asked what she wanted to do and then did it—wholeheartedly. He didn't mind staying in with her. He seemed to prefer the quieter times as well. When she talked, he listened. He even asked questions that showed he was paying attention. She got the whole spotlight when she was with Cody. He made her feel important, like the center of attention.

That meant a lot to her. His friendship and acceptance of her meant a lot to her.

But *damn*.

If he'd gone ahead with the kiss that had been brewing between them, there was no way she could have said no.

Even with her brother in the next room.

Which meant they needed something more than their rules.

The last time this had happened, when things had gotten heated to the point of making them both almost say "screw it", they'd decided to be friends. True, I-would-never-do-anything-to-jeopardize-this-relationship friends.

That had worked. Beautifully.

For a while.

Fourteen months ago or so, things had heated up again one night, and they'd barely resisted. That was when Cody had hired her as the administrative assistant at the fire house. He'd just been named chief and she'd wanted to quit her HR job desperately and they'd almost kissed again that night after his party. So he'd suggested she come work for him. Neither of them would risk their jobs by sleeping with an employee or boss.

That had worked for the past several months.

But now…

It always snuck up on them. They'd be going through their normal routines, having a normal conversation, when suddenly their eyes would meet and *bam*.

Of course, neither of them had ever been *naked* before.

That certainly jacked the heat level up a few thousand degrees.

Good thing there wasn't any peppermint schnapps around. That, combined with their chemistry, was a potent and dangerous combination.

As they well knew.

Olivia dropped her towel and turned to grab clothes from her dresser. She caught a flash of her reflection in the mirror. Yeah, the naked thing changed it a bit.

She dressed quickly, first pulling on a pair of shorts, then thinking that even though she'd worn them in front of him before, today might be a good day to cover up more. She traded the shorts for sweatpants cut off to capri length and a baggy T-shirt. She didn't always wear a bra around the house, but she definitely put one on now. She pulled her hair into a ponytail and then faced the mirror again.

She looked as dressed down as she could. She certainly didn't look like a woman with seduction on her mind.

And *seduction* was *not* on her mind. Avoiding seduction was.

With that thought, she grabbed a light, zippered sweatshirt and pulled that on as well.

She and Cody needed to rethink their strategy.

She loved their relationship. It was easy and fun and just about perfect. They shared many interests, had the same sense of humor, could tell each other anything and get honest, nonjudgmental advice—and, obviously, they both put friends and family at the top of their priority lists.

If it weren't for the fact that she wanted to jump him eighty percent of the time, Cody would be the ideal best friend.

And if it weren't for her brother, Cody would be the ideal boyfriend.

Their chemistry alone was unmatched in her experience. Add to that all the fun they had, their mutual respect, and the fact that their lives blended seamlessly, and it was almost stupid that they weren't on the fast track to spending the rest of their lives together.

In actuality, they probably were on that track—she certainly couldn't imagine another man in her life—but it would be a lifetime of baking, sporting events, parties with their friends…and no sex.

Damn Conner anyway.

Then she sighed. It wasn't Conner's fault, actually. It was hers. All hers. She had horrible taste in men. And her brother knew it better than anyone. Conner was the only person who could make her doubt Cody and her feelings for him.

She'd been in love before. Twice. Both had been disasters. But both could have—would have—been worse without Conner's intervention.

She was a trusting, forgiving, hopeless romantic. She—apparently—fell in love easily. And it—apparently—made her stupid.

Olivia took a deep breath and straightened the sweatshirt. Okay, well, if they weren't going to have hot sex up against her bathroom counter, then they needed a new plan.

And she thought she had the answer.

"Where's Conner?" she asked, stepping into the kitchen to find Cody rummaging in her fridge.

He pulled out the chicken they'd made two nights ago. "He and Shane made a run for some wiring."

"I'm surprised you didn't go." She watched him put the chicken and rice on a plate and set it in the microwave.

He pushed the buttons to start it heating, then faced her. "If I ran every time things got hot between us, I'd never be here."

Olivia pressed her lips together. They'd decided a long time ago that being upfront about the feelings they had for one another was the best approach. They didn't ignore or dance around anything.

But sometimes hearing him talk about how affected he was really got her going.

On top of the hormones still pumping through her system from the near kiss, she was definitely wound up.

She leaned against the counter across from where he stood, mimicking his pose by bracing her hands on the edge behind her. "The way I see it, we have two options here. We either sleep together or we come up with something else that will work to keep us apart."

He regarded her with the hot gaze he got whenever she mentioned anything about going for it. "Our rules have been working for a long time," he said.

"But it almost stopped working today."

He didn't say anything to that.

"Cody, seriously, a little bit ago in my bathroom I would have been fine with losing my job, and if I'd had to choose between going at it with you on my bathroom floor or never having another honest opinion from a guy about my hair, I would have picked the floor."

She saw emotion flare in his eyes and noticed that he tightened his grip on the counter.

She waited for his reaction.

"We couldn't do that," he finally said.

She sighed.

"There's nowhere near enough room on that bathroom floor."

She baited him into saying things like that. She'd admit it. Because she loved the shot of heat that always went through her when he did.

"The point is," she said after a deep breath, "we need something else to keep us apart."

The microwave beeped and he turned to retrieve the plate. "Like what?"

"I think I need a boyfriend."

He froze, his back to her. "What?"

"A boyfriend. And you need a girlfriend. If we're involved with other people, we'll never let our chemistry get out of control. We're too good for that." She tried to lace some humor into her voice but was sure she'd failed.

The idea of Cody with a girlfriend made Olivia's stomach cramp.

She knew that he dated some. She knew he slept with women. But, as his "friend", she couldn't let that bother her. Instead, she ignored it. And they never talked about it. It fell under their no-talking-about-sex rule. Except, of course, when they talked about how they *couldn't* have sex with each other.

They'd tried talking about it as friends. One of the perks of having a guy for a best friend should have been getting the male perspective on things, including how guys truly felt about and thought about sex.

But that conversation had ended quickly, with Cody going straight in for a cold shower and her going out for a run to work off some of the pent-up adrenaline.

The funny thing was, the idea of him baking cookies with someone else caused a bigger surge of jealousy than the thought of him having sex with someone else.

So the idea of a girlfriend in Cody's bed rather than a hookup made Olivia immediately begin thinking of ways to break them up.

Completely counterproductive to what she was talking about now, of course, but the plans formed subconsciously.

Cody turned to face her. "Do you have someone in mind?"

He didn't look happy about it.

"No. But I have an idea."

She hadn't had a real boyfriend since she and Cody had become friends. She hadn't been asked out much—which was a little hard on a girl's ego—but she wasn't as disappointed as she probably should have been. She didn't need a boyfriend. She had Cody. They went out together plenty—movies, parties, plays, art exhibits, festivals. And they fulfilled everything the other one needed from the opposite sex.

Except physically, of course.

Which was the root of all the problems.

"You have an idea about who you want for a boyfriend?" Cody asked. His voice sounded tight.

"Yeah." She reached to pull a brochure off the refrigerator. "And I have an idea for you too."

"I can get a girl anytime I want one," he said irritably, taking the brochure when she handed it to him.

It was true that Cody couldn't spit without hitting a female football fan who would show him all kinds of team spirit. On top of that, he was a fireman. No woman was completely immune to a hot fireman. It was a universal truth.

But Cody didn't get serious with women. She didn't know why exactly, but she did know that Cody hadn't had a real relationship—a meet-the-parents, celebrate-anniversaries, know-her-favorite-dessert relationship. At least not over the past two years. And she'd definitely been paying attention.

"I mean a *girlfriend*. Someone you feed and talk to *before* you find out if her bra matches her panties."

He scowled at the brochure. "A dating service?"

"A very reputable, highly recommended, online match-making service," she clarified.

"Perfect Pick," he read from the front of the glossy paper. He looked up at her. "Seriously?"

"One of the girls at Trudy's said she knows four people who've been set up by that service who are now in long-term, happy relationships."

Trudy's, the bar where she, Cody and all the friends, family and fans of the Hawks hung out, was the source for every kind of information possible.

"I don't want a long-term, happy relationship." He tossed the brochure aside and picked up his plate of chicken.

"That's because you're currently in one. With me. You need a new one."

He looked at her for a long moment, as if he was going to say something important. Then he simply nodded. "Okay."

"Okay. Come on." She ignored the twist in her stomach and the fact that she was leading Cody to the computer in an attempt to find him the perfect woman. The one who would, essentially, replace *her* in his life.

She grabbed her laptop from the coffee table, curling up on the love seat. Cody sat next to her, plate of chicken and rice in one hand, fork in the other.

"I already started your profile," she said, opening the appropriate tab and scrolling down to where she'd left off.

Cody leaned in. "You did?"

"This one is very detailed," she said, pointing to some of the topics. "But I can easily fill yours out."

"Is that right?" Cody settled back and finished off the food.

"Well, I know your height, eye color, build, interests and beliefs," she said, clicking through the various pages.

"Did you put in that I don't believe in online dating?"

"It's not really online dating," she told him. "It's a match-making service."

"Semantics." He rose to take his plate back to the kitchen. He was clearly restless.

Olivia called after him, "You have to be open-minded."

"This is stupid, Liv. You want me to get a girlfriend? I'll get one. I don't need a computer."

Hell no, she didn't want him to get a girlfriend. Her stomach cramp returned. "You have to base it on something other than how she looks."

He came back into the living room. "That's insulting."

She tipped her head to one side. "It definitely is."

He shrugged and plopped back down onto the love seat. "Yeah, okay."

She grinned. Cody was a great guy. A *nice* guy. Everyone

thought so. But he was also laid-back. He had a habit of waiting for things to happen, waiting for things to come to him —including women. And they always did. The guy didn't have to put in a lot of effort, because things always turned out for him.

But if she truly wanted to find a relationship with someone else, then Cody needed to be taken—for real, not for just a night —and she couldn't sit around and wait for the right girl to come to him. Not without constantly wanting him and comparing every guy to him. She needed to find him the right girl now so she could find the right guy for her. Finally.

"We're not looking for a hookup or a weekend thing or even just a date. We're looking for someone you can be serious about," she told him. "This is going to require a little work on your side."

"I treat the women I spend time with very well."

"I know that." She was the primary woman he spent time with. He was sweet, considerate, funny and charming. He made sure she was having a good time, no matter what they did. He offered his jacket when she was cold, made sure her glass was never empty long, pulled out her chair, put an arm around her as they walked. He was the perfect date.

As he would be for *another* woman. Soon.

Olivia swallowed and turned her attention back to the computer screen. "You'll be fine once you're on the date," she said, tucking her foot up underneath her on the cushion. "Getting you to the date stage is where you'll be a little out of your element."

Cody didn't ask women out. They asked him. Or rather, they showed up and it became a date. Or something like a date.

"I've asked women on dates before."

He sounded irritated, but she didn't look over at him.

"High school homecoming dances don't count."

"I've asked women out since high school," he protested.

"Name three." She kept her eyes on the screen. She was

clicking on the boxes next to all the sports and activities Cody enjoyed. It was nearly everything on the list.

"Katie," he said.

Olivia didn't know a Katie that Cody had dated. She couldn't keep track of all the women who'd bought him drinks, told him they never missed a Hawks game or swooned over his heroics at a fire scene, but he had definitely never asked a woman named Katie out in the past two years.

"Did you actually call her? Invite her to dinner? Pick her up at her house?"

He shifted on the seat. "That's what it takes to be considered a date?"

She finally looked at him. "You meet a woman, you find her attractive but you also talk to her for at least ten minutes and decide she seems interesting as well. You ask if she'd be interested in going out *sometime* and you get her number. Then, after a day or so, you call her. You invite her out. You take her somewhere that she'd like to go and that shows you've put some thought into it. You take time to get to know a few things about her as a person. Then you take her home, maybe kiss her—but chastely—and you go home. Alone. Then you repeat the entire thing at least a few times before you see her naked." She waited as he processed all of that. "Does *any* of this sound familiar?"

There was a long pause before he said, "Vaguely."

"Uh-huh." She tried to focus on the online questionnaire again.

"How do you think it usually goes for me?"

She took a deep breath. These were the things she specifically worked on *not* thinking about, but that she'd subconsciously stored up. She didn't look at him though. "I think that usually the woman approaches you. Probably at Trudy's, but sometimes at the field after a game or practice. Maybe occasionally they meet you at a scene and later show up at the station with cookies or something to say thanks for how heroic you were doing whatever you did." She breathed again, running her thumb along the edge of her computer as she talked. "You notice she's attractive, you ask if you can buy her a drink, she says yes. You take her to Trudy's—if you're not already there. You talk but it's really flirting. You dance. Maybe shoot some pool. Whatever. You find out she's a Randy Travis fan, and that she saw your big touchdown in the game. But she doesn't even know what position you actually play, and you have no idea what she does for a living. Still, you end up back at your place, you have hot, sweaty sex, she leaves and you jump in the shower. Rinse. Repeat."

The clock above the TV ticked several times before he spoke again.

"Tracie."

Olivia glanced at him. She knew her cheeks were pink. She'd never let herself think about Cody's women so specifically before. Emotions were churning inside her and she was trying to hold it together. "What?"

"Tracie was another girl I actually dated."

Olivia nodded. She remembered Tracie. "Is there a third?" There was a Kari. She'd really disliked Kari. Because Cody had seemingly really liked Kari.

"Yeah." He took a deep breath and let it out. "You."

Not Kari. *You.* Dammit. Her breath lodged in her chest painfully.

"And now I've finally seen you naked."

The air whooshed out of her lungs. "We're not just going to forget about that?"

"Don't see how that's even remotely possible."

Her gaze caught on his, she said, "All the more reason we need to do this dating profile asap."

She had to make him do this. They both had to do this.

She wanted to be his girlfriend. He wanted to sleep with her. Maybe they should go for it. But Conner…

Olivia sighed. People didn't understand her commitment to making her brother happy. Even her sisters didn't totally get it. Amanda had been the only other one to honestly worry about what Conner would think when she'd fallen for Conner's friend Ryan. Isabelle hadn't had much choice in the matter—her guy, Shane, wasn't the down-low, keep-it-under-wraps kind of guy, so Conner had known almost from minute one that Shane and Isabelle were together. Like it or not.

And then there was Emma. Emma had kept her budding relationship with Conner's friend Nate from her brother for about three weeks. Mostly because she honestly hadn't thought it would be more than a fling, if that. Emma wasn't any more low-key than Shane though. And she was absolutely the type to tell Conner to get over it. Then she'd gotten pregnant and, well, Conner had to find out.

But while her sisters loved Conner and understood that it was uncomfortable for a brother to imagine his friends hooking up with his sisters, they hadn't let it stop them.

It had been stopping Olivia for a long time.

She was a grown woman. She got that this was her life and that she couldn't depend on her brother forever. But there were two good reasons she wasn't going to go against Conner's wishes: Garrett and Jeff. Her two biggest regrets.

Not that there hadn't been other jerks, but Garrett and Jeff were the ones who had made her completely doubt her judgment when it came to following her heart. And men. They had definitely made her doubt men. Other than Conner, of course.

Conner had taken over as the male head of the house when Olivia was eleven and he was seventeen. Their father had died suddenly, leaving a wife and five kids brokenhearted and lost. Conner had stepped up and taken over.

From day-to-day things like home maintenance and rides to practices and appointments, to help with homework and lectures about staying out too late and being careful, Conner had been there. And, in Olivia's case, stepped in when she couldn't see that the first man she ever fell truly in love with was stealing from her or that the second man she ever fell truly in love with was cheating on her. Repeatedly.

She trusted Conner before she trusted anyone. Including herself.

Which was the reason she was still a virgin at age twenty-six.

Most people didn't know that. Most wouldn't have believed it anyway. But while she loved kissing, had enjoyed some heavy petting and had a great thing going with her plastic boyfriend in her bedside table, she hadn't let a real guy that close.

After realizing that she couldn't trust her heart, she knew that she absolutely could not trust simple chemistry.

Not that she'd been truly tempted again since Jeff. Until Cody.

The heat between them was undeniable. And she liked and trusted him.

But she knew him.

He made her hot, she sincerely liked him, and she was sure he could make her first time worth it. But Cody didn't do serious relationships. He didn't even really do romance. He was naturally attentive and charming and funny and sweet, which made it easy for him to get women and keep them from hating him after they broke up. But he didn't have a lot of…follow-through. He didn't go out of his way. He definitely didn't make big, grand gestures—or even small gestures.

And she definitely wanted big, grand gestures from whoever she fell in love with. And she definitely wanted to be in love with the man she first slept with. Old-fashioned and naive maybe, but still true.

In spite of her mistakes with men, her romantic hopes were still alive and well. She wanted a guy like the men her sisters had fallen for, a guy like in the movies, a guy who would move heaven and earth to be with her.

She wasn't sure path-of-least-resistance Cody Madsen was that guy.

And maybe that was Conner's concern too. The guys had a history. It was confusing, because Conner respected and trusted Cody in everything else. Something major had happened. Something the guys didn't talk about. Something that hadn't ended their friendship but that made Conner distrustful of Cody when it came to women. She hadn't asked more about it, and she hadn't argued. Conner had never given her bad advice or not been there when she needed him. If he asked her not to do something, she wouldn't.

Even if it meant turning to a computer matching service to find a guy who could keep her honest.

"You're really going to make me watch you have a real relationship with another guy?" Cody asked after she'd typed for a few minutes.

She made herself not react to the fact that he was obviously jealous. It didn't matter.

"You're going to be so busy with Miss Perfect, you won't even notice."

He sighed. "Fine, then let's find this perfect woman. I'd prefer to be happily head over heels before you are, if you don't mind."

There was certainly an underlying sweetness in his words, but she couldn't get past the idea of him being head over heels to truly appreciate it. Yep. This was going to be great.

"Here." She passed him the computer. "Make sure I got everything on your profile right."

He skimmed through the screens, then looked up at her. "You got all of it exactly right."

She shrugged. "It's stuff like what kind of movies you like and if you're a morning person or a night person."

He clicked on a few screens and read quietly for a few minutes. "And you nailed it on all the answers about what I'm looking for in a date."

And if he compared those answers to the ones she'd put on her own profile, he'd see they matched almost perfectly.

She grabbed the laptop back from him. "Now all we need is to pick a photo and choose a username."

"You have me in as hotguy1981. I like it."

She rolled her eyes. "That's a placeholder. I had to put something so I could answer all the questions."

"Let's keep it."

She pulled her bottom lip between her teeth and started clicking through the photos she had stored in her pictures file. She found her favorite—the night of the costume party. She'd talked him into going, but only after she agreed to his stipulation—he got to choose her costume and she got to choose his.

That night, he'd shown up grinning like an idiot.

That grin had grown even wider when he realized what she'd picked out for him.

They'd ended up at the party as Captain Hook and Red Riding Hood—the sexy versions from the TV show *Once Upon a Time* that they'd watched in marathon mode and enjoyed the hell out of together.

That photo was her favorite because of the memories it brought back. Yes, Cody looked hot and happy. But Cody often looked hot and happy. In this photo, Olivia could see his humor, his mischief. The fact that they'd both gone to the same memory for their costumes had struck her as remarkable.

She wasn't sharing *this* photo with some girl online who would only see the hot part.

Olivia clicked past the photo and found another of Cody at an Omaha Royals baseball game. He still looked hot and happy, but she also saw the guy who had overheard two little kids talking about how much they wanted an autograph from the shortstop and who had used his connections with the team's trainer to get the kids into the locker room after the game for autographs from the whole team.

She couldn't put that photo online either.

There was one of Cody at a friend's birthday party. That one brought back memories as well.

There was one of him at Christmas, but he looked too goofy—and lovable—in the Santa hat.

There was one of him holding a puppy. No way could she

put that online. Hot guys with cute baby animals? He'd have a million hits in an hour. She couldn't watch that happen.

But as she clicked through all of her photos, she realized she was never going to find one she felt like sharing with strange women who were looking for love. The one of him in his fire uniform was hot and gave her a rush of pride. The one of him in jeans and a T-shirt was hot and gave her a rush of affection for the friend who was so easy to be around, always making her laugh and taking care of her. The one of him in a suit and tie for a friend's wedding was hot and gave her a rush of desire.

This was impossible.

She must have sighed out loud because Cody asked, "Did you find a picture that will work?"

"No," she said honestly. "There aren't any good ones on here," she said dishonestly.

"Give me that." He took the computer and clicked through her picture folder. "This one will work."

It looked like a normal photo. He was standing against the wall in Ryan's apartment, holding a beer and grinning at something the camera didn't show. She remembered that photo too. It had been shortly after Amanda had fallen for Ryan but was still in denial. They'd gone over for a game night. It had been a crazy night—Isabelle and Shane had fought, Conner and Shane had fought, Emma and Nate had bickered and Olivia, Isabelle and Emma had been in a car accident.

The most memorable event of the night, however—even including the car accident—had been the dumb party game Emma had come up with. Everyone paired up and put a small rubber ball between them. The first couple to roll the ball from belly button to chin won.

Olivia and Cody had been a team.

That was the longest the front of her body had been up against his.

Irritated that even the memory of that night could make her hot, she said, "I have a better idea."

"Okay."

"Let's both sign up for the Love Is Blind program."

"Love Is Blind?"

"It's this special program through this site. You sign up without any physical description or photo. It's all about being matched with someone based purely on interests and beliefs. It's not about appearance at all. The site acts as an intermediary—the computer uses your data to match you up. You put in your favorite restaurants and what days and times you're available. It's completely objective. You don't even exchange messages or anything. The computer matches you, sends you a date, time and place to meet and that's it. After the date you decide if you want to exchange phone numbers and stuff."

"You completely trust a computer to pick someone right for you."

She forced a smile. "Your Perfect Pick."

She could see his hesitation. She turned on the couch cushion to face him. "Really? You're surrounded by beautiful, sexy women willing to fall into bed with you all the time. *This* is about finding something real. Come on, take a shot."

"You're going to do it too?" he asked.

"Sure."

"No photo of you? No description? The guys who pick you are ones who think you sound interesting and sweet and have no idea how gorgeous you are?"

He did that all the time—threw in a compliment or something charming or sexy like he was talking about making a sandwich.

She nodded. "Thank you. And yes."

He sat up, more interest in his expression now. "Okay, I like that. I can get into this then."

"It matters to you that I not put a picture up?"

"Liv, if you put a picture up, every guy on that site is going to click."

"Well, thanks, but—"

"If you're going to do this, I much prefer the idea that the guys are wanting to meet you for reasons beyond what they see."

She felt her heart melt a little. "Thanks, Cody."

"So we'll both do the Love Is Blind thing. Great."

She liked the idea too. For similar reasons. If a girl wanted to get to know Cody based on similar interests and opinions, that made her a lot more comfortable than someone who just saw the hot guy with a killer smile.

"Okay." She skipped past the photo upload and went into the Love Is Blind part of the website. "By the way, you owe me nineteen ninety-five."

"Is that the going rate for true love?" he asked dryly. "Seems like a bargain."

CODY COULDN'T BELIEVE he was letting her talk him into this. It made some strange sort of sense. As he watched Olivia type things into her computer, it struck him how stupid and how smart this was all at the same time.

He was pretty sure that he was in love with her. Or as close to being in love as he'd ever been. But Shane had asked him an important question one night when he'd confessed his feelings— *You sure it isn't because you can't have her?*

No, Cody wasn't *sure* of that. How could he be? He most definitely couldn't have her. Did that make her more appealing? Maybe. Olivia wasn't wrong when she said that he wasn't used to working very hard with women. There always seemed to be plenty who wanted to spend time with him. So, did the facts that Olivia herself hadn't fallen right into his bed and that their relationship required more from him than a charming smile and a shot of tequila make it more tempting? Possibly. Very possibly.

But it was quite established that he couldn't have her.

He didn't even blame Conner. Much. Conner knew about a

chapter in his past that was pretty unflattering and unknown to most of the people currently in his life.

Conner trusted Cody with his own life, but would never trust him to take care of Olivia.

It wasn't even all of his sisters. For a long time Conner had joked about wanting Cody to take care of Emma. Emma was…a handful. She'd given her brother more gray hair than the other three sisters, for sure. But Emma was strong and sassy and independent.

Which made her the type of woman Cody tried to hang out with. He liked women he could trust to tell him where to go if he needed it. Okay, *when* he needed it.

That wasn't Olivia.

Cody understood Conner being protective of her. Especially knowing what Conner knew about Cody's less-than-Prince-Charming behavior in the past.

Olivia was sweet and trusting and romantic and kind. But she had a strength she didn't even see. She knew what she believed, and she would go to war to protect someone she loved. Still, she was forgiving and gave everyone the benefit of the doubt. Even him. Especially him.

Because Olivia put her full trust in him, Conner took his responsibility very seriously. He would never advise her to do something that he wasn't one hundred percent sure would be safe and good for her.

Based on past experience, Conner couldn't be one hundred percent sure of Cody.

Cody hated it. He suspected that Conner even hated it at times. But it was a fact and Cody didn't know how to change it.

Cody regretted what had happened. He hated the whole ugly, lying-cheating-manipulating story. But Cody had learned an important lesson from it—that when people loved you, they gave you power. Power to hurt them. Badly.

Now he avoided women who were sweet, trusting and forgiving. He preferred sassy ones who would tell him to fuck off and completely forget his name by the next day if he pissed them off.

"Now pick a screen name."

Cody pulled his attention back to the task at hand—falling madly and eternally in love. "Hotguy1981," he said.

"It needs to be one that I don't know."

"Why?"

Her cheeks got pink. "It just does."

Cody gave her a knowing look. "You afraid you'd be too tempted to pick me?"

"I can't *pick* you," she said, avoiding his eyes. "This whole part of the site is anonymous. No names, no photos. You're not even supposed to put specifics about where you work—only what you do for a living—or where you live other than the city. It's real facts about you as a person, but nothing to identify you."

He felt a grin tug at his lips. "Then I can't imagine a reason why it would matter if you know my screen name."

"Well, you know…" She waved her hand like it was no big deal. "In case I *accidentally* saw your account and saw how many matches you've gotten. Accidentally."

He loved when she inadvertently gave away her attraction—and potential jealousy in this case. Since it could only be inadvertent, he'd take it. He nodded. "Sure, okay, that makes sense. Wouldn't want an accident to happen."

Her cheeks got redder. "I think if we're going to do this, we're all in. We play by all the rules."

"Well, I don't want to know your screen name either," he said as a thought struck him. "I don't want to be able to see how many hits you're getting."

He liked the idea of men choosing to get to know Olivia based on her wonderful personality and interests. He wanted the guys who took her out to actually take her on dates where she might have a good time.

But he hated the entire idea of her dating with a passion.

So he wasn't kidding about wanting to fall in love first. That was the only way he'd survive Olivia falling in love.

"You wouldn't be able to see that unless you knew how to get in to my account."

For once he was glad that he was computer challenged.

"Fine. Then I guess we're okay."

"Yep, guess so."

They sat quietly, awkwardly for a moment. Then he had to ask, "Are you going to tell me when you go on a date?"

She looked over. "I don't think so."

That was probably for the best. "Why not?"

"Because I don't want to know when you go on one."

Ah. Good point. Very good point.

"Yeah. Ditto. Then…good luck, I guess," he said.

She nodded. "You too."

How stupid was that? Wishing her luck on finding another guy?

"Liv," he started. Then hesitated. Who was he to give her advice?

"Yeah?"

"Make sure…he…deserves you."

The thing was, Olivia was…probably too good for *any* guy.

Emotion flickered in her eyes and she started to lean in.

"We're back!"

Olivia stopped as Shane and Ryan came through the front door, the tense moment full of emotions broken.

Thank God.

Begging her to never date anyone else and to grow old and gray going to movies and baking cookies with him was pathetic.

❧

"Too sexy."

"Well, that one's not sexy enough."

"It's a first date."

"Exactly. She can't look like a Sunday school teacher."

Olivia sighed and waited for Emma and Amanda to stop bickering. Then she'd put on the purple dress that she'd bought and loved.

This was the best method for dealing with her sisters, hands down. She had to let them both have input—there was no way to stop either of these women from giving input anyway—then she did whatever she wanted to.

"Sunday school teachers are not the only women who dress conservatively and tastefully," Amanda told Emma.

"Okay, she can't look like a college professor."

Amanda narrowed her eyes. As a grad school instructor, Amanda definitely dressed more conservatively than yoga-instructor Emma did. "She's making a first impression here on a guy she's never met." She held up a very pretty peach-colored dress.

"And she doesn't want her first impression to be June Cleaver meets Sarah Palin," Emma said, holding up a little black dress. Emphasis on *little*.

"But she also doesn't need to look like she might run down to the street corner to make a few extra bucks after the date," Amanda said, holding up a pair of black pants and a scoop-neck, royal-blue top.

"And she doesn't need to look like she's going to going to deliver the address at the Stick-Up-Their-Butts National Convention," Emma said, showing Olivia a shimmery silver dress that was less fitted than the black but would show more cleavage.

Amanda sighed and tossed the dresses on the bed. "Maybe you should tell us about the date itself," she said to Olivia. "Where are you meeting and what are you doing on this date? That might be more helpful than trying to dress for a guy you know nothing about."

Amanda wasn't thrilled about this date, and Olivia understood that. All three of her sisters had fallen for guys they'd known before dating them. The idea of Olivia—the sweet, innocent baby—venturing out into the great, big world of unknown men made her sisters nervous.

Thank God they hadn't told Conner.

"I know stuff about him. Important stuff. He gets along great with his family—"

"So he says," Emma interrupted. Even the less conventional, more daring of her sisters wasn't entirely supportive of this.

Olivia went on anyway. "He has a full-time job where he's in charge of several employees. He likes outside activities like hiking and running. He loves to cook and bake. We have a ton in common. We were a ninety-seven-percent match."

"I can't believe you don't know what he looks like," Emma said.

"It's not supposed to matter," Olivia said. "He doesn't know what I look like either. It's a match based on other things. More important things."

"Well, where are you going?" Emma asked, as if maybe *that* would save this whole thing from being ridiculous.

"We're meeting at Cliff's."

Amanda was clearly surprised. "Cliff's is nice." It was the swanky bar and restaurant downtown, across from the posh Britton Hotel.

Olivia had listed it as one of her favorite restaurants in her profile and had been pleased when the computer had chosen it as the site of the blind date.

"And it's a nice public place where nothing bad is going to happen," Olivia said, pushing up off of her bed and taking the new purple dress from her closet. "It's not a place where I need to look like June Cleaver, but the black number might be a bit much. Or should I say, not enough?" She grinned and held the purple dress up. "This, on the other hand, is perfect."

Neither sister could argue with that.

"Okay, Cliff's is nice," Emma agreed.

She took Olivia's vacated spot on the bed and ran a hand over her tummy. She was four months pregnant, and anyone who didn't know her would have no idea when she had a loose top or baggy sweatshirt on, but those close to her could already see a little bump. It made Olivia grin every time she noticed.

"What happens after Cliff's?" Emma asked.

Olivia shrugged. "We're going to play it by ear."

"You're not going anywhere with him in his car," Amanda said, rummaging through Olivia's shoes. "You have to promise you'll drive your own car."

"I think you need to stay at Cliff's. Talk, get to know each other, whatever, but then call it a night," Emma said. "If it works out and you want to see more of each other, there's always another night."

Olivia met Amanda's eyes and they both burst out laughing at the same time.

"What?" Emma sat up straighter.

"*You*, Miss Up All Night, New Guy Every Weekend, you're giving advice to stay put, clothes on and just talk?" Amanda asked. "Wow."

Emma looked offended. "First of all, I was never up all night with a guy I just met and had never heard of. And second of all —" her expression gentled, "—keeping the same guy around for several weekends in a row isn't all bad."

Olivia went to her and hugged her tight. She didn't know if it was the falling in love with Nate or the pregnancy hormones or what, but Emma was softening up. "I'm going to be fine. I'm not going to go anywhere with him. It's drinks. That's it."

"But he's a ninety-seven-percent match," Amanda said.

Olivia turned to her. "You think this whole thing is silly."

"I think there are a lot of nice guys you could go out with without needing a computer to tell you that you'll get along."

"Yeah, well, it's been a long time since a guy actually asked me out," she said, frowning as she thought about it. "But the guys I meet are either firefighters—and off limits because we work together." Yeah, that made sense. "Or they're guys that I meet at Trudy's, which means they either play for the Hawks or they work at St. Anthony's."

Trudy's Tavern was the popular bar across from the hospital where Conner and Ryan, Amanda's fiancé, were paramedics. The entire clientele was made up of St. Anthony's employees, their friends and family, or fans of the Hawks.

"So? At least you know who they are, or you know someone who knows who they are," Amanda pointed out.

It was mostly okay that she didn't get asked out much—or at all for several months, now that she was trying to remember the last time—but it would still be nice for there to be a guy who was interested once in a while.

"And they have all kinds of assumptions about me." Or they had. Back when guys actually asked her out.

Her frown deepened as she realized she couldn't remember a guy asking her out since sometime last April. And he hadn't called again after their one date.

"Assumptions like what?" Emma asked.

"They either assume I'm a party girl like you and Isabelle," Olivia said, "or they assume I'm the sweet, innocent girl Conner claims I am."

Amanda was watching her closely. "And you don't like either of those assumptions?"

"Neither is true," Olivia said. "Em, I love you, but I'm not like you. I don't want to party and meet new guys all the time and win drinking challenges." Emma was—or had been—well-known as the wild child of the Dixon clan. "But I'm not as inno-cent as Conner would like to think. I want…" She sighed. This was why she didn't mind not getting asked out more often. She was waiting for something specific…and special. And she knew that it wasn't easy to find. But she was going to sound like a teenage girl who had watched too many romantic comedies. "I want romance. I want someone to treat me like a princess. I want to feel my heart pound and my stomach flip…and I want…" She looked at her sisters. "Can I tell you something corny?"

"Cornier than the stomach-flipping thing?" Emma asked.

Olivia could tell by her expression that Emma was touched by what she'd said though.

"Yeah. Really corny."

"Sure, honey," Amanda said, sitting down next to Emma.

"I want a guy who's a combination of all of your guys. I want a guy to respect me like Ryan respects you," she said to Amanda. "Someone who will see the strongest parts of me and support them fully. And I want a guy who's sweet and crazy like Shane is with Isabelle. Someone who will go over the top to show me how he feels. And—" she looked at Emma, "—I want a guy who makes me feel wanted and sexy like Nate does with you. The way he looks at you could start the place on fire if you're not careful."

Both of her sisters were blushing. And smiling.

Her sisters had found love. The true, no-matter-what kind of love. She wanted that. And it wasn't going to happen with the guys at Trudy's. She could feel it.

Amanda cleared her throat. "And you think Mr. Ninety-Seven-Percent might be that guy?" she asked.

"I hope so," Olivia said with a shrug. Heck, at this point it might be good just to remind herself what going on a real date was like. "But it's what I asked for, and he was the one at the top of the list of matches."

Emma looked like she was fighting tears. The hormones were making her nuts.

"I don't know if Nate and I would even match at ninety-seven percent," she said. "Go for it."

"I hope this date is with Prince Charming," Amanda said, reaching for Olivia's hand. "But if it's not, keep looking. You deserve to have exactly what you want."

Olivia nodded. "I agree. And I think he's out there somewhere."

The thing was, she had a feeling that this perfect guy—whoever he was—was going to remind her a lot of Cody

Madsen.

He'd never been stood up before.

Cody swirled the liquor in the bottom of his glass and thought about that. Most of the women he'd spent time with in the past two years had approached him just as Olivia had said. So getting stood up was impossible. The woman initiated the conversation, he bought the drinks and they ended up back at his place.

No chance of being stood up.

He preferred that.

Sitting at a bar waiting for a date to show up—fifteen minutes past the time they'd agree upon—sucked.

"Another?" the bartender asked.

Cody checked his watch. "Nah. Guess I'm driving home."

Perfect Pick his ass.

He put more than enough money down to cover his tab, then swiveled on the barstool, prepared to head for the door. But his gaze landed on a beautiful blond in a purple dress. A beautiful blond he'd recognize anywhere.

"Olivia?"

She was too far away to hear him. She was sitting at one of the small tables across the bar area, nursing a drink—Amaretto and Coke, he'd guess—and messing with her phone. Probably checking her e-mail or Facebook.

She had to be meeting a date here.

Had she chosen someone from Perfect Pick?

He'd specifically not asked her about how many matches she'd been given or if she'd been out with anyone. They'd worked together all week without him asking.

But it had been killing him.

She hadn't seemed abnormally happy—though Olivia was a perpetually happy, upbeat person, so it would be hard to tell if she was unusually so. She wasn't glowing from true love—or great sex—either, so he'd told himself that she hadn't found her perfect pick. Yet.

There was no date sitting with her, so Cody headed over.

If nothing else, he needed a close-up of this dress.

He was only halfway to her when she lifted her head and saw him.

Her mouth curled into a huge smile and he felt the warmth that always hit when he saw her. She was always happy to see him. Always. And it was clear in how she looked at him. He loved that.

"Hey, gorgeous," he greeted her, stopping by her table and slipping a hand into his pants pocket. He was going to be—or at least act—nonchalant about her date.

"Hey, yourself. Wow, a jacket, huh?" Her gaze traveled over him, taking in the dark gray slacks, the white dress shirt, the jacket and the gray-and-black tie. "Very nice."

He liked having her eyes on him.

"Thanks. Trying to make a good first impression."

She smiled. "Thank you."

"For what?"

"For taking this seriously."

He hadn't felt like he had a lot of choice in the matter when he'd been at her house and she'd been putting his info into the Perfect Pick site. But as he'd thought on it later, he could admit that it made some sense. They were in a holding pattern. Could he happily go along for a few more years as nothing more than Olivia's best friend? Maybe. They were good together. But the urges to kiss her were becoming stronger and more frequent. And it wasn't fair to her.

She wasn't dating. He'd selfishly loved that for nearly two years. But he couldn't keep telling himself that it was okay, that somewhere down the road—far down a very long road—she'd meet the right guy and fall in love. Olivia was a romantic at heart. She wanted an amazing love story, and she had high standards for relationships. And as long as Cody was firmly by her side at every party, event or night out—and glaring at guys who looked like they were thinking about asking her to dance or to buy her a drink, or flat-out telling them to get lost—she wasn't going to find the guy. It was pretty hard to imagine a guy who could meet all of her criteria, but Cody rarely let them close enough to even try.

And he couldn't be the guy.

If he gave her an ultimatum—him or Conner—she'd pick Conner. He knew that.

It made him a little crazy. Yes, he felt a loyalty to Conner and knew that Conner wasn't entirely wrong—Cody wasn't good enough for Olivia—but in a him-or-me ultimatum from Olivia, Cody would dump Conner in a heartbeat.

In fact, if he were absolutely positive that he could be the guy that she had built up in her mind as the one guy she should be with forever, he might risk whisking her off to some faraway place where they could be together in spite of her brother.

But he wasn't absolutely positive he could be that guy.

He would, of course, do everything he could to be the right guy and to make her happy, but he also knew Olivia's ideal was…intimidating. He knew what she found attractive, what she found romantic. He'd watched more than enough movies and TV with her, read magazine articles she showed him and listened to the stories she collected from people she met about real-life love stories to know that she had the dream guy built up pretty big. Any girl would fall for that guy. He was awesome.

Far more awesome than Cody.

He couldn't convince her to take a chance with him and then fall short. He'd fallen short once before with a wonderful girl who'd thought he was amazing. He couldn't do it again.

Looking at Olivia now, he wanted her so damned much while at the same time being sure that she deserved the very best —and that wasn't him.

He cleared his throat and gave her a smile. "Does the tie make me seem like I'm taking this *too* seriously?"

She shook her head. "Not at all. You look like a guy who wants his date to think this is important to him. And Cliff's? I'm impressed

"I'm not the only one looking good tonight. New dress?"

She glanced down. "Yes. It was the only thing that Amanda and Emma agreed on."

He forced a laugh. "Your sisters were trying to dress you for this?" His chest hurt at the idea of Olivia's whole family getting excited about her date.

One huge thing the perfect guy would need would be to get along with Olivia's family. They were tight. They had each other's backs.

Cody got along with every single one of them.

"They gave their opinions," Olivia said of Amanda and Emma. "Of course."

He continued to smile but it felt more and more stiff. "Well, I'd better leave you alone. Don't want Romeo to come in and see you with another guy."

Except that he did kind of want that.

Her smile faded. "Actually, I don't—"

Cody immediately straightened. "What?"

She huffed out a breath. "I don't think he's coming."

"What?" What kind of idiot wouldn't show up for Olivia?

She glanced at her phone, then looked up at Cody. "How long has to go by before you're officially stood up?"

He wanted to kick the guy's ass, but he made himself shrug casually. "I figured I was stood up after about fifteen."

Her eyebrows rose. "*You* were stood up?"

"You didn't let me put a picture on there, remember?" he teased. "Clearly I'm not as appealing as you thought I would be without a photo."

Her expression darkened and he knew he'd said the wrong thing. She shoved her chair back and stood. "That's ridiculous.

You're totally appealing. You have everything going for you," she said emphatically. "You don't need a photo. You're charming and funny and interesting and a gentleman and—"

He took her hand and tugged her toward the bar, chuckling. "Okay, okay, you're right. I'm amazing. She's passing up the date of a lifetime."

Olivia was tense, still clearly offended on his behalf as he nudged her onto a barstool.

"Well, you are amazing," she said.

Cody took the stool next to her. Usually when she said stuff like that, he let it sink in and puff up his ego a bit. A woman like Olivia thinking he was awesome was hard to ignore. But tonight, with thoughts of her looking for someone else amazing and Ashley, who had also thought Cody was amazing—and had been wrong—well, his ego wasn't gaining any girth tonight.

"Ditto, by the way. Clearly this guy's a jackass." He signaled the bartender. "You drinking a margarita?"

Olivia shook her head. "I got stood up for the first time ever."

He nodded. "Me too."

"I think that calls for more than a margarita."

"Whatever you want."

"You'll call us a cab?" she asked the bartender.

"I have my car here," Cody said.

"Me too. But we're not going to be in any shape to drive home," she told him. She turned to the bartender. "Four tequila shots. To start."

The bartender grinned. "You got it."

"Tequila?" Cody asked, watching the guy pour. "You do remember tailgating at the Nebraska football game with tequila?"

Olivia picked up a shot glass and swiveled to face him, holding the glass up. "Actually no, I don't."

"Exactly. We didn't even make it into the stadium. You were passed out in the backseat within thirty minutes."

"Sounds good to me." She toasted him with the shot, then tipped it back.

Cody smiled and shook his head, watching her. Well, it wasn't a *bad* idea. It was Friday night and neither of them had to work the next day. The bartender would be sure they had a cab. Why not? They'd both been stood up by blind dates.

He took one of the shots, shuddering as it went down. He didn't love the taste of tequila, but he did love the effects.

Thirty minutes later—and three shots in—they both felt a lot better.

"I'm not upset," Olivia said. "I mean, I don't even know him."

"And he's a jackass," Cody said, for at least the fifth time. Though he meant it more each time. What guy stood Olivia Dixon up? Even without seeing her, she was a catch. Perfect Pick didn't have a better girl. He knew. He'd looked all over that site.

Part of him desperately *wanted* to find a girl that he'd look forward to seeing as much as he did to seeing Olivia. He'd finally settled on someone who came close. They shared many of the same interests. She even had the same top five favorite bands. He'd actually made himself admit that this date could be a good thing. He'd convinced himself that he was interested in meeting the woman on the other side of the profile he'd read.

And he'd gotten stood up.

Karma was such a bitch.

"You're better off never having met him," Cody declared with as much sincerity as the tequila would allow.

He wasn't drunk. He was just buzzed enough to not fully think through everything he was saying before opening his mouth. But this was Olivia. There wasn't anything he couldn't say to her. That was the thing about best friends.

"You're awesome," he told her, lifting a lime slice to his mouth and biting down.

"Thanks. You are too. Completely, totally awesome," she said, also with tequila-enhanced-sincerity. "Your Perfect Pick is an idiot. A shallow, stupid…" She seemed to be searching for a word. Finally she said "idiot" again.

Cody grinned. "Thanks. I try."

"What I don't get," Olivia said, blinking at the shot glass in her hand, "is why someone would even sign up for a dating service if they didn't intend to show up? I mean, he didn't have to agree to meet me. Which would also be stupid, though, I guess. If you choose to be part of the Love Is Blind program, then you know you're going to be set up on *blind* dates. It's right there in the name! You're on a dating service to get set up on dates, right?"

"Or to, you know, keep from ravishing your best friend," Cody said.

She turned to look at him, and he waited for her to chastise him. It didn't help to talk about it. They'd learned that.

Instead, she started laughing. Laughing so hard he took the shot of tequila out of her hand before she dumped it all over the bar. This was a nice place and they were drinking top-shelf booze here. If he was picking up the tab, all of the expensive liquor was going to be *inside* one of them.

"What's so funny?"

"You're here to keep from ravishing me, and here we are sitting together getting drunk."

He set the shot glass down, trying to brush her comment off. "We've sat together and gotten drunk before."

"And we've almost kissed every time."

It was true. And probably not a good topic of conversation right now.

"Do you remember the first time?" she asked.

The first time they'd been alone together with a bottle of liquor? Uh, yeah. It was also the first—and only—time he'd ever actually kissed her.

He'd never forget it.

"Maybe we should switch over to water."

He raised his hand to signal the bartender, but Olivia grabbed his wrist. He looked at her.

"Do you remember?" she asked again.

"Of course I do."

"You were comforting me that night too."

Yeah, yeah, he remembered. She'd gone out with a guy a couple of times and then she'd seen him somewhere with another girl. Cody had gone over to her place to pick up a cooler that Conner wanted to borrow. He'd found Olivia working out her frustrations in her kitchen. She'd been trying to come up with a unique Christmas cookie recipe for a local charity backing contest. There hadn't been any mistletoe in sight. But there had been peppermint schnapps.

That had been the night she'd discovered he could bake.

And they both discovered that the chemistry they *thought* they felt was real.

The sight had been adorable—at first. Her ponytail was hanging half out of the elastic band and she was muttering and swearing as she mixed. She wore an apron and powdered sugar and red icing and green granulated sugar and a bunch of other ingredients on her clothes, skin and lips. That last had been the problem. When she'd turned to face him, cheeks pink, and he'd focused on her big blue eyes and the smudge of chocolate on her lips, the sight went far beyond adorable.

He remembered asking, "You okay?"

And she'd told him about her idiot boyfriend and his new girlfriend and the whipped cream they'd been buying together and ended with, "What's wrong with me?"

He'd rushed to assure her that there was nothing wrong with her. That she was amazing and the guy was a jackass.

A lot like tonight.

While he rescued a bowl of innocent caramel mocha cookie dough from her and gave suggestions for the eggnog cookies she was trying, he had to keep reminding himself that the gorgeous woman bending to put cookie sheets in and out of the oven, who smelled like vanilla and sugar, who kept *licking* things, was *Olivia*. Olivia was the little sister of his best friend. The best friend who would *never* be okay with Cody dating his sister.

Then she'd told him that she wanted to kiss him.

He'd reminded her it was a bad idea.

But he was only human. And he'd made a mistake.

He'd said, "You're gorgeous and sexy and sweet and any guy would be a damned fool if he didn't kiss you every chance he got."

She'd looked him straight in the eye and said, "Prove it."

So he had. He'd put her up on the countertop and kissed her. And he would have done a hell of a lot more than that if her sisters hadn't come in. Thankfully, they'd come in the front door or they would have seen Cody feeling their little sister up.

They'd met the next day at a busy, public mall food court where there was no chance of romance or kissing. They decided that being friends—good friends who would never make the mistake of thinking the with-benefits-thing could happen without complications—was the way to go.

"You made me feel a lot better that night, Cody," Olivia said, still holding his wrist.

Uh-huh. He hadn't even done half of the things that could have made her feel—

He shook his hand and pulled his hand away. Damn, the girl was like a drug. He became flat-out stupid around her.

"Have another shot," he said, pushing the shot glass in front of him over to her.

She licked the salt, drank the tequila and bit into the lime slice. Then they sat quietly for a few minutes. Olivia had her chin propped on her hand, and she traced the rim of her shot glass with a finger. "I had to go get more shaving cream for tonight. That might be what ticks me off the most," she finally said.

"What?"

Her eyes were still on the empty glass. "I shaved one leg and ran out of shaving cream. So I had to rinse off, get dressed, go get more and then get home and back into the tub to shave the other leg. That was a lot of hassle for nothing."

She looked almost sad and Cody sighed. He knew this woman. "You're not disappointed because you wasted your time getting more shaving cream."

"I'm not?"

"You had this all built up in your mind," he said. "You were intrigued by the idea of some guy picking you based on interests and personality only and you were excited to walk in here and wow him with the visuals too."

She sat up straighter on the stool and looked at him. "I—" Then she must have remembered who she was talking to. "Maybe a little," she admitted. "I'm not naive. I know that the chances of this guy being Mr. Right were slim, but yeah, okay, maybe while I was doing my hair it occurred to me that I might be on my way to meeting…" She trailed off and her cheeks got pink. "Someone special," she finished.

He chuckled. Yeah, he knew her. "You thought you might be on your way to meet your future husband."

God, he hated that idea. But he loved how sweet she was. Even more, he loved that the guy hadn't shown up.

She sighed. "I know it's so stupid. I know. But all the husbands and wives out there had to first meet sometime, right?"

"That's true."

"And I know that Amanda met Ryan and Emma first met Nate and had no idea they would end up together—but I remember when Shane met Isabelle. It was so obvious he was smitten from the first minute."

Cody grinned. "Smitten?"

She smiled too. "It's a great word. It fits Shane perfectly."

Cody couldn't argue. Shane Kelley had no problem making an ass of himself over the love of his life.

And maybe that was exactly how it was supposed to be.

It was how Olivia wanted it to be, he knew.

He should have seen this coming. They all should have. The woman who was all about true love and Prince Charmings had watched the three women she was closest to experience their versions of the fairy tale. Now Amanda and Ryan were getting married. Of course this would have pushed all of Olivia's I-want-some-of-that buttons.

"You want a guy who acts like Shane?"

Olivia shook her head quickly. "Shane's...a bit much," she said.

Cody couldn't argue there either. Shane was the kind of guy who could exhaust even the most extroverted person.

"But," Olivia went on, "I want a guy who feels like Shane so obviously does. And how Ryan feels and how Nate feels." She sighed wistfully. "I guess I've always been a romantic, but seeing it happen up close with my sisters showed me that all of those movies and stories can come true."

Cody wasn't sure that everything in those relationships had been Hollywood-worthy, but he admitted that those three couples seemed to know how to be in love. They were happy. No question. And it was the kind of happiness that made everyone around them want a little bit of it.

Putting that kind of love in front of a woman who had made Valentine's Day her own personal holy day was just asking for a renewed sense of earnestness to find it for herself.

"You'll have it too, Liv. I know it. This guy wasn't it, but that doesn't mean anything. And," he said, finally allowing himself to look her up and down, "you look amazing. You are, without question, the whole package."

Didn't he know it.

"Thanks," she said. "I do work hard on my ass."

He snorted. "What?"

She nodded solemnly. "I work hard on my ass. I've always run, but I've been taking this butts-and-belly class at the gym and I'm *firm*."

Holy crap. The naked thing the other day and now they were

going to talk about how firm her ass was? Sure, this was a great idea.

"Good for you," he said slowly. What did a guy say when a woman commented on her own ass?

She pivoted to face him, her knees knocking against his. "Are you telling me that you've never noticed my ass?"

"When I'm with you, I specifically work on *not* noticing things like that," he said with all seriousness. That wasn't easy either. Olivia was curvy in all the right places and he saw her every day. He was a damned saint for keeping his eyes on only appropriate body parts. "Unless, of course, you step out of a room naked," he couldn't help but add.

She gave him a half smile. "But then you only saw the front of me."

And every gorgeous inch of her front flashed before his eyes with that reminder.

"Really, you have to check this out." She slid off the stool and turned. "What do you think?"

What did he think of her ass? He'd have to look at it to tell, and he felt the need to make one more protest before he looked.

"I can't have this conversation with you."

"I'm not asking you to *feel* it," she said. "Just look at it."

Talking about *not* feeling it put the idea of feeling it in his head. Dammit. "Liv."

"Cody, look at my ass."

He had to get points in the Good Guy column for trying so hard not to, didn't he? He finally let his gaze drop to the back of her skirt.

The purple fabric molded gently over the sweet curve of her butt. The skirt wasn't too tight, but the perfect—and, yes, firm— shape was easy to appreciate.

She looked over her shoulder. "Well?"

"Spectacular," he said, putting a hand over his heart. "Best I've ever seen."

It was. It went perfectly with her breasts. But he had to ham this up or he'd end up spreading her out on the bar and appreciating all of her curves up close—and without purple silk between them.

"Thank you." She looked genuinely pleased as she reclaimed her seat at the bar. "Like I said, I've been working hard on it."

"It shows." Now maybe they could move on to a new topic. Any new topic.

"Spectacular," she repeated. "I like that."

"Feel free to quote me." Maybe *now* they could move on.

"I might even get a pair of shorts that says *Cody approved* across the butt."

He closed his eyes and groaned. "Olivia?"

"Yeah?"

"Shut up."

"You got it." He could hear the smile in her voice.

He knew that she sometimes said things to mess with him. He did the same thing. They mostly succeeded in staying away from conversations that were too risqué…or tempting. But every once in a while he felt the need to check that the spark was still there.

It was stupid. But it always made him grin.

They sat quietly for a few minutes, neither drinking any more, both apparently lost in thought. It was nice.

She sighed, the sound tired and a little sad.

He looked over at her. "I'm sorry that you didn't get to have drinks with your Perfect Pick," he said honestly. He wasn't upset that she hadn't met and fallen madly in love with her soul mate tonight, but he was sorry she was disappointed.

She gave him a small smile. "Actually, I was thinking that I *am* sitting here having drinks with the perfect guy."

He felt a flash of desire go through him, and it wasn't the passionate, physical desire he was used to where she was concerned. It was a desire to be exactly what she'd said—the perfect guy for her. He cleared his throat. "I'll admit to being awesome, but I'm not sure I quite pull off perfect."

She laughed softly. "Well, perfect for me."

He didn't know what to say to that and wasn't so sure he could speak past the tightness in his chest right then anyway.

"I mean, think about it. You and I have so much in common, like so many of the same things. I kept thinking as I typed the stuff into the computer that the guy I was describing seemed an awful lot like you."

The tightness near his heart increased. He knew exactly what she meant. The woman she'd created for him on paper—or on her computer screen anyway—had seemed very familiar.

"I actually thought, wouldn't it be weird if *we* got matched up?" she added. "I mean, I'm sure that's nearly impossible. The chances of that have to be astronomical. But then, if you start taking out all of the people who *wouldn't* be a good match, that narrows it down a lot, I'm sure. And we do have *a lot* in common."

His heart kicked and his mind started whirling. What *were* the chances of that? Slim, at best. But what were the chances they would set up a date on the same night? At the same restaurant? And *both* be stood up?

He faced her on the barstool as the thoughts continued to swirl, finally combining into a question. Had Olivia set this up somehow?

He only knew the basics about how the Perfect Pick site worked, and Olivia had started his account. Maybe she'd somehow made it so she could get back into his account whenever she wanted to and had made sure the computer matched them.

He looked at her looking at him with wide, curious eyes.

Or was he totally full of himself?

Would she go to these extremes to date him? She could certainly tell Conner that it had been an accidental date, that they hadn't exactly *chosen* to go out with one another.

They were, essentially, dating anyway. They went to nearly

every social event together and he saw her every weekend. So what would she have gained from doing this?

That answer hit him hard.

Conner approved of them spending time together. Because he trusted that it wasn't naked time.

The only difference between what Cody and Olivia already did and what she could do with an online beau was obvious.

He stared at her. Was that what this was about? Was this her way of getting what she wanted—what they *both* wanted? Was this a loophole?

He welcomed the nagging questions. They distracted him from dwelling on the fact that her dress was in his favorite color. And that she knew he liked her hair twisted up like it was tonight. And that, now that he'd allowed himself to notice, her dress had thick straps that ran over her shoulders and left her arms bare and had a deep V-neck that plunged between her breasts and showed off the delicate silver chain with the crescent moon charm she wore. The necklace that he'd given her for her birthday last year.

If she was dressing for a date with *him*, she'd nailed it.

CHAPTER
THREE

CODY CLOSED HIS EYES—OBVIOUSLY the only way to keep from taking a thorough inventory—and swiveled his stool to more fully face the room. He opened his eyes only when he was sure Olivia would be out of his line of sight. He looked around the softly lit lounge.

"Did your date suggest this place?" he asked casually.

"No, the computer picked it. My date and I must have both put it down as a favorite."

"That's…interesting." Cliff's was a special place for them. They'd discovered it together. They were the only ones in their group who ever came here, and the chances of running into someone from work or the Hawks were almost zero.

"Interesting how?"

"The computer obviously picked this place for me and my date too."

Olivia shrugged. "So?"

"This is a great place."

"It is."

"Do you remember the night we first came here? It was my

birthday and they'd messed our reservations up at the other place. We were walking by and this place looked so nice. We came in and discovered the best shrimp scampi in town."

"I remember." Of course he did. He remembered every time he spent with her. It had been the night he'd given her the necklace she wore. If he and Olivia were going to go on a real date, this was definitely the place.

Dammit. She was his Perfect Pick.

That had to be it. Not many people their age would put Cliff's down as a favorite, as it typically catered to an older, wealthier crowd. Besides, the chances of them both being here on the same night, then stood up were ridiculous.

Should he tell her? She'd be thrilled. She'd take this as a sign they were meant to be. She'd build this up into something huge.

Looking into her big blue eyes, his heart twisted. He wanted this to be something huge.

She must have seen something strange in his expression because she frowned. "What's wrong?"

"I think we were matched up."

"You do?"

"It's the only thing that really makes sense."

"Um…wow…that's…" she stumbled.

She seemed legitimately surprised.

"We were a ninety-seven-percent match," she finally said. "That's almost unprecedented."

But he wasn't surprised. "Told you my dream girl sounded a lot like you."

That was a stupid thing to say. He knew it the moment he said it and her eyes changed. The look in them went from surprised to something much softer—something very tempting. He labeled it *affection* rather than anything more complicated.

"So we *were* set up with one another," she said.

"Looks that way."

"Well…crap."

Not exactly the reaction he'd been expecting. "What?"

"This is a mess. We did this to stay *away* from each other and then we get set up? That's perfect."

She actually looked bothered by this turn of events. Okay, so maybe she hadn't set this up.

Cody felt a streak of annoyance. "Well, clearly we're *perfect* for each other," he said. "This isn't schnapps induced or because I accidentally saw you naked in the hallway. An objective computer program thinks we should be together."

She sighed. "I know. Geez, we can't even get away from one another this way."

His scowled. "Are you actually *disappointed* to have been set up with me?"

"More…perturbed."

"You're *perturbed* that I'm the perfect pick for you based on things like beliefs and interests and not on looks or the fact our only kiss almost set the place on fire?" he demanded. "Out of all the guys on that site, *I'm* the one that is obviously the best match for you and that *perturbs* you?"

She was looking at him like he'd announced he was going to compete in the Miss America pageant in drag.

Finally she nodded slowly. "Yes, I'm perturbed that I paid money, spent time carefully filling in our profiles, did my hair and got a new dress to be set up with the guy I spend more time with than I do with anyone else, that I already know better than I know anyone else, and who I *can't be with*."

That was a great point.

Still he said, "So the fact that I think you look fucking hotter than hell but you know I will keep my hands to myself, listen to all your stories and have a real interest in your new recipe for wild berry blintzes doesn't matter at all?"

He sounded like an idiot. He was trying to sell himself as the perfect guy for her? What was that going to get either of them but more frustration?

But she didn't have to seem so put out about spending the evening with him.

"Thank you for the compliment," she said. "And sorry, but… yeah. The whole leg-shaving thing is even worse now that I know I did it for a guy who won't ever know how smooth my legs are."

He narrowed his eyes. "This other guy, a total stranger who you would have just met, would have found that out?" He didn't like *that* at all.

"Well, at least he wouldn't be sitting here promising to keep his hands to himself," she shot back.

"He better have been at least *thinking* that. You don't need to be going out with someone who's feeling your legs on the first date."

"But it would be nice to be out with someone who might feel my legs *at some point*."

"I'll feel your legs," he said tightly. "You can rub them over any part of my body that you want. I promise I'll appreciate your shaving effort like crazy."

They sat staring at each other. Cody's heart was pounding and he could see that she was breathing harder.

They never fought or argued.

And he couldn't exactly say he disliked it. She looked gorgeous all wound up.

"Oh, sure. Great idea," she finally said. "Let's make this even worse."

He growled—literally—at that. "Being set up on a date with me is *bad* and the idea of me rubbing your legs is *even worse*?"

She shook her head. "You know what I mean. This is crazy that we were set up when we were trying to stay away from each other. A dumb computer glitch and here we are—"

"Dumb?" He hated the way his voice rose on the word but he couldn't help it. "Computer *glitch*? Where's the girl who believes in soul mates and fate and true love?"

Her lips parted and she blinked at him in clear surprise. "You think we're here tonight because we're soul mates?"

Well…*that* might be pushing it. But…

"That seems like something *you* might be thinking."

She regarded him carefully. "That does seem like something I would think."

"So why didn't you jump to that conclusion now?"

She lifted a shoulder. "Because it's you."

He felt his eyebrows rise and was strangely offended. "Why couldn't *I* be your soul mate?"

"I'd hate to think that my soul mate would be the one man I couldn't be with. That's depressing as hell."

Yeah, it was.

"You think someone else out there is your soul mate?" he asked. Wow, he fucking hated *that* idea.

She took a deep breath. "Honestly, Cody? I hope so."

There was something in her voice, though, that made him press on.

"You would be disappointed to find out it was me? You'd really, truly be upset if I was your actual perfect match?"

She pressed her lips together, and the look she gave him was so sad that he almost took it all back. Then she nodded. "I'd hate the idea that we were both living our lives with someone who was second best. And that *they* were also living without their soul mates. I'd rather not know. I'd rather keep believing that if we *were* meant to be together, then there wouldn't be this problem with Conner, and he'd give us his blessing and we could live happily ever after." She took another breath. "But that can't happen. So I choose to believe that we're *not* true loves."

Fuck. He should let this go. He needed to let this go.

"What I'm having a hard time believing," he said, definitely not letting it go, "is that there's another woman out there who I could feel as strongly—or *more* strongly—about than I do about you."

Olivia swallowed hard, then licked her lips. "The romantic movies are starting to rub off on you," she finally said.

He gave a humorless laugh. "That must be it."

That wasn't it. Or was it? Those frickin' movies…

"We should watch a *Die Hard* marathon or something," she said with a shaky smile.

"Bruce Willis took on the terrorists in *Die Hard* mostly because his wife was being held hostage. Even though they were estranged, he still loved her enough that he would go through hell and risk his life to save her."

Dammit. Where had that come from?

Olivia looked surprised. "That's true." She paused, looking torn for a moment. Then said, "We should go."

Of course they should go. This was all ridiculous. "Why?"

"Because of two of our rules."

Their rules. Right. "We're drinking together," he said.

"Yep."

"What other one are we breaking?" She looked sexy as hell the way she was dressed, but it wasn't actually skimpy or revealing. They weren't talking about sex. Exactly. And they weren't avoiding each other. Quite the opposite. That only left…

"I have a feeling we're about to break another rule," she said softly. Her gaze flickered to his mouth.

Cody felt the heat shoot through him. She was simply *talking* about kissing him and he got worked up.

"Yeah, well, our rules don't work worth a shit anyway," he said. "We can follow them all to a *T* and I still want you more than anything I've ever wanted. I get hard when I smell your hair and when I hear you laugh and when you put lip gloss on and when you wear sandals."

He stopped talking when he realized she was now looking at him like he'd announced that his talent for the Miss America pageant was clog dancing.

He took another shot of tequila. Because why not? This was already out of control.

"What?" he finally snapped when she didn't say anything.

"I… You…you get hard when I wear sandals?"

Apparently he also got hard when Olivia talked about him

getting hard. He shifted on his chair. "Yeah. And tennis shoes. And boots. And heels. Definitely heels."

They both looked down at her feet. Her heels were sexy, and he knew that he'd make her keep them on in bed.

If they were ever going to be in bed together.

Which they weren't.

She went back to staring at him.

"*What?*" he asked, exasperated. And horny.

"I want that."

"What?"

"A guy who loves the smell of my hair and my lip gloss and who…wants me like that."

He tamped down the urge to say, *See? I'm your guy.*

Because he wasn't, dammit. He couldn't be. He could try, of course. But he'd never been very good at *trying*. Conner could attest to that.

Still, for a moment, it would have been nice to have the most romantic woman he'd ever met assume that they were written in the stars.

The worst thing was that he wasn't sure any guy would try hard enough for Olivia.

He turned to her suddenly. "Liv, you have to promise me something."

"What?"

"You will *insist* that whatever guy you're with treats you like —" He broke off as a proper analogy failed to come to him.

"Like what?" she prompted.

"Hang on. I'm trying to come up with the right example."

She looked amused but stayed quiet.

"Not Prince Charming," he said, thinking out loud. "That's what everyone says, right? That they're looking for Prince Charming. But you know what? He was kind of a douche. Who decides to marry a girl from *dancing* with her? It takes more than that. Though," he went on, his thoughts spinning, "the Prince in the Drew Barrymore version was good. He at least got to know her and *kissed* her. Do you know how many romantic movies show people falling in love without ever even kissing?" he asked her. "*While You Were Sleeping, Sleepless in Seattle, You've Got Mail…*"

"*When Harry Met Sally,*" she offered. "As long as we're talking about Meg Ryan."

"No, they kiss. They sleep together," he said.

"But they were in love by then."

"But they didn't know it."

She was quiet for a moment. "They often don't know it, huh?"

"Almost never."

"Well," she said, brighter again. "How about John Cusack in *Say Anything*?"

"I like his passion," Cody agreed. "He was determined. And he kissed her."

"He knew he was in love with her," Olivia said.

"Yeah, but he was kind of awkward," Cody said. "You need someone with confidence."

"How about John Cusack in *Serendipity*? He had it all," she said. "Confidence, knew he loved her…"

"He hadn't kissed her. And he let her get in the damned elevator without him?" Cody hated that movie. It was sweet how they'd kept thinking of one another and tried to find each other again, but that guy should never have let the girl go in the first place. "What a dumb ass."

Olivia laughed softly. "Okay, so we only like the ones that go after what they want from the beginning."

"Right."

"Okay." She was clearly amused now. "Like who? Are we talking Bogart in *Casablanca*?"

"Hell no," Cody said adamantly. He hated that movie too. "He let her leave. After everything. In fact, he *made* her go."

"It was out of love," Olivia protested. "It was what was best."

"Dumb ass," Cody said firmly.

"Let me get this straight. You think Rick Blaine in *Casablanca*—one of the best-known and critically acclaimed movies ever—was a dumb ass?"

"Yes."

She shook her head and laughed.

"You deserve someone who refuses to live without you." Which, of course, counted *him* out. Speaking of dumb asses…

"Well, I know you don't like Hugh Grant in *Notting Hill*."

"Pussy," Cody said bluntly. "Should have gone for it *way* before he did."

"How about Ryan Reynolds in *The Proposal*? Or Ryan Gosling in *The Notebook*?"

He nodded as he thought about those. "Gosling could have stepped up a little more." Then the right guy hit him. "I've got it." He smacked his palm on top of the bar. "Leo in *Titanic*."

"Jack Dawson?" Olivia asked. Then she nodded. "Okay, I see what you mean."

"Jack knew what he wanted and he went for it. He was confident, but romantic and down to earth. Jack's the guy for you."

"Too bad he's fictional. And would be about a hundred and twenty years old now."

"But you hold out for a guy like him," Cody said, taking her hand. "That's what you deserve."

She looked into his eyes. She wasn't smiling or laughing now. "Okay, Cody. That's what I'll hold out for."

"You two ready for a cab?"

Cody pulled his attention from Olivia to the bartender. Bartender. Cab. Right. He and Olivia had been drinking tequila. No wonder he was getting all these mushy meant-to-be feelings. Olivia Dixon was amazing. She was everything he'd ever want in a woman—if it were possible for him to have her.

But she wasn't his soul mate or his destiny or his other half or any other romantic illusion someone in Hollywood or Harlequin could conjure.

People were attracted and fell in love every day. And he and Olivia would do the same thing. With two *other* people.

"Yeah, that's probably a good idea," he told the bartender.

Olivia nodded her agreement.

Cody held her elbow as they made their way to the front doors. The cab arrived as they stepped out onto the sidewalk, and he helped her into the backseat.

He gave the driver her address and they settled in for the trip, neither talking the entire way.

They pulled up in front of her condo and Cody got out to escort her to the door. She slid across the seat and took his hand when he offered it. He didn't let go as they walked to her front door.

At the door, they stopped and faced each other.

"Well, I am definitely relieved to know that I wasn't stood up," she said.

He smiled. "I'm glad to know that too. Thinking there was a guy that stupid out there was draining my hope for humanity."

She smiled, but it didn't quite reach her eyes.

"You okay?" he asked.

They couldn't pursue this, but she had to be okay. Cody couldn't handle her not being okay.

"I can't believe I'm standing here, looking at the perfect guy, in a new dress, after a romantic restaurant, and I won't even get a kiss goodnight."

He looked down at her, his stomach in knots. Affection and desire warred with exasperation and plain old fear. Fear that whatever he did at this moment would be wrong. Fear that he'd ruin everything with the wrong word or action. Fear of losing her.

"You had high hopes for tonight," he said.

"Yeah."

"Sorry."

"Don't be." She squeezed his hand. "I could never not be happy after being with you."

He squeezed her back, then dropped her hand before he pulled her in and gave her the kiss she wanted.

Because he wanted more than that from her.

"Night, Liv."

"Night, Cody."

He made himself turn and walk back to the cab. He turned back before he got into the car and saw her still standing on the top step. "You got your key?"

She held it up.

"Okay. Then…goodnight."

"Goodnight."

She didn't move, and as Cody got into the car and gave the driver his address, he knew exactly what he had to do.

It couldn't last. It couldn't be everything forever and ever. But *tonight* could be perfect. Tonight she could have her big, romantic, swoon-worthy, movie moment. And he wanted to give her that. Enough that it scared him.

Still, as the driver put the car into drive, the anticipation swirled in Cody's gut. And as the car began to pull away from the curb, his excitement mounted and his grin grew.

When they got a half of a block away, Cody said, "Stop."

The cab driver braked. "What's wrong?"

"Pull over."

The cab pulled toward the curb again and Cody wrenched the door open, got out and jogged back to Olivia's door.

She was still standing there, now with huge, wide eyes.

He took the four steps two at a time.

"Cody, what are you—"

Before she could finish the question, Cody took her face in his hands, tipped her chin and covered her mouth with his.

Emotions swirled through him as she immediately adjusted to the kiss, pressing closer, gripping his forearms, sighing happily.

It was better than any movie moment he'd ever seen.

He kept his lips still for the first several moments, relishing the feel, absorbing the moment.

It's been too long.

It was a ridiculous thought for something that wasn't supposed to have *ever* happened and had only happened once, but it had, and his body, his heart, his *soul* had never forgotten.

Eventually, though, his lips couldn't stay still and he moved. Slightly, a small parting, but Olivia's lips followed, soft, yet eager, and when he felt her sigh again, he knew he needed to hear—and feel—her moan.

He traced her bottom lip with his tongue, the taste the sweetest he'd ever had. Then he dipped inside, stroking along her tongue as his thumbs stroked along her jaw. She opened for him, pressing against him with a willingness and excitement that humbled him. Olivia Dixon wanted him. It made him want to claim her and show the world that this woman would give him everything she had if he asked. Because she trusted him.

That thought was precisely what made him finally pull back.

He didn't let go of her just yet though. He wasn't *that* strong.

He worked to catch his breath. The kiss had been relatively sweet. Their hands were still outside of each other's clothes. But he felt as if they'd shared something much more intimate.

He supposed they had. That kiss was the admission that this was what they both wanted. Not simple friendship, not crazed, tear-our-clothes-off-to-hell-with-the-consequences-until-morning desire, but the sweetness and tenderness too.

Tenderness was something he hadn't had with a woman since Ashley. And that had turned out to be the worst thing he'd ever done.

That memory was enough to finally get him to let go of Olivia.

Cody dropped his hands and stepped back.

She stared at him, lifting her hand and running the pads of her fingers over her lips. "Wow."

He gave her a smile. "Yeah."

"Better than the movies."

"You think so?"

"Right up there with the kiss at the end of *Never Been Kissed*."

He chuckled. That was her favorite movie kiss of all time. "Quite a compliment."

She watched him for several heartbeats. Then she dropped her hand to her side. "But not wanting to do it again would be a lot easier if you weren't so good at it."

So she already knew that it wouldn't happen again.

Cody thought fast. Her realization was good, but he didn't want that to ruin an otherwise magical night's end. He stepped forward and took her face in his hands again. "You mean, it would have been better in some ways if I'd done something like this?" He put his mouth over hers again, but this time wide open, his tongue sweeping in large, sloppy, not-entirely-on-target arcs, her entire lower face getting wet. He made plenty of smacking and slurping sounds too, and by the time he'd gotten her nice and slobbery, she was laughing and wiggling and pushing against his chest.

"Yes," she gasped. "Yes, that would have definitely helped."

He stepped back, soaking in her wide grin and sparkling eyes as she wiped his dog-worthy sign of affection from her face.

He smiled, filled with a multitude of emotions for this woman. "Goodnight, Olivia."

She took a big breath, but her smile held. "Goodnight, Cody."

He successfully did *not* pull a Rhett Butler and sweep her into his arms to stride up the steps to the bedroom—no matter how many times that scene played in his head on his way down the sidewalk to the still-waiting cab.

He even successfully resisted looking back at the best and worst date of his entire life.

Olivia awoke the next morning with a huge grin on her face. That lasted for thirty seconds.

Thirty seconds in, she realized she had a problem.

The one man her brother had forbidden her to date was the man who had laid the kiss of all kisses on her.

She'd dreamed about that kiss all night.

And not only the kiss itself, but the way he'd made it perfect. Leonardo DiCaprio would be proud.

Now she needed to figure out what to do about it. It had been a big enough problem that she liked and trusted Cody. It had been enough trouble that he was someone she was always happy to see, someone who really knew her, someone she could be completely herself with. It had been hard enough to *want* him so much physically. Now that was all rolled together with the fact that he got her. He understood that it was important to her and he'd cared enough about that to make the night end perfectly.

She threw back her blankets and reached for her phone on the bedside table. She texted three people the same message: *I'm making French toast.*

Amanda, Emma and Isabelle would be over within an hour. Olivia being willing to make breakfast on a Saturday morning meant she needed to talk.

As she quickly showered and started the French toast, Olivia was surprised but pleased to find that she wasn't feeling the effects of a morning after too much tequila. She did, however, drink three cups of coffee as she prepared the bananas Foster French toast and brown sugared bacon.

Cody must have kissed the poison right out of her system. She giggled at the thought.

"You're laughing at bacon?" Amanda asked, coming in the back door. "This is worse than I thought."

Of course she was the first to arrive. Amanda would be the most concerned that Olivia needed a sister powwow, especially the morning after a blind date.

"Not the bacon," Olivia said, removing the strips from the baking sheet. "Just thought of something from last night."

"You okay?"

"I'm…" Fantastic. Terrible. "Confused."

"Was the date awful?" Amanda filled a cup with coffee and took a seat at the kitchen table.

"The date was…interesting."

"Interesting how?"

"If you're up this early the day after a date, it was either over by eight p.m. or you eloped and had to tell us all right away."

That was how Emma Dixon came through the door.

Isabelle was right behind her. "Shane wants to know if he needs to kick anyone's ass."

Olivia had to appreciate the offer from her almost-brother-in-law. "No ass kicking needed."

She dished up the food and waited until everyone was settled around the table.

"Olivia was about to tell me what was so interesting about her date," Amanda said.

Isabelle bit into the French toast and moaned in approval. After she swallowed, she said, "Okay, I'm ready."

Olivia sat up straighter. "The night was interesting in that my date stood me up, Cody was there instead, we realized *we* had been set up and then he gave me a kiss that I will never, ever forget, as long as I live."

There was a long pause without a sound.

Emma was the first to break the silence. *"Finally."*

"Finally?" Olivia repeated. "Are you serious?"

"Yes. You finally realized that being with Cody is more important than disappointing Conner."

Olivia frowned at her sister. "I'm not worried about disappointing Conner."

Emma snorted.

"I'm not *just* worried about disappointing Conner."

Emma leaned back and crossed her arms. "Then what are you worried about?"

Olivia looked at Isabelle and Emma, two women who she

knew would do anything for her. But, in spite of how close they were, they didn't know *everything*.

She glanced at Amanda. Amanda did know everything. At least about Olivia. Her oldest sister gave her a smile.

Olivia took a deep breath.

"Cody can't be my soul mate. It's not fair. That's not how this is supposed to work. How is it possible that the universe matched me up with the guy that my brother forbids me to be with? How can it be destined that I love a guy I can't have?"

Her sisters were all looking at her with varying degrees of surprise and worry.

"Who said soul mates?" Emma asked.

Olivia bit the inside of her lip. Then she sighed. "Cody did."

Amanda's eyebrows shot up. "Cody used the term *soul mates*, referring to the two of you?"

"Well, he was offended to find out that *I* didn't think he and I are soul mates."

"You don't?" Isabelle looked shocked.

"I *can't*." Why didn't they understand this? Denial was a great emotion. It was strong and when properly applied could keep all kinds of nasty, depressing, confusing and difficult stuff out.

But it only worked until someone brought things front and center and forced you to look at it.

Like now. She'd been happily denying that she and Cody could ever be more than friends. Yes, they had great chemistry. But she'd convinced herself that it simply meant there was another man out there who would be even better, more amazing, more tempting, more…everything. Because she and Cody were *not* meant to be. Her *perfect* guy would be someone her brother loved, respected and trusted and would give his unwavering blessing to, complete with a big old smile and a pat on the back.

Now her sisters were acting like they'd been waiting for the day when she'd throw herself into Cody's arms and he'd whisk her off to a happily ever after.

"Did you hit your head or something?" Emma asked.

"You're going to think I'm crazy," Olivia said.

"For letting Conner decide who you date? Uh, yeah," Emma said. "I mean, I get it. I was ready for him to lose his mind about me and Nate. But he didn't. And he helped Shane pick out Isabelle's engagement ring."

Isabelle nodded. "I think you need to tell Conner that this is what you want. He wants you to be happy, Liv."

Olivia knew that made sense. But whenever she thought about going for it and letting Conner just deal with it, her stomach hurt. It didn't feel right and she couldn't ignore that. She didn't want Conner to deal with it. She didn't want him to get over it. She wanted him to be *happy* about it. She knew he wanted what was best for her, and she wanted to know that he felt her husband was the best man for her.

Of course there was a chance—a teeny, tiny, almost microscopic chance—that Conner would come around.

But it was a huge risk. Telling Conner would ruin what she and Cody had now. If Conner knew they were hot for each other, he wouldn't want Cody anywhere near her. Things would be tense for all of them. It was an all or nothing situation—they either told Conner what was going on and risked both her and Cody's relationships with him, or they did nothing and stayed only friends. There was no in-between.

Bottom line, she trusted Conner. Cody seemed perfect, but if Conner didn't think so…she couldn't ignore that.

"I know you think I'm all for following my heart and trusting fate for love," Olivia said. "But…I don't trust my own feelings. Not after Garrett and Jeff."

Amanda opened her mouth, shut it, then said, "Cody's never…mistreated you. Has he?"

Emma straightened. "What do you mean by 'mistreated'?"

Olivia looked at Isabelle, then Emma. They knew of Garrett and Jeff, her most serious boyfriends to date. Her sisters also knew that the men had turned out to be jerks and she'd ended the relationships. But they didn't know the details.

Olivia took a deep breath. "Garrett stole about three thousand dollars from me over the course of several months. And Jeff was—" She swallowed hard. Amanda reached out to squeeze Olivia's hand.

Olivia sniffed and gave her sister a smile. "Jeff was controlling and critical and cheated on me. Several times."

Emma's eyes narrowed. "Tell me more."

She smiled. Not about her dysfunctional relationships, but about the murderous gleam in Emma's eyes at even the hint of one of her sisters being unhappy.

Olivia hadn't told Emma or Isabelle about what had happened. They were both so together, so independent, so confident—she hadn't been able to admit to them that she had been none of the above. Amanda, however, had always been incredibly insightful and watched her sisters like a mother hen. She'd noticed something was wrong, and Olivia had finally confided in her.

"Jeff started off sweet and romantic and attentive. But over time, as I kept putting him off for sex, he started cheating. He always apologized profusely, made lots of great promises, but it kept happening."

"But you kept forgiving him?" Isabelle asked.

She nodded. She wasn't proud of it now, of course, but four years ago she'd thought she was in love with him and believed his cheating was partly her fault. "I wouldn't have sex with him. It just didn't feel right. I wanted to wait and I wanted a guy who thought I was worth waiting for. He said that's why the other girls were so tempting—because he wanted me so badly."

"Asshole," Isabelle breathed, her eyes wide.

"I know that now," Olivia said. "I know everything he said was a lie and he would have cheated anyway and I didn't deserve it and it wasn't my fault. But…it took me awhile to get there."

"He still works at the bank downtown, right?" Emma asked, starting to stand.

"Sit down, Em," Amanda told her. "Liv is fine now."

Olivia nodded. She was definitely fine. Better than fine.

Isabelle looked equally pissed. "So Conner figured it out and helped you see what was going on?"

Olivia took another deep breath. "No. Not for a long time. Conner and I argued about it. Especially as I kept forgiving Jeff. But eventually Conner got sick of it, and he physically removed me from Jeff's apartment one night. He made me listen and then, when I finally decided to break things off with Jeff, Conner made sure that he took it…well."

Isabelle's expression softened into a smile. "Oh, really?"

Olivia smiled too. "I was all ready for Jeff to fight me on it, but he accepted it all very graciously. Has never contacted me since."

Emma's shoulders relaxed a little at that. "Good. Though if I happen to run into him downtown sometime, I'm not responsible for my words—or actions."

Isabelle patted her arm comfortingly, Amanda shook her head and Olivia grinned.

"So, what you're saying," Isabelle said, "is that Conner now gets to decide who you do and don't date?"

Olivia shrugged. "Not entirely. But if he has a reservation about someone, like he does about Cody, I can't just ignore that. And…" she started, then thought better of it.

"And?" Amanda pressed.

Olivia knew that Amanda was torn on this issue. Amanda knew personally that Conner's misgivings were often overly dramatic. But she was also concerned about Olivia and couldn't deny that Olivia hadn't always made the best decisions in her love life.

"I have some reservations about Cody too," Olivia admitted.

"Like what?" Isabelle wanted to know.

"He doesn't do relationships." Olivia held up a finger. "He

could very easily lose interest after we sleep together." She added a second finger. "He could decide that monogamy isn't for him long-term," she said as she put up her third finger. "And he doesn't want to ruin his friendship with Conner either," she concluded, extending a fourth finger.

"Well, first of all, Cody doesn't do serious relationships because he wants *you*," Isabelle said.

"And second of all," Amanda added. "There is no way he'd lose interest in you. He's been interested in everything else for two years. You add in sex and you've got him for good."

Olivia felt her stomach flip at that. She liked how that sounded.

"All I know," Emma said, "is he better have a damned good reason for putting Conner before you."

Olivia knew her sister was trying to be supportive. "He must. Right? I mean, it must be something big to be more important than me and how he feels about me," she said, expressing a thought—and concern—she'd had for a while. What if it wasn't all that big and important? What if it was just more important than *her*? Did she really even want to know?

But she did. Desperately. "I need to know what happened between Conner and Cody," she said. "I need to know what Conner's problem really is and why Cody's letting it get in the way."

Amanda looked at Emma, who looked at Isabelle.

Isabelle shrugged. "I don't know the story."

"All I know is that it's something that happened when they lived together in college," Amanda said.

"It's about a girl," Emma said.

They all looked at her.

"A girl?" Olivia asked. "What do you mean?"

"I don't know much more than that," Emma said. "And I only know that much because one night we were all drinking at Trudy's and some girl came in and Cody commented that she looked a lot like someone named Ashley. Conner turned to him and said, 'I can't believe you said her name. We promised to never talk about her', and Cody goes, 'Sorry man. You're right'."

Amanda shook her head. "That doesn't really mean anything."

"There was something about their reactions. It was suddenly majorly tense." Emma shrugged. "But yeah, that doesn't tell much. Sorry."

Olivia *hated* the idea that there had been a girl at the center of the strain between her brother and the man she was pretty sure she was in love with. But it made some sense.

"I need this whole story," she said.

"Conner's never going to tell you," Amanda told her. "And if you ask, he's going to suspect why you want to know."

"That's okay," Olivia said. "I want to hear it from Cody anyway."

Olivia felt her heart rate kick up. She'd never asked Cody about the story. Another thing she'd simply ignored, hoping it would never matter. But now that she was going to hear it from him, she was equally nervous and excited.

She looked around the table. "So will you help me?"

Isabelle was the first to say, "What do you need?"

"I need you to find out Conner's side of the story," Olivia said to Amanda.

"Me? Why me?"

Amanda was the most responsible, the one who had taken a lot of the worry and burden from Conner without him even realizing it when they'd been growing up. He trusted Amanda to share his concerns for their younger sisters. And he'd let himself be the most vulnerable with her. If anyone could get Conner to open up, it would be Amanda.

And if that didn't work, Emma could wear him down and trick him into telling her.

But that was plan B. Because Olivia needed Emma here.

"What do we do?" Isabelle asked.

"I need you to help me get Cody over here."

"You can't call him?" Isabelle asked.

"I know this man," Olivia told her. "He will not want to come to my house and spend time alone the day after that kiss."

"Afraid he won't be able to control himself?" Emma asked.

"Exactly," Olivia confirmed.

They all grinned at that.

"You want me to call him?" Isabelle asked.

"I'll have Emma call him." She turned to Emma. "Tell him I've got my hands full in the kitchen with a baking project we're trying out for your baby shower, and I need his help."

"I thought we were doing vanilla and lemon cupcakes with…" Emma trailed off as she caught on. "Oh, right. It's just a way to get him over here."

Olivia smiled. "Right."

"And he'll drop everything and come right over to help you?" Emma asked.

"He'll ask if you're going to be here too," Olivia said, knowing that Cody wouldn't trust himself—or her—if they were alone. Which gave her a funny thrill.

"And I should tell him yes?" Emma asked.

"Yes. You won't be lying. You'll be here when he first shows up," Olivia told her. "Then you'll leave."

"What can I do?" Isabelle asked.

Olivia grinned at her. "You can borrow a set of Shane's handcuffs."

CHAPTER
FOUR

CODY LET himself into Olivia's house an hour later.

Olivia had the hand mixer running, clearly too busy to do more than greet him with a "hi" when he stepped into the kitchen. Which was a relief. Because even dressed down in a pair of old yoga pants and a T-shirt with an apron over her, she looked gorgeous. And he immediately flashed back to the night before.

Thank goodness her sisters were here. He had to keep his hands to himself and get Olivia firmly back on the best-friends-only track, and his only hope for the first few times seeing her after that kiss was to have other people around.

Eventually, he'd get his control back.

Probably.

Then she turned and dipped a finger into the bowl she held and lifted the glob of cupcake batter toward his mouth. "Here. See what I have so far."

He wanted to strip her down, dump that bowl all over her and lick every drop of it off.

He was absolutely sure, however, that it would taste perfect when eaten that way.

Cody dipped his own finger into the bowl instead of licking it from her finger. He was at least *that* smart. She gave him a knowing look but didn't say anything. He tasted the batter. "What's the problem?" It tasted like really good dark chocolate cake batter.

"If we want chocolate, banana and coconut cupcakes do you think we should do banana frosting and put the coconut in the batter or the other way around?"

He completely lost his train of thought when she put her finger in her own mouth and sucked the batter from it.

That mouth. He'd felt it, tasted it, dreamed about it.

Damn.

"Uh," was the best he could do.

He heard a soft laugh and felt two hands push him gently backward until he was sitting in one of Olivia's kitchen chairs.

Olivia stepped close, her knee bumping his. "Coconut in the batter or the icing?"

He cleared his throat and gripped the edge of the chair seat. "Icing."

"Then bananas or banana extract in the batter?"

Cody watched her dip another glob of batter from the bowl with her finger. Before she could lick it off, some of the chocolate slipped down the length of her finger, and when she did follow it with her tongue it required a longer swipe.

He had to fight not to groan as he was vaguely aware that her sisters were still in the room with them. Not that he should be groaning out loud even if he was alone with Olivia. But she knew how he felt. He couldn't risk her sisters finding out that he wanted her. One of them might slip to Conner.

"Cody? Mashed bananas?"

He made himself focus on her question. Of course they should use real bananas instead of extract. It would make the batter really moist and heavy though. They might have to adjust other liquids.

"Yes. Definitely. And…" He forced himself to concentrate. "What about peanut butter frosting instead of coconut?"

Her grin was wide. "Oh, yes. Perfect."

"We can use that recipe we made—"

"—for the PB and J cupcakes."

They finished each other's sentences at the fire station and in the kitchen. He'd grown used to it a long time ago.

Isabelle moved into his line of sight. "Wow, that's weird how you do that."

They'd heard that from the firefighters at Fire House Three for over a year.

"Tell me more about these PB and J cupcakes," Emma said.

"They're vanilla cupcakes with strawberry extract in the batter and jam in the middle, then frosted with peanut butter frosting," Olivia said. "Cody came up with the jam in the middle idea."

He grinned. Those cupcakes had rocked.

"Make those," Emma said. "I want those for the shower."

Olivia looked at her. "I thought you liked the lemon. They have custard in the middle."

"The peanut butter frosting sounds amazing."

Cody was paying much more attention now. "You already decided on lemon? I thought these banana and chocolate ones are for the shower."

Olivia and Emma exchanged a look that was hard to decipher.

"Oops," Emma said. Quickly she leaned over and grabbed Cody's left wrist.

He heard a click, then Isabelle took Emma's hand and started tugging her toward the door.

"See you later!"

And they disappeared.

Cody looked down at his wrist.

He was handcuffed to the chair.

He stared at the silver cuff for a moment, having trouble processing what it meant for a second. He tugged, and it sank in that Emma had handcuffed him to the chair.

What the hell?

"Olivia," he said, putting plenty of warning into his voice. "Unlock me."

She shook her head. "Can't. We need to talk."

He tugged again. These were real cuffs. Heavy metal, no give. He looked up at Olivia. If the conversation required handcuffs, he absolutely did not want to have it.

"You want to talk about the kissing."

"I want to talk about you and Conner."

Well, shit. That wasn't any easier.

"No."

Olivia didn't look surprised by that answer. She leaned past him and set the bowl of cake batter on the table beside him. The motion stirred the air around him and filled it with her scent combined with the aroma of chocolate.

He closed his eyes and did groan out loud this time.

She moved back and he reluctantly opened his eyes. She was standing with a hand on her hip and looking far too serious.

"I want to know what happened between you and Conner. What is it that makes him not trust you with me?"

When she said it like that, he felt a little stab in his heart. Conner *didn't* trust him with Olivia. But Cody didn't like to think about it like that.

"I don't want to tell you."

She sighed as if she'd been expecting that response. "I understand that," she said, dropping her hands to her sides. "But you have to understand that I need this."

"I understand why you want to know. But…I don't want you to know."

She nodded. Then straightened and reached behind her to untie the apron. "Then I'm going to have to force the issue."

She tossed the apron to the side.

"What are you doing?"

"I'm going to ask you questions. Every time you say no or refuse to answer, I'm going to take a piece of clothing off."

His mind raced. Seriously? Why would he even think of answering anything other than no? But as he took in her attire—four pieces of clothing, assuming she was wearing underwear—he realized he was in trouble. "I've, um…" He had to clear his throat again. "Already seen it all."

She shrugged. "And once I'm naked, I'm going to come over there and sit on your lap."

He only had one hand fastened to the chair. And it was his nondominant hand. His right hand was free with full range of motion.

Bad idea, bad idea, bad idea.

"I can stand up and carry this chair out of here," he said, realizing it for the first time himself. He was handcuffed to a simple wooden chair.

"How are you going to drive with a chair connected to your wrist?" she asked.

"I'll walk."

"You live ten miles from here."

"I'll…"

She quirked an eyebrow.

Dammit.

It wasn't like he was all that serious about leaving anyway. It probably was time for her to know this story. It wasn't going to make him look good at all. One big reason for never telling her before this. But that might be a good thing. If she realized what an ass he really was, maybe she'd want to stay away from him.

However, the *whole* story also made her brother look…naive. At least.

Which was the reason he and Conner had agreed, over beers nine years ago, that they were never going to talk about it.

Of course, they'd also agreed to never let another woman come between them and, well, here they were.

"Who's Ashley?" Olivia asked.

Cody was jerked back to the moment by the mention of Ashley's name. "How do you know her name?"

"So there is an Ashley? Emma said she overheard the name once when you and Conner were talking. Who is she?"

Could he really tell her this? He hated thinking about it and he hadn't talked about it in years.

Olivia pulled her T-shirt up and over her head, tossing it on top of the apron.

Her bra was cotton. White with green polka dots.

Cody really liked it.

Dammit.

"Ashley was my high school girlfriend."

Olivia looked suspicious. "You met Conner in college. Did he know Ashley?"

Cody nodded. "He met her." That was an understatement.

"Start at the beginning," Olivia said.

She looked determined. Everyone knew that Olivia was sweet and accommodating, but he knew she could be indomitable when she made her mind up about something. She was a Dixon after all.

"Ashley and I dated for two years in high school. She was the girl I thought I was going to marry. Everyone thought she was the girl I was going to marry."

Olivia's eyes narrowed and he couldn't help but smile at the flash of jealousy he saw there. She propped a hand on her hip again. "What happened?"

"We went to different colleges after graduation. We were about two hours apart. She didn't like it, but we both got scholarships—me for football and her for volleyball—so we didn't have a lot of choice if we wanted to play."

"*She* didn't like it? What about you?" Olivia asked.

"I wasn't too worried about it," he said honestly. "I knew I'd be busy and wrapped up in football stuff and I knew I was going to love college. I didn't really think I'd be sitting around missing her, you know?"

"That's not very nice."

"No, it's not." He shrugged. "This isn't a story that makes me look good, Liv."

"So, you went off to college and never called and she eventually broke up with you?"

He coughed. That would have been easier. "Uh, no. Not exactly."

"You went off to college, had a great time, and you broke up with her."

"No." That, too, would have been a lot easier.

"Cody, what happened?"

This was where he was going to look like a jackass. And he suddenly couldn't do it. "Actually, that was pretty much how it went. We were both crazy busy with practices and games on the weekends. We went for two solid months without seeing each other, and I finally said that it wasn't working out."

Olivia sighed and slipped her pants off. Cody's mouth went dry as she kicked the yoga pants to the side. Her panties were green with white polka dots, the opposite of her bra. They were also small, dipping low under her belly button and arching high on her hips.

"Liv," he said, his voice sounding strained.

"I'm also going to take an article of clothing off every time you lie or fudge the truth," she said. "I know you, Cody. I know when you're not telling me everything."

Damn.

There were now two tiny pieces of cotton and elastic keeping Olivia from being completely bare. But there was nothing between his eyes and an awful lot of sweet, smooth, bare skin.

He felt his breathing speed up and could not, for the life of him, tear his eyes away from her thighs. They were toned from running, the skin lightly gold from the sun. Olivia was built like her sisters, but she was shorter than Amanda and Emma and curvier than Isabelle. She had hips and a butt that looked amazing in blue jeans. And out of blue jeans. She ran almost five miles a day, and the thought of tracing the lines and ridges of each muscle in her legs with his tongue made a certain muscle of his nice and tight as well.

"I can keep going," she said, interrupting his thoughts. "Or *you* can keep going."

His body and mind warred. He wanted her. She knew it and would welcome his touch, his kiss, *his* body. He knew that and it was almost too much to think about. He also didn't want her to know this story.

But if they got involved, she would hear the story eventually. From Conner. And he appreciated that she'd come to him instead of going to her brother first.

The bottom line was, and always had been, Olivia was his friend. A woman he respected, liked and trusted. If she was going to learn ugly truths about him, at least it should be from him.

"Fine. I'll keep going," he said.

Olivia almost looked disappointed.

He fought a grin. Well, once the story was out, if she still wanted to take a few tiny scraps of cotton off, he wouldn't object. At least not too much.

"I was having a great time. Football was going well, I was working my way toward a starting position, I liked my classes and my roommate was cool."

"Conner."

"Right."

Cody knew there had been arguments between Conner and their mother about Conner going to college. Conner felt that he needed to stay home to help her out while she felt he deserved the chance to get away and to play football at the college level. He'd been awarded a scholarship—which helped the family out immensely as well—for football at a small school about an hour away. It had been a great compromise. He was close enough to help out with family stuff, but also had a chance to be a college kid and blow off some steam after being a responsible father figure to four younger sisters for two years.

"And you didn't miss your girlfriend?" Olivia asked Cody.

"I, um…" He shifted uncomfortably on the chair. "I had a lot of female attention."

She rolled her eyes. "I'm shocked."

He shrugged. "It was a small school. I was a football player. I showed up at most parties. I was…popular."

"And Conner was right beside you?" Olivia guessed.

"A lot of the time," Cody agreed. "He went home as much as possible, but yeah, in those first few months, there wasn't much chance for him to get away with our game schedule, so he went to plenty of parties and stuff too."

They'd had a great time. He and Conner had clicked right away. Conner had shared a lot about his experiences losing his father, taking care of his sisters, looking out for his mom. Cody had respected the hell out of him right away.

He couldn't say that the respect had necessarily been mutual though.

"And what happened with Ashley?" Olivia asked. "She found out about the other girls?"

Cody's gut clenched. "I treated her badly, Olivia. Okay? That's the bottom line here."

"Badly how?"

He sighed. "After not seeing each other for a couple of months, she started talking about breaking up and saying maybe that would be best. But I didn't like that. She was beautiful and smart and fun. I was sure there were all kinds of guys wanting her."

"Like there were all kinds of girls wanting you," Olivia said.

He nodded. "But I knew that she was completely in love with me and was an honest, sweet person. I knew that all I had to do was tell her I wanted to stay together and ask her to be faithful."

Olivia raised an eyebrow. "And she said?"

"Of course."

"So you asked her to stay faithful to you and not date anyone else, while you were partying and going crazy with a bunch of girls two hours away?"

"Pretty much."

"You were only flirting though? You didn't actually cheat on her, did you?"

He blew out a breath. "You know the answer to that, Liv. Of course I did. I cheated on her repeatedly. And I barely called her. I never visited her campus. She missed a big school dance because I couldn't go as her date, but asked her not to go with anyone else."

"Why didn't she break up with you?" Olivia asked, her eyes wide.

"Because I was good," he said, feeling like an even bigger ass than he'd expected to. "I knew how to keep her dangling. I sent her flowers, wrote the occasional sweet card or e-mail…just enough to keep her from really seeing what was going on."

"You kept telling her you loved her?" Olivia's expression said she didn't really want the answer.

He nodded anyway. "I knew her really well. I was the only boyfriend she'd ever had. I was her first love, the first—and only—guy she'd slept with. I knew I had her wrapped around my little finger, and it didn't really take much to keep her there."

Olivia looked disappointed. "You didn't want her but you didn't want anyone else to have her?"

"I did want her. On one hand. I knew that all the football craziness and college fame and fun would eventually end, and I knew that when it was over, I wanted a sweet, honest, completely-in-love-with-me girl waiting."

Olivia gave him a wow-you're-a-dick look. Good. He'd been waiting for her to realize that.

Though the cramp in his gut got worse.

"How did Conner get involved?" she finally asked.

The wow-you're-a-dick sentiment was about to get worse. "I didn't answer her calls. I'd let it go to voice mail, then I'd e-mail her, but I couldn't talk to her without feeling guilty."

"Wow," Olivia muttered.

Her look of disapproval almost made him forget she was standing in front of him in only her underwear. Almost.

"One night she was calling me over and over, so I went out for a run."

"Uh-huh." Olivia crossed her arms. It was clear that she'd gone from jealous of Ashley to defensive on her behalf.

"Conner was studying in the room and finally got sick of it and answered. It turned out that her grandmother had passed away and she needed someone to talk to. They talked for almost two hours." He'd finished his run and then stopped by a house full of guys who always had a keg tapped and a video game hooked up, avoiding going back to Ashley's voice mails as long as possible.

Olivia's expression softened a bit. "Conner's a great listener."

Cody nodded. "Ashley thought so too. Conner told her to call anytime she needed to talk. And she did. They started talking every day. I didn't know at first, but after about a week, Conner was starting to act like a jerk toward me. I couldn't figure out what was going on. One night he said, 'Have you noticed Ashley hasn't called you in almost a week?'" Cody took a deep breath and avoided Olivia's eyes. "I had noticed. At first I didn't think much of it, but then started to wonder if she was pulling away, so I sent her flowers. She'd gotten them that day."

Olivia didn't say anything. Her arms were still crossed, and when he glanced at her face, he saw that she was watching him with a combination of fascination and offense. "You still didn't know about her grandmother?"

"Right."

"So those flowers probably seemed really insensitive."

"Probably."

"Go on."

"When Conner asked me if I'd noticed the no-call thing, I said something like 'yeah, it's been nice and quiet' and Conner was on me like that." Cody snapped his fingers. "He grabbed me by the front of the shirt and pushed me up against the door and got right in my face. He told me I was a scumbag and how could I treat her like that and on and on." Cody took another deep breath. "He hadn't even known about her for a few weeks. When he'd found out I had a girlfriend from home, he'd asked about her but I told him it was really casual and no big deal. Well, obviously Ashley filled him in on the truth. Conner was pissed."

Olivia nodded. "I can see that. He's always very quick to come to any woman's defense."

It was one of the things Cody liked best about him. Conner had a huge respect for women and treated them all very well. He seemed to have a knack for knowing how to best get on a woman's good side. Some went for the perfect gentleman, some for the flirtatious playboy. Whatever they responded to was what they got from Conner.

"Anyway, I told him to mind his own damned business. He said it was now his business and that I had one hour to call her and tell her everything or he would."

The fascination on Olivia's face seemed to overshadow any other emotion at the moment. "What did you do?"

Cody shrugged. "I got the hell away from him."

"Did you call her?"

He shook his head. He wasn't proud of any of this. But he'd been a nineteen-year-old kid. He'd been full of himself and, frankly, had been a jerk. A big one. He liked things easy. Confronting Ashley, being honest, telling her what a dick he really was and breaking her heart would *not* have been easy.

"So Conner called her," Olivia said.

"Right. And spent like two hours on the phone with her, then got in his car and drove up to see her."

"He drove two hours to her campus?" Olivia asked.

Cody nodded. "I didn't know about that until a while after. But yeah, he was worried she'd do something stupid if he didn't go up there."

"Stupid like what?" Olivia asked. "Like she'd be suicidal?"

Cody took a deep breath. "No. I think he was more worried that she'd get drunk and then try to drive down to see me. Or she'd call my mom. I don't know. I don't know if *she* even really knew what she would do. Ashley was sweet and we'd never even fought before."

"She was easy to take for granted then," Olivia said. "Right? You figured she'd always be there. That you couldn't screw up enough for her to break up with you. That she'd always forgive you."

That was exactly it. "I was the first guy to pay attention to her in high school. I was very romantic. She thought I was awesome."

Olivia snorted softly. "What happened with her and Conner?"

Cody shifted on the chair. Her words about Ashley applied to Olivia too. Every one of them. That she was easy to take for granted, that she'd always be there, always forgive him. He could hurt her. Big time. And while hurting Ashley still bothered him, hurting Olivia would haunt him forever.

"Conner drove up there to comfort her. They already had a little crush going, I think, over the phone, and she'd been dumped and he was pissed at me and…they…"

Olivia's arms dropped to her sides. "Conner *slept* with her?"

"Yes."

"But…uh…wow."

That pretty much covered it. "And it gets worse."

"I've never even heard of Ashley, so it couldn't have been too serious," Olivia said.

Cody hated to tell Conner's secrets. But Olivia deserved to know the whole thing. "They started seeing each other. Conner thought it was serious. She…was using him to make me jealous. It seemed perfect, I'm sure. When she came down to visit him, she ended up staying in our room."

"I'll bet that was awkward."

"I stayed away."

"It didn't bother you?"

"I felt bad about it. Still do. But no. It didn't bother me. Once I got used to the idea anyway. I knew Conner would treat her well. And I, obviously, wasn't truly in love with her."

In truth, then and now, he wished that Ashley had actually fallen for Conner. Conner would have taken care of her. Her life wouldn't have spiraled out of control. And Cody wouldn't still be blaming himself ten years later.

Olivia frowned. "So what happened? Like I said, I've never heard of her."

Cody fidgeted again. Then said, "When she realized it wasn't bothering me, she tried to get my attention in other ways. Drinking and partying, e-mailing me photos, calling me when she was drunk. Sleeping around."

"She used Conner." Olivia's voice was harder now.

Now they were talking about her big brother. *That* would bother her.

"Yeah. She dumped him and got out of control. She got kicked off the volleyball team and lost her scholarship. She didn't go back the next year."

Olivia looked conflicted now. She wouldn't like Ashley because of what she'd done to Conner—and maybe even Cody —but she would also be concerned about the girl messing up her life. That was Olivia. Sweet to a fault.

That was the entire problem with him being with her in a nutshell.

"She eventually cleaned up and finished school," Cody said. "At least according to Facebook and my parents. Who, by the way, ended their friendship with Ashley's parents after we broke up."

"Why?"

"Because my mother has always been convinced that I can do no wrong. So it seemed to her that it was all Ashley's fault somehow and I'd been treated poorly and wrongly accused."

"You've got to be kidding me."

"I'm not." This was probably important for her to understand too. "I've never been held responsible for anything I've done wrong, Liv. My parents thought I walked on water. The things I did well, I got praised and rewarded for. The things I did wrong…they always found an excuse."

"You were a bratty little kid, weren't you?" she asked.

"Big time. I've been a dick since I was two or three, I'm sure. Always got my way, never had to say I was sorry."

"You're not a dick now."

"Thanks to your brother, I'm a reformed dick," Cody conceded. "But it's really easy for me to slip back into my asshole ways. Trust me."

"What did Conner do?"

Cody took a deep breath. This was the basis for the friendship that was keeping him from being with the woman he was in love with. "Mostly he was a role model. Your brother does the right things for the right reasons. He's a good guy."

Olivia's expression softened. "No arguments from me."

"And he didn't write me off. I mean, there were about six months where we didn't speak or hang out. But in the end, Conner realized that…I have some issues and some potential."

"You're a great guy now. Everyone knows it. You're the nice guy, the good guy."

"I work at it," he said with a shrug. He did a lot of charity work, he was there for his friends, he was trying to get over his propensity for thinking he could get away with anything.

He was trying to be a grown-up. And a good guy.

He treated women much better than he used to. He gave

sincere compliments, was a serial monogamist, never forgot important dates.

But a relationship with another woman who had a big heart and thought he walked on water was a level of good-guy he wasn't sure he could do. He needed a girl who could look out for herself when he messed up.

However, the little blond in front of him—who thought he was awesome—was making it harder to remember that than it had ever been.

"Conner's not so perfect," Olivia said. "He still holds this against you, right?"

Cody nodded. "He tries not to, but yeah. He can't get over how I treated her. How I chose the good time and the popularity over the long-term relationship I had with her."

"You were a kid," she said. "And it was a long time ago."

"I know. But it messed up my friendship with your brother for a long time. We stayed roommates and tried to be civil when we were around the football team and coaches. The coaches would have been annoyed if they find out we were fighting about a girl. But we didn't talk and spent no time together other than when we were sleeping."

"But you're friends now," she pointed out.

"We ran into each other at a bar one night about six months later. He was really drunk. I offered to take him home. He said he'd rather I get drunk with him. So I did and we called a buddy later to pick us up. Once we were liquored up, we talked about everything and decided we'd both been jerks and promised to never let a girl come between us again." He looked Olivia directly in the eye. "I really don't think either of us would have guessed the next girl we'd be torn over would be one of his sisters though."

"So Conner's going to worry that you'll treat me like you did Ashley?" she asked. "That's ridiculous."

"Maybe." He would never *want* to hurt Olivia. He would

never *want* to take her for granted. And there was no way he could ever want to be with another woman if he had her.

But…Olivia was sweet and trusting and loyal and good. Like Ashley times ten. She saw the best in him for sure. Even when he wasn't sure it was really there.

"He doesn't trust you with women?"

"He doesn't trust me with women he thinks are easily influenced by charm, good looks and romance. He used to joke about me and Emma going out, but I always knew that if I did ask her out, he would have been okay with it. Amanda too, probably."

"Because he thinks they can take care of themselves."

"Because they'll bust my balls if I do something they don't like."

"But I won't?"

He laughed. Olivia was definitely not the ball-busting kind. "You'd make me muffins and want to talk about it. And you'd give me a dozen chances to get it right. Emma would throw me out on my ass at violation number one. Even for an alleged violation."

Olivia chewed on her bottom lip. He could tell she wanted to deny it, but she couldn't. Olivia was forgiving of most people. She saw the good in everyone. With him? The rose-colored glasses were a deep, dark pink. He could get away with anything. Even hurting her. Whether he wanted to or not.

He'd screw up. For sure. And she'd be there to take him back, every time.

Conner wasn't wrong about that.

Fuck.

"I can't make you any promises, Liv," he finally said. "I mean, I *could*. I want to. But I can't honestly tell you that I'll treat you the way you deserve."

"Everyone makes mistakes, Cody. And you're older now. And you learned from that situation," she told him.

He smiled even as a sadness gripped him. He really wasn't good enough for her. He was a guy who had always taken a mile when given an inch. He'd grown up believing that it was easier to get forgiven than to get permission. His mother had been exactly like Ashley and Olivia. He could do no wrong in her eyes, and she made excuses for him and never stayed mad, never punished him.

He would try his damnedest to be the man Olivia believed he was, but inevitably he'd say or do something without thinking it through and he'd hurt her. That would kill him.

And then Conner would kill him.

"See, you're doing it already," he said. "You're spinning this to make me look good."

"You're not an asshole," she said firmly. "You're a great guy. You have a big heart. You're…my best friend."

He nodded. "Ditto, babe. But friendship is different. Be honest. I have more leeway as a friend than as a boyfriend."

She pressed her lips together and studied him for a long time. Long enough Cody began shifting again.

Olivia Dixon, the most amazing woman in the world, was standing in front of him in her underwear telling him that he was a great guy.

It was pretty much the best and most painful moment of his life.

"Here's the thing," she finally said. "I think you're going to have to step up."

"Step up? What do you mean?"

"I know you don't want to hurt me," she told him, moving closer. "And if you walk out of here without kissing me, you'll hurt me for sure."

Cody stared at her. "That's very…"

"Honest?"

"I was going to say manipulative."

She smiled, clearly not bothered by that at all. "Not quite ball-busting though, huh? I'll have to work on that."

Cody snorted. He couldn't help it. Olivia couldn't be a ball-buster. It wasn't possible.

"Cody?" she said softly, stepping closer again. They were now knee to knee. He could reach out and touch her. If he wanted to.

He *always* wanted to. But he'd gotten good at resisting.

"Yeah?" His voice sounded as tight as his throat felt.

"You have a choice to make," she said.

Hell.

"None of that story bothered you?"

"Of course it did. I'm not very proud or pleased with either you or Conner," she said. "But I know you both, and you're not those guys anymore."

He knew she wanted to see him a certain way, but damn, when she said stuff like that, *he* started to believe it. He wanted to be that guy. He wanted to prove to her that she was absolutely right about him.

"What do you think we're going to do here?"

She smiled and reached behind her, unhooking her bra and letting it fall away from his favorite pair of breasts *ever*.

He should have seen that coming.

That was going to become his new mantra.

"Liv," he said hoarsely.

"I'm going to show you that you are the guy that I want and need you to be, right here and right now."

She moved closer, braced a hand on his shoulder and straddled his knees, settling her sweet ass on his lap.

She threaded her fingers through the hair at the back of his head and leaned to put her lips against his ear. "I need you to touch me, Cody. So much. It doesn't matter who you've been or who I've been before this. It's you and me, right now, just as we are this moment."

Damn, that sounded good.

Somewhere in the back of his mind he acknowledged the fact that he was great at making—or taking—any excuse to get what he wanted.

But he was also very good at ignoring important insights

about himself.

Then something not-clear-at-the-back of his mind took over. The part that registered Olivia's scent, the feel of her fingers in his hair, the hot weight of her on his lap, the beaded pink nipples that made his tongue tingle with the need to taste.

A good guy would have dumped her on her pretty butt and gotten the hell out of there.

He wasn't a good guy. Anyone who wondered about that could ask Conner Dixon himself.

Cody put his free right hand on Olivia's ass, cupping her cheek, soaking in the feel of the soft cotton warm from her body. He curled his fingers into the firm flesh and lifted her slightly, bringing her forward, her breasts pressing into his chest.

Now his mouth was near her ear.

"This is a stupid, dangerous, terrible idea," he said huskily. "But I tend to make very bad decisions when something feels good, and you'll forgive me for anything anyway."

"If that means I should go ahead and take my panties off, I'm in favor," she said, sounding a bit breathless herself.

And the bad decision was made just like that.

"Last chance to avoid believing in an asshole."

"I can't believe in an asshole," she told him. "I believe in *you*."

Her words shredded his resistance. He turned his head and captured her lips with his.

She sighed against his mouth, both of her hands going to his head so she could press closer, and lust rushed through his bloodstream, lighting his nerve endings on fire.

"Uncuff me," he murmured against her lips.

"Not yet," she whispered.

"Liv, there are some really great things I plan to do—with both hands."

"Give me a second here." She leaned back and licked her lips. Her fingers went to his shirt, and she tugged it up and over his head. He slipped his free hand from the sleeve, and she let the shirt fall to dangle from the chain of the handcuff that held his wrist to the chair.

She ran her hands over his chest. "You know, I've never touched you like this," she said softly.

He knew that. He was absolutely, one hundred percent aware of that fact. Her touch was gentle but he felt like he was coming out of his skin. Every cell in his body was yearning to feel her hands, her tongue, her body against it.

She kneaded her fingers into his shoulder muscles, then ran her palms down his upper arms to his elbows, then back up to his shoulders and down over his pecs and lower.

He watched her face as he absorbed the feel of her hands on him. She looked as turned on as he felt, and that gave him an even bigger surge of adrenaline.

"Liv—"

"I love touching you like this. I can't imagine what it will feel like to kiss you all over."

"Girl…"

"Almost done."

She ran her hands over his stomach and the muscles tensed under her fingers. She explored the bumps of his abs, seemingly fascinated. But surely she wouldn't…

Her fingers trailed down over the rock-hard erection behind his fly and he swore, his hips bucking.

The sly look in her eyes when she met his gaze was as potent as the fingers that again traced over the straining bulge, this time with more pressure.

"Olivia Ann," he said firmly. "Uncuff me."

She flattened her palm against his cock, pressing and dragging up and down the length.

"Now."

Her smile was pure feminine power, and any chance of resisting her that might have been lingering flew out the window.

She pushed herself back, stood and retrieved the key from a

coffee cup on the counter behind her. She returned to his lap, legs spread wide over his thighs, and leaned in to reach the cuff. The move pressed her breasts and nipples into his chest, and he sucked in a quick breath.

The moment his hand was free, he reached for the bowl of batter sitting on the table next to him.

"Best cupcakes you've ever made." He scooped a glob of batter up with two fingers and painted a stripe of chocolate over her right breast. As he ran his fingers over her nipple, she gasped and wiggled on his lap.

There were a thousand things he should probably say or do or ask or at least think about, but all he could do was wrap his hands around her rib cage and lift her to his mouth.

He licked up every trace of chocolate from the gorgeous swell before fastening his mouth on her nipple and drawing all of the stickiness from the stiff point. He knew the sweetness he was going to crave forever was all Olivia and had nothing to do with the sugar in the recipe.

Her fingers dug into his scalp, and he relished the breathy moans and the "oh, Cody" that he pulled from her.

Finally settling her back on his lap, he took in the dazed look in her eyes.

Not letting himself think too hard or long, and needing to keep her from saying anything that might pull him from this moment, he slid his hand down, around the curve of her butt, over the silky skin of her thigh and around to cup her mound.

She gasped. He kept his eyes on hers as his finger moved past the elastic band of her panties and met the wet heat that would have sent him to his knees if he hadn't been sitting down.

Her hands dropped to his shoulders, her fingers digging in again, but she said nothing to stop him. She simply pulled her bottom lip between her teeth and seemed to be holding her breath.

He pressed his finger forward, her slick folds parted and he eased in, her body welcoming him, holding on tight as he stroked in and out.

Olivia puffed out a breath and tipped her head back. "Wow," she breathed.

Wow. Three letters, but they were perfect.

She looked perfect, she felt perfect, she sounded perfect.

He moved his fingers deeper and faster and felt a surge of satisfaction when her hips moved with the rhythm. He leaned in and sucked on a nipple, feeling the response around his finger. Then he looked up at her as he brushed his thumb over her clit.

She cried out, clutching at his shoulders.

The look on her face was one of the prettiest sights he'd ever seen.

He did it again, with more pressure this time. Her thighs clenched on his, and her inner muscles tightened on his finger.

"Cody," she gasped.

"Anything, Liv."

"Never stop."

He grinned and happily added another finger, deeper strokes and faster flicks over her clit.

She was tight. It was a snug fit for two fingers, and Cody groaned at the thought of how she would feel around his cock. He'd have to be careful not to hurt her.

Though the delicious sounds she was making and the way she was moving against his hand, seeking the relief he was holding just out of her reach, made him doubt his ability to go slow with her. He'd have to be sure she came at least a couple times before he took her completely.

Darn.

Then she reached for his unoccupied hand and lifted it to her breast.

"Please."

"What, Liv?" He wanted to hear it. "Whatever makes you feel good."

"Play with my nipples. I love that. It makes me come faster."

All the blood in Cody's head drained south. Holy hell. He would have easily assumed that hearing Olivia talk dirty would be hot, but…

He took a deep breath. He'd so firmly steered away from anything that made him look at her sexually that everything about being smack dab in the middle of such a hot moment was a surprise. A pleasant, erotic, I-want-to-do-this-over-and-over-and-over surprise.

He took her nipple between his thumb and forefinger, tugging, then squeezing, making her grind closer to his hand and give a hissed "yes."

"God, you're gorgeous," he said, watching her with awe.

And then she was coming. Her head fell forward and she gripped his upper arms as her pussy clamped down hard.

He didn't hear his name, but otherwise it was perfect. And there was always next time.

The ripples of her orgasm hadn't even quieted when he pulled his hand free, cupped her ass, stood and turned to deposit her on the table.

"Lie back."

He started unbuttoning his pants. He'd make her come again, this time with his tongue, and then he'd have her—in the first of the dozen or so positions he needed her in.

He'd barely opened his fly when his phone rang.

He froze.

Fuck no. This couldn't be happening.

She must have seen something in his expression because she sat up on the edge of the table. "Is that your work phone?"

It sure fucking was.

"Son of a bitch." He yanked the phone from his pocket. "What?" he barked a moment later.

"Fire. Downtown in the old warehouse on Tenth."

Fuck. The warehouse they'd converted into upscale studio apartments.

He disconnected and started rebuttoning, a task he did carefully over the raging hard-on he still had. Dammit-fuck-hell.

"I have to go."

Olivia nodded. "I figured."

She was perched on the edge of her kitchen table, half-naked. Her cheeks were flushed, her hair tousled, and she had remnants of chocolate cupcake batter on her right breast.

He paused in the process of reaching for his shirt. "I don't think I've ever wanted anything more than I want you right now."

Her eyes widened at the unexpected comment. "You know where to find me when you're done at work."

He nodded. But it was very possible that he'd come to his senses by the time he was done with work tonight. Whether he liked it or not. He was good at ignoring his conscience, but it broke through a hell of a lot more often than he wanted it to as he got older. And grew up. Somewhere along the way he'd become an almost-adult. Most of the time.

"And Cody?" Olivia added.

He shrugged into his shirt. "Yeah?"

"I'm not going anywhere."

He paused, the double meaning crystal clear.

What was he going to do with her?

Nothing was, of course, the answer he was supposed to come up with.

And she was right in saying he'd changed since college. Now he had a sense of responsibility. He liked to help and protect other people. And he had an appreciation for deep, lasting friendships.

"I'll talk to you later," was all he said as he finished dressing.

Because, of course he would. She was his friend. They had a standing Wednesday night baking date. And she'd promised to see Michael Bublé with him—and tell everyone *she* was making *him* go. And the next time Melanie Carter flirted with him at Trudy's, Olivia was honor bound to save him.

He glanced at the bowl of batter on the table next to Olivia's hip, then turned quickly and headed for the door.

Of course, he was going to have to bake with a painful erection from now on. But hey, a true friend was worth a little pain.

Like the pain of never finding a woman to measure up to the one he'd just left in green-and-white polka-dotted panties.

CHAPTER
FIVE

CODY PULLED up to the scene fifteen minutes later and quickly took in the details as he grabbed his hat from the seat next to him and bailed from his truck.

The structure was big, taking up a full city block. There weren't as many units as in a typical apartment complex, but they were big, wide-open studios. There was only one floor of living spaces above the craft store and art gallery on the street level, but a fire in one area could easily spread to the entire warehouse. It was an old building, made mostly of brick. The wiring and plumbing had been updated when it had been converted to lofts, but the walls, floors and ceilings were original.

There were already three engines on scene and a ladder truck extended against the side of the building. As he strode toward the command truck, where his assistant fire chief, Tom, would be running the scene, he noted two ambulances and several police cars keeping the curious public back from the area.

As always, he hoped Conner, Ryan and Shane were some of the personnel on scene. They didn't always work the same shifts, of course, but when they did, everything was better.

Tom saw him coming.

"Go," Cody told him as soon as he was close enough to hear the man's rundown of the situation.

"Search teams have been in and out. They cleared all the apartments, but we had a fireman go down. A couple paramedics went in."

"Who went down?"

"Greg."

Dammit. He was a new guy. "What happened?"

"There are some archways in the living spaces," Tom said, pointing to the upper-level windows. "Mostly decorative, made of lightweight stuff. One collapsed and smacked him in the head. He was knocked out."

Cody glanced around. "They got him out?"

"Yeah, he's en route to the hospital. Had a pretty good gash on his head."

"No civilians left inside?"

"The lofts were all cleared. Fire is under control on the south side, but we're still fighting on the east."

Cody zeroed in on his friend Ryan. So Ryan and Conner's crew was here. Awesome. But then Cody frowned. Ryan was holding on to their crewmate, Gabby, by the arm. It looked like he was holding her back.

"Who were the paramedics that went in?" Cody asked, his gut telling him already that Tom was going to say—

"Dixon was the first in."

"Fuck." Cody started in Ryan's direction. "Kaye," he said as he got closer. "What's going on?"

Gabby whirled to face him before Ryan could reply. "He's still in there."

He'd known it. Cody worked to control his reaction. He had to handle this. Conner was a professional too. He had to trust Conner to do the right thing.

"What happened?"

"We went in after the firefighter. He was out cold, so we had to assess him and stabilize his neck before we carried him to the door, but as soon as Ryan and Sierra took him, I turned back and Conner was gone," Gabby said. She looked pissed. "If you don't go in after him, I will."

"Calm down," Cody said with a frown. The last thing he needed was two paramedics inside the burning building his crew was working to save.

"He radioed that he'd heard someone cry for help and that he was going back in," Sierra, the fourth member of Conner's crew, said. Her face was tight with worry. "But when I replied and asked for more detail, he wasn't there. He isn't answering."

Cody took a deep breath and forced himself to relax his shoulders. Conner's crew needed him to be in control right now. His own crew needed him to take charge.

But he was going to kick Conner's ass as soon as he pulled it out of the fire.

Two of his men approached, dragging their helmets off, their faces coated with soot. "We located Dixon."

"And why the fuck isn't he with you?" Cody's gut cramped. He knew why. Not exactly, of course, but he knew it meant that they couldn't get to him for some reason. His guys would never leave someone inside.

"He fell. A chunk of ceiling fell, dropping a chandelier straight through the floor. He went through with it."

Cody's entire body went cold. He heard Ryan's muttered "fuck" and Sierra's gasp. But he couldn't worry about them right now. He couldn't worry about anyone but Conner.

"I need equipment!" he shouted to the crew at the truck.

"There's a lot of smoke. The stairwell is six paces to your left when you step through the door," Gabby began as someone came running with what he needed and he started pulling on pants, boots, jacket and helmet.

He appreciated the information. Once he was inside, he wouldn't be able to see.

When she didn't go on, Cody looked up. She had her arms crossed tightly and her lips pressed together.

"Then what?" he asked.

"I don't know," she said, still looking pissed but with worry at the edges. "I don't know where he went from there."

Right. Dammit.

"Okay." He turned to the firefighters who'd told him about Conner's fall. "Where do I go from the staircase?"

"You can't go in there," one of them protested. "You can't see a fucking thing and a lot of the floor gave way. You'll go right in too."

"Then I'm gonna need a harness," Cody said. He *was* going in there. But he had to use his head. Plunging into a smoke-filled building with a hole in the floor was a dumb-ass move. "Where'd he go down?"

"Keep on past the staircase. Probably one hundred feet," one said.

"Did you see Dixon fall?"

"He was behind us, the chandelier came down, the floor gave, then he wasn't behind us," the firefighter said. "We kind of assumed."

They didn't know if Conner was conscious, hurt or worse. Dammit.

Someone brought a harness and rope. "You're going to have to lower me down," he told his men. "Everyone we can spare. As far as we know, Dixon is the only person still inside. We need to get him out."

His crew got into position, ready to hold the rope and lower Cody into the hole to Conner. But the man at the front of the line was Ryan Kaye.

"You need to keep trying to get Conner on the radio," Cody told Ryan.

"Screw that," Ryan said, clamping the gigantic metal hook onto Cody's harness. "I'll let you be the big shot since you're chief, but you don't get all the hero glory."

Cody knew very well that Ryan didn't do any of the things he did for the glory. None of them did. He was as worried about Conner as Cody was.

"Fine. I can't think of someone I'd rather have at my back," he told the paramedic.

"Let's go fish Dixon out of there," Ryan said, nudging Cody forward.

They approached the building carefully.

"Keep trying to get Conner on the radio," he told Sierra. "At least I'll be able to hear you talking on his radio as I get close." He turned to his men. "I'm going in. Alone to start. But stay ready."

Tom was out here running things, so Cody could afford to go in. And he had to. Not because it was Conner—he'd go in after anyone left behind and he wouldn't ask his men to do it. But it *was* Conner.

He strode to the door and shined the heavy-duty flashlight into the smoky entryway. Thank God it was daylight. That always helped.

He stepped through that door carefully. The fire was supposedly focused on the other side of the building from this stairwell, but something was burning overhead to cause that fixture to drop. He didn't want to go through the floor himself, and he sure as hell didn't want to get clocked in the head by something falling.

"Conner!" he hollered once he was through the door and in a hallway. "Dixon!" he bellowed again, turning left as Gabby had instructed. No answer.

He reached the stairwell and peered into the smoke. He could make out the edge of what was, obviously, a hole in the floor.

"Conner!" He kept yelling but he moved carefully forward. He hadn't looked at the blueprint of the building, which was stupid and something he never did. But getting in here had been his only concern.

Dammit.

He grabbed his radio. "Somebody give me a general idea of what I'm doing here," he said. "I'm heading east down a long hallway. Two doors opening off to the north."

"Those are going to be storage. The lofts are above you to the north," the voice crackled back. "We cleared them. The hallway chandelier came down just beyond that second door."

"How are we doing on the flames, boys?" Cody asked.

The second loft would share a wall with the loft where they were still battling the fire.

"We're on it, boss," the voice—he thought it belonged to Trevor Wilson—said. "But we've got a ways to go."

Terrific. He approached the edge of the hole in the floor. He jerked on the harness that wrapped around his chest. If the floor suddenly gave, the harness—and the men outside—would keep him from falling to his death. That didn't mean he wouldn't swing into something that would hurt. And it didn't mean that it wouldn't freak him the fuck out.

"Dixon!"

He didn't hear anything at first. He stepped to the edge of the hole, listening, scanning, *feeling*. He was sure it sounded ridiculous, but he trusted his gut in these scenarios. If something felt wrong, it was.

But this didn't feel wrong. It felt like he wanted to not be underneath a ceiling that was potentially falling, but...

"Cody."

The voice was weak, but it was there.

Cody felt his heart thud. "You gotta help me out here, man," he called out, leaning in and trying to scan the depth of the hole with the flashlight. Conner had clearly fallen into the basement. "What's going on down there?"

"Boring as hell actually. I just woke up."

Cody's heart squeezed. So he'd been unconscious. Okay. At least now he was joking. That was a good sign. "Can you see my light?"

"Yeah."

"Is it hitting you at all?" Cody couldn't see a damned thing in there.

"Yeah, my boot."

"You hurt?"

"Uh, I think so."

Cody frowned. "You're not sure?"

"I'm kind of…under some stuff."

Fantastic. "What kind of stuff?"

"I can't tell. It's dark. But whatever it is weighs a ton. I can't move it. And my head's killing me."

Cody radioed back to the men outside on the other end of the rope. He felt them increase the tension and he eased himself to the floor, then to the edge of the hole. "I'm coming down," he told Conner.

"I sure as hell hope so."

Cody turned and let himself down through the floorboards with his arms, like getting into a swimming pool—though there was no water buoyancy to help him now. Damn, he didn't like this.

Finally, he had to let go and trust the harness and his crew to keep him in the air.

They eased him in slowly. He twirled at the end of the rope, but the descent was gradual and he finally felt his feet touch something solid.

There was significantly less smoke down here, and his high-powered beam lit the area nicely.

It was most definitely a basement. The walls were brick, the floor was brick, and it was packed with stuff. Shelves lined two walls, stuffed full of boxes and books and odds and ends. There were also huge canvases he assumed belonged to the art gallery, as well as glass cases, chairs, tables, mannequins, crates and boxes, old furniture and even a refrigerator.

"I don't suppose you found an old stash of moonshine while you've been hanging out down here?" Cody asked, locating Conner easily now that he was on the same floor. He was about twenty feet away, on his back, covered in dust, a huge, solid-looking piece of wood across his legs.

"Been a little busy, actually," Conner said.

Cody could see he was gritting his teeth. Cody began picking his way over the debris littering the floor.

"Busy, huh? Making your Christmas list?"

"Coming up with various horror-movie scenarios for this basement. And that was before I saw the mannequins. Glad I didn't have any light down here."

Cody chuckled. Conner sounded pretty fine to him.

"You know what day it is?" Cody asked him. He had to determine if he was dealing with a bump on the head or a concussion or a more serious head injury.

"Saturday."

"Where are you?"

"Under a pile of rubble." Conner even chuckled at that.

Cody moved around the remnants of the chandelier. Damn, what a mess.

"Your ears ringing?" Cody asked Conner.

"Yep. And I'm sick to my stomach."

Conner knew the questions Cody was going to ask and why.

"You feel dizzy?"

"Probably. I can't get up to tell," Conner said.

"You can't get up because stuff's on top of you or because you're hurt?"

"Both. I don't know how hurt," Conner said.

"Can you move any of that crap off of you?" Cody got to him as Conner tried to shift whatever way lying across his lap.

Cody could see one of Conner's legs, but not the other.

Plaster and wood moved as Conner pushed, but something heavier was on him. In the dim light, Cody couldn't tell what it was.

"What's your pain like in your head?" he asked.

"Ten out of ten. Hey, fuck!" Conner jerked back when Cody shined the flashlight in his eyes. His pupils were dilated.

"When are your sisters' birthdays?" Cody reached out and felt the object pinning Conner's legs down. It didn't feel like a ceiling beam or a piece of the ceiling. What the hell?

He looked up to find Conner apparently concentrating to answer his question. He couldn't do it. Cody could tell.

Conner had a headache, nausea, dizziness, and ringing in the ears, and he couldn't concentrate. He had a concussion, if not something more serious.

"Did this thing hit you in the head?" He reached for Conner's head and found a huge knot on the back.

"Guess so." The words weren't exactly slurred but neither were they clear and articulate.

Cody shoved at the wooden beam. It was heavy. "Where the hell did this come from?"

Conner lifted his head, looking down at his legs as Cody shone his light on it. "No way." He started laughing. "It's a totem pole."

Cody blinked. "What?"

"It's a totem pole." Conner repeated, still chuckling. "Stupid fucking thing. It's decorative. I assume. I don't know if it came down with me or if it was down here and fell over on me."

That sounded more slurred. Dammit.

He crouched next to Conner and radioed out. "I've got him. I'm gonna need some help getting him out, guys. He's under a heavy wood pole. Bring a saw." He went on to direct them to the hole, the distance down and what to expect when they got into the basement.

"Roger that, boss."

"They're gonna send some tools," he told Conner. "Keep talking to me. We need to keep you awake and focused."

He'd been tuning the crackling sounds out, but they were hard to ignore a moment later when another large portion of the ceiling from the floor above dropped. Cody lurched to the side, the chunk of ceiling narrowly missing him.

"Dammit." He peered up through the hole.

"You know what I was thinking?" Conner asked him, sounding a little sleepy. Or drunk.

"What's that?" Cody put both his feet against the totem pole and tried shifting it, but when it did move, Conner swore in pain. Well, shit.

After he'd quit cursing, Conner said, "I was thinking that I could die happy. All my sisters are taken care of. Ryan and Shane and Nate would take care of their girls and you'd take care of Liv. So it wouldn't matter if I died down here."

Cody scowled at his friend even though Conner couldn't see him. "What the hell are you talking about? You're not going to die down here."

Cody stubbornly ignored how his heart pounded when Conner had said that he knew Cody would take care of Olivia. He also ignored the twinge of guilt he felt about where he'd been —and what he'd been doing—when he'd been called to the fire.

"Well, not now that you're here," Conner agreed. "But I thought for a little while there that the whole roof was going to cave in and bury me here. But the girls would be okay."

He definitely sounded drunk—which, considering the lack of moonshine, meant he had knocked his brain around.

"My crew is the best," Cody told him, feigning offense. "I can't believe you thought they'd let this roof cave in."

"Sorry, man," Conner said, definitely slurring.

"And your sisters still need you," Cody told him. He had to clear his throat before he went on. "It doesn't matter that they're in love and have men in their lives that love them. You're still important to them."

Even if it was possible that Olivia—for example—could get caught up in a moment, a kiss, a confusing mess of emotions, when push came to shove, Conner was the man whose feelings and opinions mattered most.

"Yeah, I'm important," Conner agreed in his punch-drunk voice. "But it's good that they have all you guys."

Cody swallowed. This was so not the time for this…

"You know that I care about Olivia a lot."

Conner nodded, then groaned when the motion obviously caused some pain. "I know. It's not just any guy who would do all the things you've done to be her friend." Conner tried to shift and winced.

Cody knew he should let it go. Conner had a concussion and he'd been lying down here in the dark, alone, contemplating his humanity. It might not be the best time to get clear, rational answers from him.

But frankly, if Olivia's big brother was going to give Cody permission to be with her, he didn't really care if it was the result of a brain injury or a death scare. He'd take it.

"I'd do whatever I could to make sure she was happy."

"I know," Conner said. "I'm glad she's got you."

Cody felt his chest tighten. "She sure does, buddy."

"So you promise me that you'll make sure the guys treat her right." Conner still sounded like he did after about four beers.

But Cody didn't care. He needed to know what this was about. "What do you mean?"

"If I'm not around, you'll have to be sure the guy she picks appreciates her." He tried to shift again and grimaced, then swore.

"You're going to be around. We'll get you out of here soon, Conner," Cody promised him, glancing up at the hole in the floor above them. They'd better be moving out there or he was going to chew some ass.

"I know. Maybe today's not my last day. But if that happens before Liv is in love, you have to promise to be there to make sure he's the right guy." Cody had to remind himself that Conner had fallen on his head.

"You want *me* to help her find the right guy?"

"Yes. Liv's special. And you know that best. All of my sisters are beautiful and smart, but Amanda, Iz and Em are like…"

He trailed off and Cody wondered if he was fading.

"Con—"

"Plastic tumblers."

Cody looked up at the hole in the ceiling. It was a long fall but wow. "Conner, maybe we should—"

"They're like those big plastic glasses Trudy got for the big Hawks celebration last month. They're colorful and fun, but they're durable, tough. You can bounce them around, you know, and they're just fine. Liv is like…a wine glass. The glass ones. She's also fun, but she can be broken if you're not careful…"

Conner trailed off as if the deep thoughts had sucked his energy.

Cody rubbed his forehead. The headache was contagious apparently. Though the cause was much different.

"Hey, boys, somebody need a saw down here?"

Cody was relieved to be interrupted, but when he looked up to see Sierra being lowered into the basement with a harness and rope like his, he scowled and got to his feet. "What are you doing down here?"

"The fire is under control and they figured it made sense to send a paramedic down. Turns out I'm the lightest one who was standing around with nothing to do." She grinned as she got her feet under her and held up the saw. "Gabby talked the guys into letting me down so I could also see about his injuries."

"I can't believe Gabby didn't come herself," Conner said. "She's always jumping in."

"She's heavier than me," Sierra said with a shrug. She picked her way over the debris as well, clearly sizing up the situation as she spoke.

"Women talk about how much they weigh?" Cody asked. That was *not* his experience.

Sierra laughed. "Gabby's the most practical person ever. She knew a paramedic should come, and I'm easier to lower than her or Ryan."

Made sense to Cody. "Give me the saw."

It was actually a chainsaw.

"You're not putting that thing next to my leg," Conner said as Cody fired the machine up.

"We're fine. Sierra's here now in case I cut it off," Cody hollered over the noise of the saw.

He grinned at Conner's put-out expression. Okay, a chainsaw right on top of his leg in a dark room might make him a little nervous too, but he couldn't get any more personnel down here, and they had to get the totem pole off of Conner so they could get him out.

"Pretty good concussion. Maybe more," Cody told Sierra as she moved past him to check Conner out as best she could with the wooden statue still pinning him down.

"Gotcha," she said.

Cody got into position to apply the saw and quickly cut the totem pole into smaller, more moveable pieces.

Twenty minutes later, the pole was no longer an issue, Conner was as bandaged up as he was going to get in the hole, and Cody was directing the effort to get the three of them up and out. The crew upstairs pulled Sierra up and then lowered a scoop stretcher for Conner. Several men were needed to haul Conner to the first floor, and finally Cody was pulled back up.

He crawled out of the hole and gratefully followed the stretcher and his friend out of the smoke-filled building.

As they stepped into the sunlight, Cody heard a big, deep voice boom.

"Holy shit, Dixon, this is the best fucking day."

Mac Gordon, the big bearded and tattooed, ace paramedic on the other primary ambulance crew from St. Anthony's, was striding toward Conner's stretcher.

Cody grinned. This was going to be good.

"I almost died, Gordon, you dick," Conner said.

"I know. But you didn't. Which means I get to enjoy taking care of you. Somebody get me a needle for an IV. A big one. Blunt on the end, preferably."

Cody came up next to Ryan. "You going to step aside while another crew takes care of your friend and partner?"

Ryan turned to him with a grin. "Conner deserves every bit of this."

It was true. Conner had been flirting—unabashedly—with Mac's wife, Sara, ever since he'd first laid eyes on her. Even after finding out about her husband. And having said husband threaten important parts of his body.

In fact, knowing Mac was Sara's husband made it more fun for Conner.

Until, of course, he was strapped down and concussed.

But if Mac and the rest of the crew weren't damned good at what they did, Cody knew Ryan would be shoving them out of the way.

Dooley Miller, another of the paramedics on Mac's crew, stepped up next to Conner's gurney, holding his phone up.

"Smile, Dixon," he said.

"What're you doing?" Conner asked.

"Showing all the girls at the hospital that you actually aren't as good-lookin' as they all think you are." Dooley snapped a couple of pictures with his phone.

Conner was covered with dust and soot, he had a gash on the side of his head and he was definitely missing his usual cocky grin.

"He was knocked a little loopy," Cody said to Ryan. "He might not even remember Mac treating him later."

"Yeah, Sierra said he was goofy. But I have a feeling he'll remember this." Ryan chuckled. "He'll be okay."

Cody finally drew in a deep breath and let it out. Possibly the first he'd taken since finding out his friend had plummeted into a basement in a building on fire.

"Fuck," he sighed. "This has already been a long damned day."

"Yeah," Ryan agreed. Then he slapped Cody on the back. "Let's go rescue Conner from Mac and the gang."

But they already had him hooked up and loaded in the back of their rig.

"We've got him," Sam Bradford told them. "You guys hold things together here and we'll head back over after we dump him off."

"Do *not* call my sisters!" Conner yelled to them as Sam and Kevin Campbell slammed the back doors of the ambulance.

Ryan and Cody turned to look at each other.

"Do we call them?" Ryan asked.

"Hell if I know," Cody said. "You're engaged to one of them. Will you be in bigger trouble with Conner for telling or Amanda for not telling?"

Ryan groaned and pulled his phone out. "Hey, babe," he said a minute later. "I have to tell you something about your brother."

Cody chuckled. Ryan was damned if he did and damned if he didn't. That sucked.

Then the air lodged in his chest and he had to cough to breathe again.

Wasn't he in exactly the same spot?

This had most definitely been a long damned day.

Olivia was at Fire House Three when the guys got back. She was always there when they came back from a big call, if she could be. Occasionally, of course, they had calls in the middle of the night that she wasn't aware of until the next day. But since she'd gotten the emergency scanner that sat on her bedside table three months ago, she hadn't missed one.

She liked having the lights on and the place smelling like comfort food when they got back. Even before she'd gotten to know the guys individually, she'd admired and respected what these guys did for a living. It was the least she could do to have soup or lasagna or a chicken casserole ready for them when they got back.

Now that she knew them better one-on-one, she was aware that her tendency to mother them was met with various reactions. Some found it sweet and amusing. One guy—Frank, a tough, grumpy, older guy who didn't like *anyone*—felt she was babying them all. Of course, he was usually the first to come back for seconds on her cooking. And then there were the vast majority of the young, single guys who apparently found it sexy that she would cook for them and take care of them.

She'd been happily unaware of it until Cody had taken two by the fronts of their shirts—at the same time—pushed them up against the wall and told them they were eating frozen burritos for a week until they could learn how to properly appreciate her efforts to help them out.

Then he'd told her to stop doing it.

She hadn't, of course, but since then Cody had hung around longer and closer than he had before.

Not that he needed to. Having Cody tell them to back off had been enough. None of the men, even grumpy old Frank, did anything other than smile and ask her how she was and compliment her food now.

It was a little irritating. Some of the younger guys were cute, and flirting with them had been fun. She hadn't for a moment worried that any of them would do anything that would make her uncomfortable. But she knew that Cody's warning had been effective not because he was their boss, but because it had been very clear that he would have gladly pounded anyone who didn't listen.

"You didn't eat very much," she said, stepping through the door to Cody's office without knocking.

He'd come straight over to her when he arrived at the fire house and asked if she'd talked to Amanda. She had, of course. She knew that Cody had pulled Conner out of a burning building and that Conner was at St. A's with a concussion and a bloody leg—that had somehow not broken. However, they were most concerned about the dust and smoke he'd inhaled. They were keeping him overnight, but he was going to be fine.

She would go over, of course. But Amanda and their mother were there now. There was only so much female fussing that Conner would tolerate at a time.

"I'm not very hungry."

Cody was sitting in front of his computer. He'd been scowling when she walked in.

She set a plate of cornbread on his desk near his elbow. Maybe he hadn't been hungry for the chili she'd made, but this was his favorite cornbread. It was his recipe.

"You're avoiding me."

He looked up at her, then sighed. "Yes."

"Because of what happened in my kitchen?"

She knew what he was going to say before he answered, but she *hated* that he was going to say yes.

He leaned back, resting his linked hands on his stomach. "Yes."

"And because my brother almost died today."

The flinch was slight but she saw it. Her own heart clenched when she thought about that, but she was simply going off of what everyone had told her about what had happened to Conner. Cody had seen it.

"Ryan said you went in after him. Without even thinking about it."

"They would have gotten him out if I hadn't."

"I knew you were the one who went in after him even before they told me." She hadn't known anything more than it was a fire until Amanda had called. Amanda said Conner had been trapped in the building and they'd had to go in after him.

Olivia had known that Cody had been the first one through the door.

Cody took a deep breath, then let it out. "Of course I was the one who went in."

She swallowed hard. She had to tell him the conclusion she'd come to. "I'm glad it was you. Because I know that was the only way you and Conner were okay. And I don't mean physically," she said when he looked like he was about to respond. "I mean that *you* were only okay emotionally if you could be right there with him and see him and talk to him. And I know that Conner was relieved when he heard you coming for him. As soon as he knew it was you, it comforted him. Because he trusts you. He trusts that you will do anything for him. And knowing that he was comforted by that made me feel comforted."

She had been focused on Cody's chin as she talked, but when she lifted her gaze to meet his, she found him watching her intently.

"So, thank you," she added. "For being the guy that Conner can trust. The guy who will go into the building for him and to do whatever it takes to make sure he's safe and—" Her voice cracked slightly and she stopped. She pressed her lips together and blinked rapidly. When she could go on, she said, "That means a lot to me that my brother has someone like you."

She'd always appreciated and enjoyed her brother's friends, but Conner was the kind of guy to have lots of friends, lots of people who liked being around him. He was friendly and funny and smart and trustworthy—and a whole bunch of other adjectives that made him someone everyone liked.

But she'd never really thought about what his close friendships meant to him.

Olivia didn't have many girlfriends. Her sisters were her best friends, and she had inherited friendships with the guys who were Conner's friends and were now her sisters' fiancés. She took those relationships for granted. Had anyone asked her *Does your brother have people he can depend on?* she wouldn't have hesitated to say yes.

But today, she knew how much it meant to *her* to have people who cared about her brother and had his back.

"I can't mess that up, Cody."

He didn't reply immediately, but finally he nodded. "I understand."

Had she not been worked up about her brother's accident, she might have been irritated that he didn't try to argue. But it was for the best.

"Okay, so…" She started to turn away, at a loss for words with Cody for the first time in nearly a year. They always had plenty to talk about. She was more comfortable with him than almost anyone. She pivoted to face him again though. "Thank you for telling me the story today. And don't forget that you *are* the guy Conner wanted you to be back then. You're…awesome."

He gave her a single nod.

She let herself out of his office, closing the door behind her. Having him avoid her for a bit sounded good.

She went straight to her computer and logged on.

Cody Madsen was awesome…but he clearly wasn't her soul mate.

Or, if he was, she needed him to be her brother's friend even more.

She logged in to the Perfect Pick website and found five matches and suggested dates waiting for her.

There was a ninety-eight percent match.

She stared at it.

There he was—the guy who was even more perfect for her than Cody.

She'd never thought she'd see that.

With a deep breath, she hit the Accept button.

Two nights later, when Olivia looked up from her Coke at the bar at Cliff's, she realized she wasn't all that surprised to see Cody walk through the door.

He must have seen her through the window because his steps didn't falter as he made his way across the restaurant to her.

"Did you change your profile and user name?" she asked as he came near.

He nodded.

Well, of course.

She sighed.

"Are you telling me that you're Miss Ninety-Eight Percent?" he asked with a grin.

"Who else could it be?" she asked. She pivoted back to face the bar as Cody claimed the stool next to her.

"Tequila?" the bartender, the same one from the last night they'd been here, asked.

"No!" they both said quickly.

He smiled and refilled Olivia's soda.

"I'll take a beer," Cody told him.

Olivia's head spun as the bartender opened a bottle of imported beer for Cody. Here they were again. Matched up. *Again*. A ninety-eight percent compatible match.

The odds of that were astronomical.

This was unbelievable.

She'd gone back in to her profile and changed some key things, thinking that would make it less likely she and Cody might get matched again. Just in case.

She'd thought about switching dating sites entirely, but Perfect Pick was the only one that offered the blind date option and she really liked that. She liked the idea of being matched up based on personality and similarities first. Lord knew she made bad decisions when it came to basing relationships on feelings— like love and desire.

And Cody was her perfect match anyway.

Even more so now that she'd changed her profile under *Do you want kids?* from *maybe* to *definitely* and *Do you believe in soul mates?* from *definitely* to *maybe*.

Moving from *maybe* to *definitely* didn't seem like a huge change, but on those two questions it was. Definitely.

It was true that she'd been all in for this after their first setup.

It made her nervous, but fate, destiny or good old dumb luck had brought Cody into her life. She'd be stupid not to be thrilled about that…and want to do something about it.

Then Conner had fallen into a hole.

The day she'd decided to go for it with Cody.

That sounded so stupid, but it was the truth.

Some people might say it was a sign. She didn't care one way or the other. The truth was, their setup had prompted her to push for the story of Cody and Conner's history. Which had sparked her protective instinct for Cody. Which had prompted her to take off her clothes and plop herself down on his lap. Which had prompted a whole bunch of delicious things that had nothing to do with cake batter.

If Conner had fallen into that hole and Cody had pulled him out *before* she'd known what had happened between them and before she'd felt that surge of emotion that made her want to take care of Cody and make sure he was happy, she might not be so convinced that she needed to leave him alone.

But part of Cody being happy was having a friendship with Conner.

Cody needed to know that he was good enough, that he had changed, that he could be forgiven and trusted.

Him going down into that hole had been as good for him as it had been for Conner.

Whether or not the whole burning-building-the-day-she-finally-made-out-with-Cody was a sign from the universe, she didn't know. But it had put front and center how much *she* cared about the relationship between Cody and Conner.

It was even more important to her that Conner and Cody have their bond than it was for her to have anything more than a friendship with Cody.

And now here he was, her ninety-eight percent match, her Perfect Pick for the second time.

Damn, Fate was a bitch.

"You know, I get it, but your continued obvious disappointment about being set up with me is starting to sting."

"Well, this sucks."

"Seriously, babe, my ego's in good shape. No need to keep me in check."

She turned to face him. "Seriously, babe," she repeated. "This is not good."

"Maybe it's just a funny coincidence," he said, clearly trying to keep things light.

"Really, Cody?" she demanded. "Or maybe it's proof that I'll never find anyone I can be deliriously happy with." Or that she'd never find anyone *other than him*.

He finally turned to her, his light, joking expression now a frown. "You were pretty frickin' deliriously happy the other day on my lap."

Heat flooded through her. *Deliriously happy* wasn't quite right. It wasn't quite *enough*. But it was very, very close.

"Exactly," she said, rather than deny what they both knew was true. "I can be deliriously happy with *you*. Except for the fact that it would ruin an incredibly important relationship for both of us. I know that my sisters are right and that Conner shouldn't make my decisions for me, but *I'm* making this decision. You are too important to him for me to take you away. And his trust is too important to you for me to take that away."

Cody leaned in, and she could see in his eyes that he was completely serious now. "Liv, I let you walk out of my office the other night because it was an emotional night for both of us, and it was easier. We both know that I like do things the easy way. But that doesn't mean I don't know how to do things the hard way."

He reached for her, cupped the back of her head and pulled her to his mouth.

Her reaction was instantaneous. She'd talked herself into believing this was never going to happen again and that she'd be fine, but as she gripped his shoulders and opened her mouth she realized she was an idiot.

How could she ever be fine without this? Without him?

He kissed her like he'd been starving for her. His lips were firm, his tongue possessive, his hand holding her without any chance of escape. As if she'd want to escape. Ever.

She was sizzling and stunned by the time he finally pulled back.

She swallowed hard at the look in his eyes. It was greedy and hot and she loved it.

He stared into her eyes. "Glass not plastic," he muttered, almost to himself.

Olivia blinked. Then repeated the words in her head. Nope, still didn't make sense. "What?"

"Just a reminder to myself." He tossed a few bills onto the bar, took her hand and tugged her from her barstool.

"Where are we going?" she asked as she tried to follow his long strides with her three-inch heels and short legs.

"I think you know the answer to that." He shoved the door of the restaurant open and stalked out onto the sidewalk. He barely paused at the curb before he crossed the street against the light.

Olivia knew exactly where they were headed. To the Britton Hotel.

It was the nicest hotel in the city, and it was directly in front of them.

Her stomach swooped as her heart thudded in her chest.

Conner needed him. She knew that. But in that moment she also knew that there was no way Conner needed Cody more than she did.

She couldn't trust herself maybe, but she could trust fate. Surely. And if not fate, then an objective computer system that knew nothing about her past or what her heart and libido were feeling, a computer that would match her up with the right guy for the right reasons. "*Yes,*" she murmured.

But he heard her. He stopped on the sidewalk in front of the

Britton and swung to face her. He was breathing a little harder than a walk across the street should cause, and the look in his eyes held a myriad of emotion. But one stood out from the rest—determination.

He suddenly tugged her forward, one big hand going to the back of her neck, and again kissed her senseless.

When they parted, she said breathlessly, "I could get used to that."

His jaw tightened as if he was fighting saying or doing something. He abruptly pivoted and pushed through the rotating door, dragging her after him.

Olivia barely paid attention to anything Cody said to the woman behind the front desk. She heard "suite" and "just one night" but other than that her mind was too busy swirling with what was happening and what was about to happen.

She was going to make love to Cody. He was going to make love to her. She was going to have sex. With Cody. For the first time.

With *Cody*.

She actually shivered from excitement. Every nerve ending was jumping and popping, like fireworks were going off throughout her body and she was having trouble standing still.

She knew all about sex. Her sisters were very forthcoming with information, and Olivia was a naturally curious person. She'd read extensively, listened keenly and never once shied away from visiting Tease, the lingerie and adult toy shop downtown, with her sisters.

And what she knew best was that she had been waiting for *this* with *this* man her entire life.

Finally the front desk attendant handed over key cards and Cody headed for the elevators.

She almost had to jog to keep up with him.

That made her want to laugh with joy. Cody Madsen could have any woman he wanted—had had many. But right now he was almost as eager to get upstairs to a hotel room as she was. Almost. No one could possibly be as excited as she was.

Cody punched the button for the twentieth floor, and the moment the elevator doors swished shut, Olivia turned to him. He'd done a lot of kissing her tonight so far. It was time she kissed him.

He faced her, but looked hesitant for a moment. Did he think she was changing her mind?

Then his expression turned to one of resolve. "I always do things the easy way, Liv," he said, his voice rough. "Always. I'm not good with facing consequences or making apologies. I have almost zero experience with either thing when it comes to my relationships."

"Co—"

"But," he went on, "for once in my life, with you, I want to do things the hard way. I want to go in knowing there will be consequences and that I'm ready to face them. Because, babe, there's no way in hell I will ever apologize for this."

OLIVIA WANTED TO CRY. She wanted to tell him she loved him. She wanted to deny that this could be anything other than perfect.

Instead of any of those, she pulled him close and stretched onto her tiptoes. "The harder the better."

She kissed him, absorbing his groan, relishing the feel of his hands gripping her hips and pulling her against him, the hunger in his kiss. She meant it. Yes, this was going to be complicated. They might both have a few regrets. But there was no stopping this now.

The kiss was as hot as the ones before, but sweeter, not as frenzied, not as desperate. This kiss said they were both here, now, in this moment for better or worse.

The elevator arrived at their floor and they reluctantly parted. The suite was at the end of a long hallway, and they hurried toward the door without talking.

She'd worn the peach-colored dress Amanda had initially approved. It had made her feel feminine versus seriously sexy, and that had been, she'd assumed, perfect for meeting her ninety-eight percent match. She'd had no intentions of having this dress end up on a bedroom floor tonight.

How wrong she'd been.

As Cody fumbled with the key card, Olivia slipped her heels off.

Cody was dressed up again too, though had left the tie at home. Still, it was obvious that he'd approached tonight's date seriously, and suddenly Olivia was hit with a wave of jealousy. Another woman might notice how good he looked—okay, she *would* notice how good he looked—but she wouldn't *appreciate* how good he looked. Only Olivia knew how much he hated dress shirts.

Finally the door swung open. She started to step forward, but Cody turned and picked her up, putting her over his shoulder.

She giggled even as her blood heated. It was a very caveman move and she loved it.

He kicked the door shut behind them, then turned to face it, pulling her down the front of his body, every inch of her sliding against every inch of him. She wrapped her legs around his waist and her arms around his neck, hanging on, memorizing the feel of his hard body against her.

"I've imagined this so many fucking times," Cody muttered. "I can't make it one more step."

"*Good.*" She started unbuttoning his shirt as he reached for the zipper on the back of her dress.

He let her feet touch the floor so he could push her dress off before going for the front closure to her bra. "I have to have you now."

Her nipples beaded from his words and the heat in his gaze as her bra fell away.

Cody groaned. "I'll do anything you want. Give you anything. However you want it."

Oh, that was a long menu. She knew it would shock him. She couldn't wait. Then he unzipped his pants and dropped them to the floor. Okay, she could wait a little bit.

She might be a technical virgin, but she was very aware what the ache between her legs meant and how to relieve it.

"You," she simply. "That's all I want."

He toed off his shoes, yanked off his socks and kicked out of his pants.

Then they were down to their underwear only.

"Those are in my way," he said, eyeing the silky, peach-colored panties she wore.

She'd completely forgotten about undressing as he slid his boxers off and reached into his pants pocket for a condom.

He'd seen her naked, but she'd never seen him before.

And wow, what a view. She needed a minute.

He was big and thick and hard. Very hard. And big. And thick.

She licked her lips. She wanted to taste him, feel him against her tongue, make him moan as she sucked…

"Liv." Cody's groan pulled her gaze to his.

"What?"

"That look on your face is going to make this go even faster."

She grinned and hooked her thumbs in the elastic of her panties. "Can't help it."

But she had no more time to appreciate the view. As her panties dropped to the floor, he pressed her up against the door, kissing her like he'd never get enough. His hands were all over her—at her hips, her waist, down the outside of her thighs, over her ribs, cupping her breasts. He teased her nipples, plucking and squeezing, and she felt the sparks streak from there to her clit, the ache between her legs building rapidly.

He let go of her only long enough to sheath himself with a condom. Then his big hands were back on her, touching every-where at once, it seemed.

Olivia could only hang on.

Her fingers dug into his shoulders as he lifted her against the door. She wrapped her legs around his waist, the tip of his cock sliding between her hot folds. She was ready for him. So ready.

"God, Liv. I feel like I've been waiting forever for this."

She knew what he meant. "Me too."

He pressed forward, sliding a few inches in. It was the closest she'd ever been to anyone, and the fact that it was Cody made tears well up.

This was how it was supposed to be. Someone who cared about her, someone she loved and totally trusted.

Cody stopped, panting. "Damn, you're so tight."

He gritted his teeth, like he was trying for restraint, and pressed again.

Olivia's body adjusted slowly, taking him in. The stretching wasn't entirely new, but the heat and friction of real human flesh —even inside latex—versus plastic made her catch her breath.

It was a snug fit but her muscles softened, the wet heat letting him sink further and further.

It didn't hurt. There was an ache, but it was more an ache of *need* than of pain. An ache like hunger or thirst.

She tried to move, knowing that he had to be deeper to touch the place she most needed him, but pinned to the door with her legs around his hips, she was at his mercy.

"So good," he said tightly. "You're squeezing me so good. You feel so fucking good." He pulled out and pressed in again. It was a few centimeters at best, but he groaned. "I want you to feel every inch. Take me, Liv."

The sexy crooning made her squirm, wanting to press closer, or pull him deeper, or something.

She wanted to. She wanted all of him. "Cody," she gasped.

"You're killing me." He thrust again. "I want all of you. I want you screaming my name, begging me to take you. I want you losing your mind as I touch every hot, wet inch inside you."

The dirty talk definitely worked. She felt a swirl of desire twist through her pelvis, her inner muscles clamping down on him.

He groaned. "I need all in." He turned swiftly, her butt

cradled in his hands. Without losing contact, he lowered them both to the floor.

Olivia was on her back, but he knelt between her legs, his hands still under her butt and her hips off the floor.

"Open up, sweetheart. Let me in."

She unlocked her ankles from behind him and Cody spread her thighs wide, resting her legs on his upper thighs. He looked down at where they were joined as he pressed in, pulled out and pressed in again, sinking deeper.

"Hottest fucking thing I've ever seen," he said gruffly. He lifted his gaze to hers. "Perfect."

Then he thrust into her, burying himself deep.

The plunge pulled a cry from her, but it was more surprise than anything. It didn't hurt. Exactly. She felt so...full. And spread so wide.

Then he pulled out, the drag against her inner walls delicious, making her moan. When he drove in again, it was even deeper and he hit *that spot*. The one that made pleasure streak through her body.

Her fingers curled into the carpet on either side. She couldn't reach to touch him where he was kneeling tall between her knees. She did, however, have a fantastic view of his chest and abs clenching as he thrust, the light trail of hair leading to where they were joined. She could also see where he was driving in and out of her. The sight alone was enough to make her hotter and wetter. She whimpered softly as he hit that magical spot again and again.

Then he reached out and dragged his thumb over her clit.

"Cody," she moaned.

"I've always thought you were beautiful, Liv, but I swear this is the most gorgeous sight—you spread out, taking me over and over, all mine." He thrust deep. "All mine," he repeated huskily.

The voice—that ragged, raspy voice—and the word *mine* were enough to pull another moan from her, and she felt her entire lower body tightening and clenching.

"More," she begged softly.

"Anything, Liv," he said. "Anything."

"Harder. Deeper." She wasn't sure, actually. Her head thrashed against the floor. She'd had orgasms. She knew how this worked. She could make herself come quickly, actually—often thinking of the man who was now between her legs. For some reason, though, this climb was slow. When she was alone she could focus completely on hitting the right spots, staying there, letting it build up and sweep over her. Now there was almost too much stimulation, too much going on. The glorious sight of Cody's naked body, the feel of him filling her up, the dirty talk, the—everything. It was too much.

Cody took the *harder* and *deeper* to heart though. He spread her knees apart even further, and his thrusts increased in depth and speed.

It was all so good. Olivia put her head back, closed her eyes and let the sensations wash over her.

She felt him everywhere, and he continued to thrust hard and fast until he seemed to almost swell inside her.

"Liv, Liv," he panted. Then he shouted, "Yes!"

He paused, seemingly frozen in place, buried deep. She felt the heat increase between them and her eyes flew open. His expression was one of pure bliss, his eyes shut, his mouth open as he pulled in deep breaths.

Finally, he fell forward, catching himself on his hands on either side of her. He leaned in and captured her lips with a tender kiss, and she put her arms around his neck, kissing him back with all of the things she felt for him and the sheer joy of finally having this with him.

He let himself down on his side next to her and pulled her in close. She turned in to him, hugging him close. "Thank you," she said, kissing his chest. "Thank you, thank you."

He chuckled, running his hand up and down her back. "Unbelievable. I should have known it would be."

She snuggled close, her cheek against his chest. In this position, she was facing his soft, condomless cock. She wasn't sure how he'd taken care of the condom so quickly and easily and didn't want to think about how it was as if he'd done it a lot.

It was still big. And long. And she again had the urge to take him in her mouth.

She wanted to explore his whole body. She wanted to just stare at him.

Cody was in amazing shape. Firefighting demanded it, as did football. His regular workouts for both showed in the perfect definition of his shoulders, chest, abs, butt and thighs. She didn't know where to touch him first.

She rubbed her hand back and forth over his hard abs from one side to the other. The muscles jumped under her touch. She could trace the contours, and she felt heat and pressure start to build between her legs from even that much touching. She changed directions then, moving up and down, inching closer to his cock.

"Liv."

His voice rumbled in his chest under her cheek.

"What?"

"What are you doing?"

"Enjoying the view."

She ran her hand lower, over the head of his cock.

He sucked in a quick breath. "Liv."

"Let me touch you," she said without lifting her head.

He didn't say anything or move. She wondered if he was holding his breath. Just in case, she didn't waste any time in running her hand over his length. The flesh swelled under her hand. She smiled. She loved the feeling of power that coursed through her. He wanted her.

She dragged her hand up and down again, then curled her fingers around his girth.

A long breath hissed from Cody, but she didn't stop or look up. She squeezed gently, then drew her hand up and down. His cock responded, hardening and lengthening.

Then she moved, sliding down his torso until her lips were close to the broad head.

She flicked out her tongue, barely brushing the tip.

"Fuck." Cody's voice sounded pained.

But she knew better.

She knew this man. She loved this man. Giving him pleasure was addictive.

She licked again, like licking an ice cream cone, swirling around the end. He tasted better than any ice cream she'd ever had in her life.

She felt his fingers tangle in her hair, and it turned her on immensely. She opened her mouth, taking more of him. Her hand stroked the length that she couldn't fully take in her mouth.

"Holy… Liv… Jesus…" Cody chanted.

She slid her mouth up and down, then sucked hard.

His hips bucked and his grip on her hair tightened almost painfully.

"I can't take it," he rasped. "I can't believe it, but I need you again, already."

She lifted her head, loving the look of his cock, now hard and shiny from her mouth. "Let me do this."

"No. Now."

Without warning, he sat up, turning her onto her stomach.

His hand rubbed over her ass as he moved behind her, then pulled her onto her hands and knees.

The way he took charge surprised her and made her hot. Cody was easygoing with her. He was sweet, considerate, always let her make the decisions. But now he was commanding, handling her possessively, talking to her with pure emotion.

"I will never get enough of you," he muttered, pressing his belly against her butt.

He reached around with one hand to find her clit, while his knees moved hers farther apart. He rubbed over her clit, then dipped into her. She was wet and hot and excited and a bit nervous about this position.

"I can't wait to lick you after you come again," he told her.

She felt him moving behind her and heard the sound of a condom wrapper tearing. Should she tell him she hadn't come the first time?

Then he was back in position, one hand on her hip and one guiding his cock into her.

Talking was overrated.

When he thrust into her, all she could think was nothing mattered but this. Him being a part of her, him wanting her so much, him claiming her. She would never have guessed that Cody could be so dominating—or that she'd like it so much.

"Heaven," he said, stroking deep and sure. "Absolute heaven."

He ran a hand up and down her back, squeezing her ass, then trailing around to pinch her nipples.

Olivia felt the familiar clenching start, the tightening deep inside where she wanted to hold Cody forever. But the climb was again slow. His strokes were steady, hitting her spot perfectly each time, moving her higher and closer to climax, but it felt too far off. She really wanted to come this time. She wanted to suck him in. She wanted to clamp down on him so he could barely move in and out.

She knew exactly how to get there. She dropped her head, her hair falling forward, and reached between her legs to circle her clit. Cody was right there, thrusting, and she quickly felt the spiraling of an orgasm.

"*Liv*," he groaned. "Yes, that makes you tighten up even more." He thrust a few more times. "Taste yourself," he encouraged breathlessly.

His words made heat wash over her, and she lifted her hand to her mouth.

"Suck on your fingers."

She did, tasting herself, imagining Cody's tongue on her.

"Cody," she gasped, dropping her hand to the floor to brace herself as he thrust faster.

"I've wanted you like this for so long, but I never imagined how hot it would really be," he told her, gathering her hair in one hand and tipping her head back. "I want to do you all night, in every position. I want to break a table and knock over a lamp."

It wasn't even specifically hot or sexy phrases or words, but the images he put into her mind made her drop her upper body to the floor, her ass up higher to take him.

"Holy…*Liv.*"

And he came, hard and fast, driving into her like he was possessed.

He slumped forward over her back, then tucked her to his stomach and rolled, spooning with her on the floor.

She worked to take deep breaths, her whole body tingling.

Cody's orgasms with her were almost as good as having one of her own.

They lay together for several minutes. Cody absently stroked her hip, his breathing slowing.

Finally he said, "So maybe we should try out the bed."

She chuckled. "There's a bed?"

He rolled to his back and stretched, groaning in satisfaction. "I might have to check in for a couple of days to recover."

She rolled to face him. He was gorgeous. His dark hair was rumpled now and he wore a goofy, relaxed smile.

She was in love.

But there was a problem.

She couldn't seem to have an orgasm.

Her phone started to ring.

She glanced around for a clock and finally located one over the desk.

"You need to get that?"

"It's Emma calling to save me."

"Save you?" He propped up on one elbow.

"From my blind date. We had a deal that if she didn't get a text from me by eight, she'd call with a reason for me to escape."

He grinned and reached out, twirling a strand of her hair around his finger. "You gonna tell her that you're fine?"

She was more than fine. But… "I hadn't planned on staying out all night even if the date was going well," she said. Definitely not with her Perfect Pick date, no matter if he was a ninety-eight percent match or not. "It's sister slumber party tonight." She pushed to her feet and headed for her clothes.

Right now he was feeling good and cocky, but if she stayed around, he'd eventually figure out that she wasn't quite *there*. Or she'd have to start faking it. She wasn't sure she could pull that off. She needed some sisterly advice. She needed to decide if she needed to do something different or tell Cody about it or…

"Sister slumber party?"

She paused in pulling her clothes on, glancing at him and feeling desire hit her again hard. What were they talking about? "It's rare when all the guys are working at night, but once in a while it happens and we do a slumber party. Shane's got the night shift tonight at the police station, Ryan agreed to cover a couple of the guys on Sam Bradford's crew and Nate got called in for an emergency surgery that's going to take several hours."

"But *I'm* not working tonight."

The sexy tone in his voice made her tingle. He was grinning at her, and she was so tempted to strip down and do it all again.

But no. She needed to figure out what was she was doing wrong. Because, dammit, sex with her and Cody was supposed to be perfect. Like everything else.

And if it wasn't…what did that mean? Sex was a big deal in a relationship. She couldn't fake it forever, and she didn't *want* to fake it forever. If she and Cody couldn't set off the fireworks she knew were possible, did that mean he really wasn't the perfect guy for her?

She slipped her shoes on, carefully not looking at that grin or that body or, most of all, those eyes—those beautiful, espresso-brown eyes. He'd know something was wrong and she'd never get out of here. "I'll talk to you tomorrow," she said.

She pulled the door open and started to step through when Cody said, "Liv?"

She steeled herself and turned back. "Yeah?"

"I'm becoming a big fan of destiny."

She sucked in a quick breath. Destiny. Could he be her destiny without fireworks?

Looking at him now, she couldn't imagine him *not* being the one. She was just going to have to do something about the fireworks. And she had three very good resources to help her. If she could get out of here.

Forcing a smile, she nodded. "Destiny is a big deal."

He smiled tenderly. "I'm glad you're mine."

She stumbled over some silly words like "later" and "had fun", then turned and fled.

"Maybe I've been using my vibrators *too* much," Olivia mused.

Amanda choked on her drink. "What?"

Olivia looked over at her, completely serious. "It's not the same kind of thing, you know? Maybe my body and brain are so used to *that* kind of orgasm that the other kinds are too hard."

"Honey, you and Cody have known each other a long time, but not like this. It takes time to learn another person, to figure out what make them tick. Even in the bedroom," Isabelle said.

"So you had problems having orgasms with Shane in the beginning?" Olivia asked, knowing that was not at all the case.

"Well, um…" Isabelle looked at the other girls. "No. But…"

"Shane was better at it than Cody?" Olivia asked. "You think Shane is a better lover?" She was aware that she sounded incredibly defensive. And *she* was the one who had told them that things hadn't worked.

Isabelle gave her a wide-eyed look. "That's not what I'm saying at all."

"Then what are you saying?" Olivia knew she was riled up, but this was a big deal. Wasn't it? Maybe not. Maybe her sisters could convince her this was going to be okay.

"I'm simply saying maybe you need more time together," Isabelle said.

"More sex?" Olivia asked.

"Maybe." Isabelle didn't look entirely sure on that though.

Olivia turned to Emma. "What do you think?"

"I think I'm feeling really sorry for Cody." Emma was sitting in the chair perpendicular to them, with her feet up on the coffee table.

"Why Cody?" Olivia asked. "*He* had a great time."

Emma grinned. "I'm sure. I'm saying that you had really high expectations."

"My vibrator is too big?"

This time Amanda did spit some of her mojito out. She covered her mouth. "Sorry."

Emma's grin grew. "I wasn't talking about the size of things, Liv. I was talking about the fireworks thing you keep mentioning. You had sex built up to be this amazing thing. You had Cody built up to be this amazing thing. You put them together expecting…dynamite. It's going to be *really* hard for anything to measure up to that, you know?"

"Sex isn't amazing?" Olivia demanded. Emma had been the most active of them all before she got together with Nate, and now, whenever the two of them were within five feet of each other, the temperature in the room went up.

"Sex is amazing," her sister said with a nod.

"And having sex with the person you love and trust most isn't amazing?"

"Sex with the right person *is* amazing."

"So Cody's not the right person?"

Emma rolled her eyes. "You're not the dramatic one, Liv. You're the sweet, quiet, optimist."

Suddenly all of her indignation left her. Olivia slumped back into the love seat. "I know."

"Don't overreact," Isabelle said. She stood and went to Olivia's desk, grabbing her laptop. "You can have orgasms with a vibrator. So use it *with* Cody."

"Toys with a partner can be really fun," Emma agreed. "He won't mind."

"You sure?" Olivia asked. "What if he's offended that he can't be…enough?"

Emma shrugged. "I think he'll want you to have a good time, and he wants it to be with him. I'm sure he'll go for whatever it takes."

Olivia sat up a little straighter. "Hey, that's true. It might be me. I've never tried this with anyone else. Maybe I can't have an orgasm with *anyone*."

Isabelle looked up from where she was typing on the laptop. "You sound almost excited about that possibility."

She was, Olivia acknowledged. "If it's *me*, if I can't do that with *anyone*, then that doesn't mean Cody's not my soul mate. There's no other guy out there who's more my match, because I wouldn't be able to do that with anyone."

It was a strange thing to be relieved over the possibility that she might never be able to have an orgasm with a partner.

"Okay, it says here that some people feel you can become desensitized to other stimulation by using a vibrator a lot," Isabelle said. "Apparently, your brain can become trained to react to a specific stimulation and it dulls the ability to react to others." She looked up. "Not everyone agrees that it can happen, but some sex counselors say that it's possible."

"Does it say what to do about it?" Olivia asked, leaning forward. Her optimism was returning.

"Stop using it for a while," Isabelle read. "Or yes, use it with him. Or use it to show him what you like."

"No man can reproduce those vibrations," Emma said. "No matter who he is."

"There are cock rings," Isabelle said.

Olivia looked at her. "Huh?"

"It's a vibrator, but he wears it. Then you get both things—him and the vibration."

"That might work," Emma said, studying Olivia as if they were trying to figure out how to do her hair or if her eye makeup was working. "We could go to Tease tonight."

"What about foreplay?" Isabelle asked Emma. "She said it was hot and spontaneous. Maybe he didn't spend enough time getting her ready."

Emma turned to Isabelle. "That could be. It was unexpected for her. She wasn't in the zone. Maybe *she* needs to be the seducer. Then she'll be mentally in the right place."

Isabelle set the laptop to the side. "It would also give her a sense of control. That might be important as a virgin. She hasn't gotten to the place where it's easy to let go."

"That's possible," Emma said. "Or," she said with a shrug, "maybe all of the other women who have been with Cody have been faking it."

"Hey!" Olivia sat up straighter. She was used to her sisters talking around her or about her when she was sitting right there, but nobody talked negatively about Cody. "I'm sure all of the other women had screaming orgasms and were ready to beg him for more."

All of her sisters looked at her at once. Emma was the first to snort, but soon Isabelle and Amanda were laughing too.

"Does it seem strange that you *want* Cody to have been pleasuring women throughout the greater metropolitan area?" Emma asked her.

Olivia thought about that. Then she grinned too. "Okay, maybe that's weird." But she'd heard the talk at Trudy's. Women loved Cody. They wanted Cody. The ones who had been with him were quite happy about it and wanted more.

Amanda leaned forward and took her hand. "Can I ask you something?"

Olivia nodded.

"Did you tell him what you wanted? Did you show him how you like things or how to get things going?"

Olivia looked at her sister and thought about her questions. "Do guys not know that stuff?"

Amanda grinned. "All women are different, Liv. You have to help the guy out a little."

Olivia covered her eyes with her hands and tipped her head back. "This is complicated."

All her sisters laughed.

"But worth it," Emma said.

Olivia dropped her hands. "You tell Nate what you want?"

Emma's cheeks got pink. Olivia loved that. Nate and conversations about Nate were the only things she had ever seen cause Emma Dixon to blush.

"Come on, tell her," Isabelle said, nudging Emma's foot.

"Nate makes me tell him," Emma told her. "He loves to hear it."

Isabelle nodded. "Shane too. Especially with some of the pain issues I have, he encourages me to talk about all of that."

"Ryan likes it too," Amanda agreed. "I'm not saying he needs the help all the time, but he's completely fine with me telling him what I want and if I need something different."

Olivia felt her own cheeks heat. In her kitchen the other day, she'd asked him to play with her nipples. And he had. And she'd had an orgasm that day on his lap.

He'd played with her nipples last night too and it had helped move her closer…but not all the way. Still…

"Okay, I need to set up a seduction," she decided. Everything her sisters had said made sense. She needed to get in the zone. "Once I make this work, it'll get easier to be spontaneous. We need to figure each other out."

"There's our resident Suzy Sunshine," Isabelle said, lifting her glass. "Glad to have you back."

"There's just one thing," Olivia said.

They all focused on her. She looked at the three women she loved and trusted and who had love and sex lives that she wanted to emulate.

"I'm going to need some pointers. I've never seduced anyone before."

Emma, Amanda and Isabelle grinned at one another.

"I think we can help you out with that," Isabelle said.

"Cody's not going to know what hit him," Emma added.

CHAPTER
SEVEN

CODY KNEW EXACTLY who had hit him.

He got up from the ground slowly. Damn, that hurt. Lawrence Travis was a big guy and he was a great tackle. Not great enough to bring Cody down. Usually. But great against most opponents.

"How many times are you gonna let him take you down?" Ryan asked.

Cody didn't answer. Probably every time he got the ball today. His head was not into practice.

"Let's run it again," Conner said, his frustration clear as the guys huddled up. Because of his injuries from the fire, they weren't letting him do much and it was making him crazy. Cody's inability to hang onto the ball wasn't helping.

"Yeah, run it again!" Travis shouted before chuckling loudly. "Love that play."

"Hey, Madsen, think you can keep your ass off the grass for a play or two?" Conner asked.

"I'm tryin', man. It's a bad day."

He wasn't really trying at all. He didn't want to be at practice. Just like he hadn't wanted to be at work all day.

Olivia had called in sick today, and his stomach had been in knots ever since he'd heard the message.

She wasn't sick. He knew it.

She was avoiding him.

They'd finally had sex and now she was avoiding him. That was fan-fucking-tastic.

He'd stormed over to her house as soon as he'd had a break at work, but she hadn't been home. Probably because she wasn't sick and was avoiding him and knew him well enough to know that he'd be on her doorstep as soon as he heard she was sick.

He would have headed over to check on her even if she *had* been sick. But avoiding him wasn't going to fly. For one, they were friends, and they were now lovers. As in, it was going to happen again, and it was going to keep happening.

For another, she didn't have enough time off built up to keep calling in to work indefinitely.

And if she thought she was going to find a new job... Well, she wasn't going to find a new job.

Once he'd realized she wasn't home, he'd contemplated which of her sisters was letting her hide out at her place. Since all three were possible, he'd decided to go alphabetically and had been on his way to Amanda and Ryan's place when he'd gotten a work call.

He'd been busy at a car accident all morning, and then he'd had to do a presentation at one of the elementary schools that afternoon.

Then practice.

"Fine." Conner clearly didn't think it was fine.

Conner was a fun-loving guy, laid-back for the most part. Unless it had to do with football or his sisters.

Cody sighed. He was messing with Conner on both counts—even if Conner didn't know about Cody and Olivia yet.

But it was really Conner's fault. Once he'd said Olivia was

breakable and that it was up to Cody to find her the right guy, he'd known he would *never* be able to do that. Or let a computer do it. Because *he* was the right guy.

He'd messed up in the past—and would again. But no one would ever love Olivia like he did. No one could make him try to be a better man like she did. It wasn't perfect and Conner wasn't dead, but if she was breakable, then Cody was going to be the one protecting her.

The rest of practice went without a ball—or a tackle—coming to Cody. Thank God.

"Beers at Trudy's on me," Conner announced as they headed for the locker room.

Dammit. Cody bit back his protest. He wanted to find Olivia. He *would* find Olivia. He had to be sure she was all right, that last night had pushed them in the direction he thought it had, and that they could repeat last night tonight.

He was hungry for her. He'd slept horribly the night before, thinking and dreaming of her. Or maybe it had been the hotel bed. He'd stayed in the suite, in case she changed her mind. He'd awakened after only a couple of hours, groggy and grumpy.

She was supposed to have changed her mind. She could have slipped out of the slumber party after the other girls had fallen asleep. Or she could have told them, "Cody is naked in a suite at the Britton and I've got to go."

They would have understood.

There was only one Dixon who wouldn't. At all.

And he was offering to buy beer.

None of the Hawks said no to beer when Conner was buying. It didn't happen very often, for one thing. When it did, it meant that he felt the team needed some off-field time together. Conner was the leader of the team, no doubt, and he had an uncanny feel for the team and its players. He knew when something wasn't clicking, and he was always determined to get things back on track, no matter what.

Cody couldn't say no to Trudy's. It would be suspicious and it would piss Conner off. Especially since Cody had clearly not had his focus in practice.

But maybe Olivia would be there. He pulled his phone out as the guys headed to the showers. He quickly texted her about meeting at Trudy's, then showered and dressed.

Forty-five minutes later, she hadn't texted back and she wasn't at Trudy's.

But her sisters were.

He approached their regular booth, stopping slightly behind Emma, who was standing talking with Amanda and Isabelle, who were seated on the benches.

"She's not coming," Isabelle said. "I just talked to her."

"But she's okay?" Amanda asked.

"She said things are on track."

There was only one "she" they could be talking about. The she Cody was very interested in.

"She went to Tease," Emma said. "She texted me a picture."

Now he *really* hoped they were talking about Olivia.

"Good," Isabelle said. "She's going to use it tonight?"

Emma nodded. "Yep. She said she's having an orgasm tonight, and if Cody can't make it happen, then she will."

A rushing sound filled his ears. Then again, maybe they were talking about someone else. And another Cody.

"She's putting too much emphasis on the orgasm thing," Isabelle said. "She was a *virgin*. It will happen. I didn't have an orgasm when I lost my virginity."

"Me either," Amanda added.

"I did," Emma said. "But he was pretty experienced." She must have noticed her sisters' amazed looks. "What? I slept with Wade Morris five time and neither of us were virgins and I never had one."

"Really?" Isabelle asked. "With Wade? He's so..." She trailed off suggestively.

"I know," Emma said. "But nope. Not that it wasn't fun. I told Liv that too. Just to have fun."

Cody finally made himself accept the fact that they were, indeed, talking about Olivia. And him. And Olivia's virginity.

Her virginity.

It was as if the floor dropped out from under him. He felt off-kilter, unable to find right-side up. He couldn't focus on anything but the replay of the words Emma had said.

"I'll be right back," he heard Emma say.

He took a deep breath, crossed his arms and waited for her to turn.

"Oh, hi, Cody." Emma glanced back at her sisters.

Maybe for help.

"Come here." She was holding a glass in one hand, but he grabbed her other one and pulled her away from the table. Obviously all the girls knew what was going on, but looking one of them in the eye was going to be hard enough. Plus Emma would give it to him straight—whether he wanted it or not. But he definitely didn't want it in front of an audience.

He tugged her away from the booth and around the corner into the small hallway that led to the bathrooms.

He dropped her hand and faced her. "Your sister is avoiding me."

Emma gave him an irritating grin. "I know."

"She's not really sick."

"No."

"She wasn't at home when I stopped by."

"I know. She was shopping."

Yeah, at Tease. Because he needed help making her happy. What the fuck was that? "I'm her boss. I could write her up for calling in sick and then going shopping."

"You could." Emma took a sip of her ginger ale.

For a moment, Cody was struck by how strange that was. Emma Dixon had been the life of the party, the wild child, the tequila-shot champion of Trudy's, only three months ago. Now she was pregnant, engaged to marry Nate next month and drinking nothing stronger than soda.

But she seemed completely content, utterly happy, more confident and at ease than she ever had been.

"I'm not going to write her up," he muttered.

"I know," Emma said.

Olivia was one of the most responsible people he knew. If she was taking a day off, it was because she needed the day off. Maybe she wasn't truly sick, but she needed to not be at work.

That made *him* feel a little sick though.

He glanced around, locating Conner several feet away, talking with Shane and Nate. He lowered his voice anyway. "I understand she told you about last night."

"She sure did."

He waited.

She didn't say anything more than that.

"So she told you we're together now?" That was the most important thing here for everyone to understand.

Emma's eyebrows went up. "No, she didn't say *that*." She peered up at him. "Is that what happened the other night?"

Now his eyebrows went up. "Isn't it?"

"You tell me."

He sighed. Emma Dixon could exasperate a nun. He was far from that patient. "This is *Olivia*," he said. "Love-romance-butterflies-and-lollipops Olivia. Of course that's what happened."

"So you believe that sleeping together equals a declaration of everlasting love and a marriage proposal in Olivia's mind," Emma summarized.

"Doesn't it?"

He knew Olivia. With him, that was absolutely what that would mean. Which was one of the reasons he'd stayed away from her—or tried to—for so long. Because when they crossed that line, it would be the last line, the finish line, the point of no return.

And now that it had happened, he was okay with that. This was Olivia. He didn't need any more lines.

But he needed *her*.

Finally Emma nodded. "Yes, it does. Big time."

She kept studying him.

"I mean huge," she said after a moment. "Really, really big."

Okay, this was…weird. He knew this was big. Emma knew that he knew that it was big. Why did she keep saying that?

Cody crossed his arms and looked down at her. "Emma, what the fuck are you talking about?"

She narrowed her eyes as if she was contemplating something important.

"Yes, she told us about last night," Emma said, letting go of him. "*All* about last night. And I'm thrilled that you're taking it seriously.But there are two things about last night that I know that you don't."

"You mean the orgasm thing and the virginity thing?" he asked, proud that he didn't stammer. Or blush.

Emma blinked at him.

He took a moment to appreciate what had happened—surprising Emma Dixon was a feat.

"You heard that?"

"You didn't say it because you knew I was listening?"

"No, I didn't know you were listening."

"Yes, I heard," Cody told her.

"Oh."

"So—" He swallowed. "That's for real?"

"Yep."

"Oh."

They stood there awkwardly for a moment.

Cody felt his mind whirling. It was true. She really was—had been—a virgin. But she didn't act like a virgin. But he wasn't even sure what that meant. He'd never been with a virgin before. And there was no way Olivia didn't know all about sex. The Dixon Divas didn't even brush their teeth without telling each other all about it. She'd heard it all, he was sure. She'd been so tight, but it had felt so good. It had been like heaven to press into that tight, sweet body and…

Finally, Emma reached out and punched him in the arm. "You dick! I was thrilled you were her first. I knew she was waiting for you. And then you didn't even give her an orgasm? What the hell?"

He frowned. "I didn't know."

She raised an eyebrow. "About the virgin thing or the orgasm thing?"

"The org—"

Someone stepped into the hallway on the way to the ladies' room and he moved aside. When the woman had disappeared into the bathroom, he lowered his voice. "The orgasm thing *too.*"

"Yeah, she didn't have one."

"But…what? Each time?"

Emma gave him a don't-be-stupid look. "At all. With *you.* Her one and only. The guy she's been waiting for. The woman-izing firefighter football player. Yeah, Mr. Big Stuff. No. Orgasm."

Fuck.

Her words sank in and Cody wanted to deny them. Olivia had made those sweet, sexy little sounds. She'd grasped his shoulders so tight. She'd been breathing fast and she'd said his name…like that. Like she couldn't help it. Like he was rocking her world.

He closed his eyes and shoved a hand through his hair.

Damn. He'd truly believed he was rocking her world. He always rocked their worlds. Or so they said.

But…okay. Maybe he hadn't noticed every detail. He'd been so caught up in the moment, in Olivia, in being with her *finally* that he'd gone for it. He'd assumed she was right there with him. He'd thought that…

But no. He knew Emma was right.

"Fuck."

"Yeah."

He looked up at Emma. "Is she mad?"

Emma rolled her eyes. "Olivia? She doesn't get mad. She's sweet and trusting and in love with you, Cody. No, she's not mad. She thinks *she* might not be capable of having an orgasm." Emma pointed a finger at his nose. "And *that* might be the least cool thing of all."

His heart squeezed and he felt his face flush with heat. He'd dropped this ball. Big time. Big, big, big time.

Dammit.

"Fix this," Emma said firmly. "You're the only one who can."

He nodded. "Yeah. I got it."

"Well…" The corner of Emma's mouth curled. "Go give it to *her*."

He would. He most definitely would. Right now. Tonight.

Cody started for the door, digging his car keys from his pocket. As he crossed in front of the bar, he caught sight of Jen. Jen was a nurse at St. Anthony's and they'd hooked up a few times here and there.

He made a beeline for her, taking her elbow and turning her to face him.

Her smile brightened when she saw who it was. "Hey, Cody."

"Hey. I have a question for you."

"No, I'm not busy tonight," she said flirtatiously.

"Did you have an orgasm the times we slept together?"

He'd obviously surprised her, but she recovered quickly and gave him a sexy smile. "Well, yeah. Though I'd be happy to prove it to you. Right now in fact."

And two weeks ago, he very likely would have said yes. Now, he was never going to want a woman other than Olivia.

He was in trouble.

"Thanks," he told Jen. "I was just checking."

He saw another past fling across the room and started in her direction.

"Shari, hey."

The redhead grinned at him. "Hi, Cody."

He leaned in so he could whisper in her ear without her friends hearing.

She pulled back after he asked the question. "Yes. Of course."

"Of course," he repeated, satisfaction sweeping through him. Those two words combined with her sincerely puzzled expression, as if he'd asked the craziest question ever, were perfect. *Of course* she'd had an orgasm. Duh. "That was exactly what I needed to hear."

He headed for the exit again, ignoring the urge to ask all of the women in Trudy's that he'd slept with about their orgasms. But there were several, and that would take too long.

He kept repeating *of course* as he turned his car toward Olivia's house.

The pounding on her front door was definitely not one of her sisters.

Olivia knew who it was. And he had a key. So he was trying to make a point.

She wrapped her robe around her more tightly as she went to the door.

She'd known he would show up. She'd figured it would be tonight. So she'd called in sick so she could use the day to prepare.

She was as ready as she was going to get.

With a deep breath, she pulled the door open.

"Evenin', sunshine." His lighthearted greeting was in direct contrast to the way he'd been banging on her door. And the way he was scowling at her.

"Hi, Cody."

He held up a plastic grocery sack. "It's baking night."

So it was. It was Wednesday. They always baked on Wednesday.

"I, um…was about to…"

His gaze raked over her and his eyes reflected a strange combination of heat, anger and determination. "About to take a bath?" He met her eyes again. "Little sore maybe? You got quite a workout last night."

So that was how the whole topic was going to come up. She had been half expecting him to swing her up into his arms and carry her to the bedroom.

She raised her chin. "Maybe a little."

Anger flashed in his eyes and he stepped forward, crowding her and forcing her to step back. "A virgin? Really, Liv? That might have been something you could have mentioned."

Surprise shot through her. "Who have you been talking to?" But then she knew. "Emma." It had to be Emma.

"I should have been talking to *you* about it, dammit," he said, dropping the bag of baking items on the floor and kicking the door shut. "For fuck's sake, Liv. I could have hurt you last night." His gaze flickered over her robe. "I *did* hurt you."

"I'm fine," she insisted. "I was only a technical virgin and it didn't matter."

"How the hell can that not matter?" he demanded. "That's… a big deal. A huge deal."

She crossed her arms. "And if I'd told you, would you have gone ahead with it? No. And I wanted it, Cody. I wanted *you*."

His expression softened and he lifted a hand to her cheek. "I don't think I could have stopped. But I could have…made it…better."

She felt a lump in her throat and swallowed hard. "It was great. It was *you*. That's all it needed to be."

He gave her a half smile. "Well, thanks for that but—" He stooped and swung her up into his arms. "That's bullshit, babe."

He started for the bedroom.

She wanted to squeal with happiness. He *had* swept her up and carried her to the bedroom.

But… Hey. She frowned.

"What's bullshit? Our lovemaking is bullshit?" she asked her voice rising on the last word.

"It's bullshit that you think that's the best I can do. Trust me—you're about to have the time of your life." He tossed her onto the bed and pulled his T-shirt over his head, tossing it to the side.

Olivia felt her stomach flip at the look of hot, cocky promise on his face. She reached for the belt tie on her silky robe and pulled the knot loose. The two sides fell away, and she was gratified to see Cody pause in unzipping his pants.

"You're so damned beautiful."

His gaze traveled over her new teddy. There wasn't much to it. It was a pale pink, almost flesh colored. The silk cups on top came up barely high enough to cover her nipples, but left the upper swell of her breasts bare. The center panel dipped in at the sides, covering her with only a narrow strip of see-through lace, and the panties were the same pale-pink silk, cut high on her legs, forming a narrow *V* over her mound.

The heat in Cody's eyes suddenly made every ache in her previously well-used muscles disappear, and anticipation spread through her, making everything grow soft and ready.

"Take your hair down," he said gruffly.

She reached up for the messy bun. She pulled the clip loose, her hair falling around her on the comforter.

"Fuck," he muttered.

But she knew it was a heartfelt, good *fuck*.

"I'm going to lick, suck and kiss every inch of you."

Her body flooded with heat.

"Like I should have the other night."

"It's not like I had a *bad* time," she protested.

He looked her in the eye. "You didn't do anything wrong, Liv. It was…amazing. So amazing to be with you that I lost my mind and couldn't pay attention to anything but how fucking good you felt around me and under me and…" He trailed off and took a deep breath. "I've replayed it in my head a hundred times, and I still can't believe how hot it was. For me."

She loved all of that. It made her feel powerful and yet fully contented at the same time.

"I love that I could drive you that crazy."

"I hate that I didn't make you come. Hard. More than once."

She blew out a long breath. She was almost there now. Just lying here and having him so clearly consumed with desire and regret. It was stupid that regret could be sexy, but it was. That it mattered to him so much was sexy. That he was here now, so determined to make up for it, was sexy.

A surge of power and mischief went through her.

Her sisters had encouraged her to tell Cody what she wanted. What she needed.

She lifted a hand to her breast and pulled one of the teddy's cups away. "You know, a guy doesn't have to *make* a girl come or *give* a girl an orgasm. A girl can take care of that all on her own. I could have helped. But I was pretty overcome by everything too."

His eyes were fastened on her fingers playing with her nipple. She traced her finger around the stiff point, then rubbed back and forth over it before tugging on it. The action always made her clit tingle, and having Cody watch her do it made the tingle into an outright jolt of electricity.

"Is that right?" he drawled, moving a step closer to the end of the bed and hooking his thumbs in the waistband of his jeans, pulling them lower on his hips.

She licked her lips. "That is right. Before you go thinking that I've *never* had an orgasm, I want to assure you that is not the case."

His jaw tightened and his fingers flexed, but he didn't move.

"Tell me more," he said, his voice more gruff now. "Please."

She smiled and ran her other hand across her lower belly. "I've been well in touch with my body for a long time."

He swallowed hard. "Fingers aren't exactly the same thing."

"No, they're not," she agreed, running her hand lower over her mound. Her sisters thought she needed to be completely open and honest with Cody about all of this. Fine. "Which is why I've also got a punch card at Tease. And I went shopping today."

Cody's attention moved from her fingers to her face The well-known, well-loved lingerie and sex-toy shop downtown had a little bit of everything, from the basics up front—lacy teddies, French maid costumes, simple vibrators and soft porn—to the more adventurous items in the back.

He had to know how deep into the store Olivia had gone. And how often.

"Emma said you'd been shopping. Do I get to see what else you bought?"

"Yep." Stopping short of really touching herself, she rolled onto her stomach and crawled up the bed toward her bedside table.

"Hang on." Cody reached out and caught hold of the bottom of her robe and pulled.

She lifted one arm at a time, allowing the robe to slide from her body, the white silk slipping over her, revealing the barely-there back of the teddy and lots of soft, sweet skin that he longed to stroke and kiss and worship. The picture she made, her gorgeous ass *right there*—just like when he'd taken her from behind. Her hair fell over her back, and he wanted to grab it up in his fist and hold her still while he thrust into her.

Hell, he hadn't even been able to see her face in that position. She could have been hurting or grimacing or struggling the entire time and he wouldn't have known.

But then she glanced at him over her shoulder with a sexy, I-know-what-I'm-doing look in her eyes, and he remembered all too well how easy it had been to get completely caught up in how much he wanted her, how he *had to have her*. She had this amazing combination of sweet and sexy, of innocent and siren, that he felt the overwhelming need to take, over and over, no matter what, fast and hard.

He took a long, deep breath. He had to control himself this time. She *was* going to come, and she wasn't going to do it herself.

At least not completely by herself, he amended as she reached into the drawer in the bedside table and pulled out some toys. But he wouldn't mind being an observer for a little bit.

She turned and held them up. They were vibrators, in varying sizes and colors. The smallest was pink and shaped like a finger. The next was blue, bigger and had ridges. But the one that he was most surprised and interested to see was the purple one. It was huge. And definitely cock shaped.

She tossed the other two toward the bottom of the bed, but kept the purple one in hand. "See? Nothing to worry about as far as fit," she said. "Me and this guy have known each other for a while."

Well, that might explain why she hadn't been in a lot of pain last night. "So you…uh…can lose your virginity with a dildo?"

She lifted a shoulder. "Not really, I guess. I mean, I've never been with a guy. Until you, of course. But I…" Her cheeks got bright red as she stumbled over the words. Finally, she stopped and took a deep breath. When she met his gaze, it was clear that she was making herself look him directly in the eye. "It wasn't as painful because I've been active with vibrators. But I was a virgin in every other way."

He loved her honesty. He loved that she was comfortable—or trying to be anyway—talking to him about this. He really fucking loved that she'd never been with another man.

Cody raised an eyebrow and took the purple toy from her

fingers. "I'm feeling like I might have disappointed you in the size department."

She visibly relaxed and smiled. "Not at all. I was quite…impressed."

He chuckled. "But you didn't come. Either time," he felt the need to point out. Though why, he wasn't sure. Why keep pointing out all of the ways he'd fallen short? Maybe to hear her deny it. Maybe she *had* had an orgasm. Maybe Emma was guessing. Maybe…

"An orgasm isn't the only thing that's good about you touching me."

He groaned. She definitely hadn't denied it. "God, Liv, I'm sorry."

"Hey. You specifically told me that you would not apologize."

"I meant—"

"I know what you meant."

She looked cute—sexy and riled up—and he itched to grab her.

"I was fine last night and I'm fine now. But," she added, her voice softening, "I have an idea to make you feel better."

"I'll do anything."

"Make me come *three* times tonight."

His heart thudded in his chest as lust and love flooded through him. She was forgiving him. Of course she was. He'd disappointed her in their first time together—her first time *ever*— but she was forgiving him and giving him another chance.

A niggle of unease, the feeling of not being anywhere near deserving of her, tickled his conscience. But then she pressed close and kissed him.

She was hot and soft and smelled like everything delicious he'd ever had. And she was in his arms. In her bedroom.

He might be a jerk from time to time, but he wasn't an idiot.

He cupped her butt and pulled her up firmly against his

cock. His need for her had only intensified because of the night before.

After several long, hot, wet moments, she pulled back. She was breathing hard as she stared at him. "Maybe we don't need anything else. I've been thinking about this all day. This feels so good. Maybe we can get it…"

It was almost as if she was talking to herself but out loud.

"I've been thinking about this all day too," he told her. "I've been thinking about all the positions I can put you in and all the places I want to taste and all the noises I want you to make."

She wet her lips. "Yeah, we're going to be fine."

Something about that made him curious. He thought back over what she'd said. She moved to kiss him again, but he held her back. "What do you mean we don't need anything else?"

"Nothing. I think I was wrong. Let's do this—"

He had to hold her away with more force this time. "Hang on, sweet pea. What else do you need? I meant it when I said I'll do anything."

He wanted this to be good for her. Really good. Awesome even. Whatever she needed, he'd deliver.

And how freaky could it really be? She was a virgin.

He glanced at the vibrators lying to one side. A virgin with a punch card at a sex-toy shop.

Finally she sat back, her hands dropping to her sides. She sighed. "My sisters think that we need to have a whole big, long conversation about what I like and need and how to best get me to orgasm."

He stared at her, desire pumping through his body. He cleared his throat.

"You okay?" she asked, looking concerned.

He probably looked like he'd been punched in the stomach. Because that's exactly how he felt.

"I'm…" He cleared his throat again. "I'm so damned turned on that I can barely breathe."

Slowly she smiled. "Oh. So you *want* to have that whole big, long conversation?"

"About how to best turn you on and get you off?" he asked gruffly. "Hell, yeah."

She let a long breath out between pursed lips. "Wow." Then she shook her head. "That doesn't offend you? That I might think you need instructions?"

He gave her a slow half smile. "Babe, it's not like I blew you away last night, you know? If it means giving you orgasms, then I want to know every detail."

She looked a little sad. "I loved last night."

He cupped her cheek. "I did too. It was great. But let's make great into awesome."

She studied his eyes. "Okay. I'm…um…" She pressed her lips together and squared her shoulders. "I'm not sure I can have an orgasm without the vibrators."

That surprised him. And made him burn to know everything. "Liv, I want to know every way you've ever touched yourself, every fantasy you've had, what you think about when you're playing with your toys…every damned detail about what you need."

She sucked in a quick breath. "Okay."

He pushed her back gently on the bed. "And I intend to show you a few things that you might not even know you like."

She looked up at him eagerly. "Oh, yes, please."

"You're going to be saying 'yes' and 'please' a whole lot more tonight," he promised. He reached for the straps on the teddy, pulling them down and exposing her beautiful breasts.

"I'll say whatever you want me to say," she said, squirming as he drew the lace down over her ribs and belly.

"This isn't about what I want," he told her as she lifted her hips and he finished stripping her of the skimpy lace. "This is all about you."

She was breathing fast and looked gorgeous lying back on her bed, her hair loose, her body exposed to him.

The realization slammed into him that he was seeing her in a way no one ever had. And if he had anything to say about it, no one else ever would.

"I'm the luckiest son of a bitch in the world," he told her sincerely. "I promise to work on being worthy."

"Cody, I—"

"No," he stopped her. She was going to say something sweet about being with him. He knew her. He knew she was going to try to reassure him or tell him that nothing mattered but sharing this with him or that there was no way he could disappoint her.

"I love that I'm the one here right now," he told her. "I love that you let me be the one. And right now all I want you saying is stuff like 'right there', 'harder', 'fuck yeah' and 'you're a God'."

She laughed lightly and he leaned in to kiss her.

The thing was, he definitely could disappoint her. He appreciated that she wanted to be with him anyway, that her feelings for him were about a lot more than the physical stuff. But he didn't want her reassuring him. He didn't want her saying it didn't matter.

It mattered. A lot.

All he wanted right now was her completely overwhelmed by the way he could make her feel.

The kiss grew deeper, and he drank in the taste of her, the feel of her lips opening, her tongue against his, her arms wrapping around his neck and pulling him closer.

He ran his hand up and down her side, into the dip of her waist, over the curve of her hip, down the smooth expanse of her thigh, repeating the pattern for several strokes. Then he ran his palm up to her breast, cupping the weight, running his thumb back and forth over the hard tip. He already knew that she loved nipple play, and he relished the way she arched and moaned as he rolled the stiff nub between his finger and thumb.

He lowered his mouth, flicking his tongue over the firm point, then sucking softly, then harder as she cried out.

He ran his hand over her stomach to her mound, but paused.

"Okay, babe, this is where you start talking," he told her huskily, lifting his head to look into her face.

She had a hard time taking the deep breath. "I thought you were showing me things I didn't even know I liked."

"I'm going to show you that you might like talking dirty and telling me what to do."

Olivia moved her legs apart, and he couldn't help but glance down her body.

"Touch me," she said softly.

He wanted to. Oh, so much. But he was going to make this work if it killed him. "Show me how."

She took his hand and started to move it between her legs, but he slipped his hand free and moved hers instead. "Show me what you like."

She licked her lips and there was a long pause. But finally she moved her hand lower, her middle finger brushing over her clit. She drew it back up, stroking over the sweet spot several times.

Cody felt his own breathing quicken and he leaned in to kiss her, then scooted down the bed to get a better view.

It was like his attention gave her courage. She lifted a knee and propped her foot on the bed, then let her leg to fall to the side, opening her further to his gaze. Her finger moved over her clit, circling and pressing, then she slid lower, dipping inside and drawing the wetness up and over, continuing the circles.

She sped up her rhythm, and he looked up to her playing with her nipples as well.

Her eyes were locked on him.

She was gorgeous, amazing.

She moved her hand again, sliding two fingers into her tight channel, moving them slowly in and out.

"I can't come without my clit being stimulated," she said breathlessly.

"But you can come with your fingers?"

This was the hottest thing he'd ever done.

"It takes a long time," she said. "The vibrator gets me there faster."

"Has anyone else ever given you an orgasm?"

"You. In my kitchen."

Thank you, Lord. Cody slid off the edge of the bed and knelt between her knees. "So we know your clit and your nipples are key."

She nodded and circled her clit again.

"And we know that my fingers work too."

She pulled her bottom lip between her teeth and nodded again.

"Then let's see what else works. Besides your purple prince there," he added.

The vibrators weren't too far away. He'd get her off of those eventually, but if he needed some help right now, he could handle that. He *was* going to see Olivia come apart tonight.

He moved her hand and leaned in, pressing a kiss to her clit.

She moaned.

"Oh, it gets a lot better than that."

He licked this time, giving her a little more pressure. She was the most delicious thing he'd ever tasted.

He was doing well as far as control went. He was proud of himself. But he was only human.

When she sighed *"Cody,"* he grasped her hips to hold her still and licked harder and faster, then sucked her clit, increasing the suction slowly until she was writhing on the bed.

She was gasping and moaning…but she wasn't coming.

He could happily spend hours right where he was, but he wanted her to go over the edge for the first time *now*. He slid two fingers into her. She was incredibly wet and hot and he felt a surge of possessiveness. He'd made her that way, and no one else ever would. No one else would ever feel her like this or see her like this. No one else would ever know her taste, know what she looked like when she was squirming on the bed because of his touch.

"What do you need, Liv? I want to see you come. I want to hear that."

"I don't know," she gasped. "I'm so close."

"Then let's talk you through it." This was going to be so fun. It might kill him, but it was going to be fun.

"What do you mean?"

"Well—" He pumped his fingers in and out. "Do you like that?"

"Of course," she managed, opening her legs further.

"But do you like it as much as this?" He leaned in and licked her again.

"Cody!"

"And what about this?" He sucked hard on her clit.

"Yes, that!"

He lifted his head. "So, now which do you like best?"

"All of it."

"But you're not coming. What's going to get you there?"

She lifted her head. "Really?"

"Really," he practically growled.

She licked her lips, panting. "This is going to sound really dirty."

"*Good.*"

"Can we..."

He waited, the seconds crawling by. "Liv," he said firmly.

"Can I do this to you?"

"You want to—"

"At the same time you keep doing that."

It only took him two seconds to process. He stood, stripped, grabbed her hips and lay back on the bed, her knees on either side of his head.

Holy crap. A woman who wanted to give him a blow job to get really good and worked up? Olivia Dixon was perfect.

He pulled her hips back until he could again suck and lick her and had slid a finger into her when he felt her hand around his cock.

He froze, the sensations ripping through him as he tried to talk himself down from the edge. Olivia might need some time to get to her climax, but he was on the verge of his from simply looking at her.

She stroked up and down his length and he focused on breathing.

"I want to suck on you too," she said.

"I'm all yours, babe," he ground out.

The sensation of Olivia's hot mouth on his cock was absolutely the best thing he'd ever felt. And then he felt her pelvic muscles tighten on his finger. She was definitely into this.

He thrust another finger deep and put his mouth on her clit.

She lifted her head from licking him. "Harder," she urged. "Suck me harder, Cody."

He felt her tightening around his fingers. He did as she asked, of course.

"I love your mouth on me. The image of your tongue in me. The way you touch me. The way you look at me…"

Her muscles continued to ripple around his fingers and he could tell by her breathing and the way her head fell back that she was close.

Coaching him was turning her on.

Damn right.

"Another finger," she said softly. "Please."

He eased a third finger in and thrust in and out. Her hand worked his cock in the same rhythm.

"I love looking at you. Seeing how hard and thick you get from being with me. I want to see you come like this."

He felt his cock jerk at that. Imagining coming on Olivia's hand while he got her off with his tongue was enough to cause his balls to tighten. But he couldn't come without her.

"More, Liv. Tell me more."

"Every time I look at your mouth after this I'm going to get wet."

Her hand squeezed him as her pussy squeezed his fingers, and he worked his tongue faster.

"I'm going to walk into your office tomorrow and see you sucking on a straw or talking on the phone and I'm going to think about how it felt to have you between my legs."

And with that her breath caught and her muscles clamped down hard. She arched her back and cried out his name. Then her orgasm washed over her with the sweetest, most heartfelt "yes, Cody!" he'd ever heard.

Her orgasm sent him over the edge and he felt everything tighten, then release, his climax roaring through his body.

It was only moments before Olivia swung her leg over and turned to lie on top of him, locking her mouth with his.

He tangled his hand in her hair, holding her still, tasting her deeply, turned on in spite of his recent release. This was Olivia. He was getting dirty and hot and sweaty and sticky with Olivia.

When they finally came up for air, she rested her head on his chest.

"So maybe we don't need the cock ring I bought today."

Cody froze. He wondered if he was ever going to get used to the idea that sweet, dirty things were going to be coming out of Olivia's mouth now. He hoped not.

"You bought a cock ring?"

She reached for the bedside table. "It has a vibrator on it. That way, while we're—"

"Yeah, I get the idea," he said, taking it from her.

"But now that I've had an orgasm with you, we probably don't need it."

He looked at the red, rubbery plastic ring. He'd never worn one before. And the idea of being buried in her deep, the vibrating nub on her clit...he didn't mind the idea at all.

"Maybe we should use it a couple of times. Get you used to coming with vibration *and* me. Then work on just me."

She looked surprised. "You'd do that?'

"What do you mean?"

"You'd use something like this to be sure that I come?"

He wrapped an arm around her waist, pulling her up against him again. "Liv, I'd do anything for you. In and out of bed. Got it?"

Her eyes sparkled and she blinked rapidly. "I've always known it out of bed."

"Well, now you know the rest."

"It takes me so long to get there." She sighed. "Maybe it will get better."

He tipped her chin up with one finger. "I'm certainly not filling out any complaint forms about spending extra time naked with you."

"It doesn't make you feel like less of a man that it takes a long time to…you know?"

"A little bit ago you were saying things like 'suck me harder' and 'I'm going to think about your mouth between my legs at work'. Now you can't even say 'orgasm' to me?"

Her gaze dropped to his mouth. "I'm going to be constantly horny now. Even watching your lips move while you talk makes me feel hotter."

"Knowing that you're walking around the firehouse all hot and bothered because of me will certainly help me with my less-than-manly feelings," he told her, shifting her to the side and rolling to face her.

"So you maybe do feel less than manly?"

"Of course not." He ran his hand up and down over her hip. "You know what makes me feel manly?"

She shivered with pleasure at his touch and wiggled closer. "What?"

"That over the years, you've learned to trust me enough that I was the one you picked to be your first. That you went into Tease and walked around picking out this teddy and cock ring with me in mind. That when you came, you called out *my* name." He leaned in to kiss her, then said against her mouth, "Being with you, knowing that I'm going to get to soap you up in the shower." He ran his hand up and down again. "And that I'm the one who's going to run his hand up under your shirt while you're making copies at the station." He kissed her again. "And that I'm the one who's going to eat ice cream sandwiches with you."

She pulled back slightly. "Ice cream sandwiches?"

"Your sisters haven't told you about ice cream sandwiches?"

"No."

"Well, trust me. You're going to love it."

An hour later, Olivia flopped to her back. "Amazing," she breathed.

Cody rolled toward her, his hot, heavy hand on her stomach. "See? Nothing to worry about."

She ran her hand through his hair. "You were right."

They lay like that for several minutes. Then Cody kissed her and said, "I'm going to grab a shower. You want to come?"

She *so* wanted to come. And come hard. Dammit.

She gave him a sweet smile. "You wore me out. I can't move."

He grinned and pushed himself up off the bed. "Next time then."

The water started and she swore out loud. "Fuck!"

They'd had sex again and she hadn't had an orgasm. *Again.*

She had with his mouth. Her body flushed with the memory. She wasn't kidding when she said looking at his mouth got her going now. But now, the good old-fashioned way, it hadn't happened. She'd been tempted to grab her vibrator partway through when it became clear it wasn't going to happen, but no matter what he said, she wasn't sure Cody wouldn't feel a little let down.

But now...

She glanced toward the bathroom door. It was shut, but not

latched. Still, the shower was clearly running. Olivia quickly leaned over the side of the bed where her toys had fallen earlier when the bed had been bouncing.

She grabbed the little pink one. She just needed a little stimulation. It didn't have to be heavy duty. She lay back against the pillows and closed her eyes. Everything with Cody had, of course, felt great. And she'd felt her orgasm building. It simply hadn't gone all the way to complete.

She put the humming pink plastic against her clit and lifted her hand to her breast.

There was a tried and true method. She knew exactly how to get this to work. With this vibrator, it was setting three. This one was small but sometimes it was exactly what she needed.

The waves of pleasure started and she bumped the dial up to three. She rubbed over her nipple, the zings of sensation ratcheting up the tingles between her legs.

She felt things building and moved the vibrator tip in a larger circle.

"Let me help."

Her eyes flew open to find Cody standing next to the bed, a towel wrapped around his waist. His hair and skin was wet, as if he'd stepped out without toweling off.

His eyes were locked on hers as he reached for her purple vibrator. Her breath caught at the hot look in his eyes. There might have been some anger there too, but the lust was overriding it at the moment.

"Put it back."

She realized her hand had slipped and the pink vibrator was humming against her thigh.

"Cody, I—"

"Put it back."

Cody Madsen was a nice guy. Easygoing.

He didn't look nice or easygoing at the moment.

She felt a zing of excitement.

She moved the vibrator back into position, the pulses hitting her nerves just right. She bit back a moan.

Cody twisted the bottom of the purple vibrator, making it hum to life as well.

Another zing of excitement shot through her belly.

He put a finger against her, stroking in partway, and she felt her muscles try to hold him. But he dragged it back out, then painted the wetness on the tip of the purple dildo. Then, his eyes on hers, he moved it between her legs.

Without thinking she spread her thighs wider. Her hand was still at her breast, and she felt her nipple tighten at the intense look in his eyes as he pressed the purple plastic into her.

It filled her, stretching and vibrating in the familiar way that made her body tighten in anticipation.

Then he began to move it. He thrust it in and pulled it out in a slow, steady rhythm. With the pink vibrator still against her clit, the sensations were incredible, and she felt her climax building.

"Is this what you need?" he asked. "I'll do whatever, Liv. Anything to give you what you need. Even if I have to do it with plastic."

He didn't sound angry or bitter. He sounded sincere, and something inside of Olivia gave way. He really would. If the only way to be with her and give her full satisfaction was to use toys every time, he'd do it.

She threw the pink vibrator to the side, grasped his wrist, stopping the thrusting, and also tossed the purple one—still humming—to the floor. Then she ripped the towel off of Cody and pulled him in. He slid into her easily, the feeling completely different but so much better.

"Liv," he said gruffly, holding himself stiff. "No condom."

"Don't care." She didn't. This was Cody. He was clean, and if she got pregnant, so be it. She wanted to spend the rest of her life with him anyway.

This was *Cody*. Filling her, hooking her knees over his elbows and spreading her wide. This was Cody. The man who baked with her, who put up with her romantic notions and optimistic view of everything. The man who laughed at her inability to tell a decent joke, who knew she was secretly a horrible speller and knew that she was addicted to the TV show *Beverly Hills 90210*. This was Cody who was looking down at her like she was the most beautiful thing in the world, even though she was slightly broken in the orgasm department. Cody, who would do anything for her.

The love she felt for him welled up inside of her.

"Make love to me," she whispered.

His hands went under her butt and he lifted her, thrusting once, sliding in fully.

"Forever, if you'll let me."

Then he moved. And it was like fireworks were going off inside of her. He thrust and withdrew, thrust and withdrew, hitting a spot that made her want to scream.

So she did. She screamed his name as the most intense orgasm of her life washed over her.

Cody only thrust a few more times before he too was over the edge.

When he finally slumped down on the bed beside her and pulled her up against his side, she snuggled close.

"Sorry," she whispered.

"That might have been the hottest thing I've ever seen." Then he yawned.

She shifted to look at him. "You weren't mad?"

"Maybe a little at first. You faked an orgasm with me, didn't you?"

"Yeah. The second time. Not the first," she was quick to add.

"Don't do it again." He yawned again.

"Okay."

"I've never watched a woman with a vibrator like that before," he said sleepily.

"Yeah?" She was glad about that. Though she was sure they

were *not* going to have a long, drawn-out conversation about what all Cody had and had not seen with other women.

"It was way hot."

"Well, if you like that...I've had a lot of practice," she said lightly.

She was beyond thrilled to have had a real, true, normal orgasm. But if he wanted to incorporate toys in their sex life, she'd be okay with that.

"Oh, I liked it, and you're going to show me all kinds of stuff," he said, his eyes already shut.

"It'll be my pleasure," she said, also letting her eyes slide closed.

"Damn right it will," was the last thing she heard.

YOU HAVE *no idea how many times I've imagined you and me on your desk.*

If it involves you and a short skirt pulled up and your legs spread, then I'm right with you.

Olivia felt heat flood her as she read Cody's text in response to hers. She really had imagined a lot of delicious and dirty things happening with Cody on his desk. And in his office chair. And against his wall. And on *her* desk.

Now that she'd been with him in real life, those fantasies had only gotten hotter.

Don't even get me started on the copy machine, he texted.

Olivia had loved Cody for almost two years. Now, though, since he'd become her lover, she had no idea how she'd resisted jumping him a long time ago.

The orgasm thing was getting better. Cody made sure she had one every time—with fingers, tongue, toys or a combination. But it was important to him that she come every time. She loved it all, of course, but the ones where he was inside her were the best. They were also happening about fifty percent of the time. Still, that was good. It beat doing it herself.

She leaned back in her chair, propping her feet up on her desk, feeling cocky. Foreplay was the key and Cody was really, really good at it. They'd flirt, saying dirty things as they passed in the hallway all day long. He'd touch her whenever given the chance. Interestingly, when he took her elbow and squeezed gently, it was as arousing as when his hand ran over her butt when she was bending over to get more napkins out of a lower cupboard.

Of course, she was also bending over more than usual lately.

And she was now wearing skirts and heels around the office. And touching up her lip gloss and spritzing her body spray by her desk instead of going into the restroom like usual. The big interior windows that made up two walls of Cody's office—one that overlooked Olivia's desk—were convenient when it came to teasing him. She was also wearing lip gloss and refreshing her body spray a lot more than usual. He'd told her that it almost killed him when her lips were shiny—like they were after she'd sucked on him—and when he smelled her body spray when he walked by her desk

It was fun to tease Cody, and it definitely got her going as well. Every night after work, they barely got through her—or his —front door before they were stripping.

With her feet up on the desk, the skirt pulled up on her thighs, and she knew he could see—and was looking—from his office.

She giggled and started to text him about what she wanted him to do to her on the coffee table that night when she heard, "You have such a cushy job."

Startled, she tried to turn and put her feet down at the same time. She nearly ended up tipping out of the chair entirely. Catching herself at the last second, she looked up to find her brother in the doorway.

"Conner!" Oh crap. Damn. *Pull it together, Olivia.*

"Hey." He came forward with a frown. "You okay?"

"Yeah. Of course." She tucked a strand of hair behind her ear and smoothed a hand over her skirt. *Be cool. Be cool. He won't know anything if you don't tell him. Or act like an idiot.* "You scared me."

Her phone chimed with a new text.

And hide your phone.

She felt her cheeks heat, and she tried to surreptitiously slide her phone from her desk into her top drawer.

She shifted uncomfortably as it chimed again. She was like a trained lab animal, reacting to the sound instantly.

The sexting was the best they could do at work. The house was staffed twenty-four-seven, and Cody's office had all the windows. Nothing was going to ever actually happen at work in spite of their fantasies.

"You working hard?" Conner asked.

She made herself laugh. "Always." She got to her feet, trying to act nonchalant. "So what are you doing here?"

"Thought I'd stop and see if Cody can help me put the new dishwasher in at my place tonight."

That wasn't going to work. She had plans to keep Cody naked for much of the night.

"Uh, I don't—" She broke off, pretending to cough. She couldn't tell Conner that Cody was busy tonight. How would she know that? Why would she care?

"Finally bought it, huh?" Cody asked, stepping out of his office.

"It was on sale." Conner glanced at her.

She tried not to make eye contact. Then made a point of making eye contact since not making eye contact would seem suspicious.

"You sure you're okay?" Conner asked.

She forced a smile. Then felt like maybe it was too big and toned it down a little. Then hoped it wasn't too small. "Great. *Totally* great."

Conner raised an eyebrow at her emphasis.

Cody moved around behind him, going for the water cooler. He caught her eye over Conner's shoulder and gave her a very clear what-the-hell-are-you-doing-just-act-natural look.

Olivia focused on not looking guilty.

"Well, good," Conner said. He turned to Cody. "How's tonight? I'll grill a couple of steaks."

"How about tomorrow? Olivia asked me for some help tonight."

Yeah, help out of her panties. Help holding her up against the wall. Help having a screaming orgasm.

Conner glanced at her and she blinked at him, hoping it looked innocent.

"What do you need help with?" Conner asked her. "I could do something for you now and free Cody up later."

Gross.

She thought fast, but couldn't quite get past the disturbing idea of Conner coming over and finding her in the tight red dress with the flames on it she'd found at an online costume shop.

Then she thought about how Cody had promised to wear his fire helmet tonight.

And only his fire helmet.

"Liv?"

She realized she'd taken way too long to answer and Conner was staring at her. He looked suspicious.

"Hot…sauce," she finally said. For some reason.

Yeah. He should totally be suspicious.

"Hot sauce?"

"I'm helping her with a new recipe," Cody said smoothly. "It's a dip."

He gave her a wink when Conner wasn't looking.

His quick thinking and the way he rescued her were impressive. Hot sauce? What was she doing?

"A dip?" Conner asked.

"Yeah," Cody answered. "It's this creamy, spicy dip that is so good you want it on *everything*."

Olivia gasped, then tried to cover it with a laugh. She'd completely made that dirty in her mind.

Conner frowned at her.

She had a problem.

"We're, um, messing with the recipe tonight," she said, going with Cody's story. "So we don't know that it's that good yet."

"Oh, but all the ingredients are awesome," Cody said. "There's no way it won't be good."

"So what's to mess with?" Conner asked. "You throw it all together and mix it up."

"You'd think so, wouldn't you?" Cody asked, perching on the edge of her desk and sipping from his paper cup of water. "But surprisingly, the order you put things together in, how hard and fast you mix it, how hot you get it, all makes a difference."

Okay, he'd meant *that* dirty. Surely. Hadn't he?

Was she so horny that everything was going to sound dirty?

Possibly.

She was positive that she was so horny that when she got Cody home she was definitely going to have an orgasm. At least one.

"Oh." Conner shrugged. "Does that have to be tonight?"

It most certainly did.

And if this conversation continued, she was so giving herself and Cody away.

She looked at Cody. He was going to have to wear the suspenders, pants and boots with the helmet tonight. But no shirt. His chest and abs would look fantastic with suspenders only. And when he unsnapped them, the pants would slip low on his hips.

"*Liv*," Conner said, clearly exasperated. "Do you need Cody *tonight*?"

She nodded solemnly. "I really do. This can't wait."

"The hot sauce dip can't wait?" Conner asked.

Cody coughed and Olivia glanced at him. He'd started this. The whole thing was his fault.

"I need this dip," she told Conner. "Tonight. For sure."

"And I can't let her do this on her own," Cody said. "I mean, she's great by herself, but together it turns out better, I think. I can help her with the adjustments."

Olivia knew she was blushing, but Cody's words put images in her mind about doing things on her own versus with him.

They should not be talking like this.

With *Conner*.

"Fine. If this dip is that important." Conner rolled his eyes. "How about Monday? I have to work the next few days."

"Sounds good," Cody agreed.

"Okay. See ya."

Conner left and Olivia blew out a long breath.

"You're so naughty," Cody said, moving in close.

"*I'm* naughty?" she asked, looking up at him.

"You said hot sauce." He leaned in. "I do love your creamy hot sauce."

She couldn't help it. She kissed him.

It didn't last nearly long enough. A door slammed and she pulled back, remembering where they were. "I can't believe I just did that."

"What? Telling your brother that you and I were going to have hot dip together tonight?"

"No—well, yes. And that I kissed you. Here. At work."

He looked around. "We're alone."

She pushed him back. "For this moment. Still, we're going to get caught. They're all going to wonder why I breathe fast while making copies."

"Why do you?" he asked with a little grin.

"Because of yesterday."

"The text about bending you over it?" he asked. "I really do love that black tile behind it. It would work like a mirror. I'd be able to see your face as I—"

She slapped her hand over his mouth. She liked the foreplay. But she didn't want it to culminate in the office with him talking to her...and she was close. She wanted him naked too—except for the fire helmet of course.

"Not that one," she said of the text.

He pulled her hand away, then pressed her palm to his lips, then flicked his tongue out, running it along the line in the middle of her hand.

She made a quick fist, the tingles shooting from her palm to her nipples. Damn.

"So you mean the text about sitting you up there without your panties and photocopying your sweet pussy?"

Typically that word made her flinch. But when Cody said it, it made her hot.

"That one," she confirmed.

He gave her a grin that told her exactly how much he loved making her panties wet at work.

Yeah, well, she wasn't going to be the only one worked up and uncomfortable for the rest of the shift.

"Look in my second desk drawer."

He gave her a funny, sweet smile, then leaned to pull the drawer open. He pulled out the folded piece of paper and held it up. "This?"

"Yep."

"For me?"

"Yep."

"I know what this better be."

"It is."

He opened it slowly, then sat staring at it. Finally he lifted his gaze to hers. "Holy shit."

"That's why I breathe faster every time I make copies."

It was a photocopy of her sitting—without panties—on the copy machine.

He looked at it again for a long moment. Then he folded it and tucked it into his pocket.

He sighed and met her gaze. "I want you every second of the day."

"Me too."

And it was more than physical. It was like when that barrier broke, everything else they'd made up to keep them apart crumbled as well. She was fully in love and she wanted everything—waking up late on Sunday morning beside him, dancing with him—and only him—at Trudy's and being free to press as close as she wanted to and whisper naughty things in his ear and feel his hand run up the back of her neck and into her hair.

She wanted to be free to be in love with him, to let the world know it.

"I don't want to hide it. I want to kiss you and touch you and tell you how I feel all the time," he said, as if reading her mind.

Her heart melted at that. "Me too," she said softly.

"Which means we need to tell your brother about us."

Yeah, they did.

Dammit.

"I know."

"So how should we do it?"

"I think we should take off for Hawaii and send him a postcard."

"Meaning Hawaii is where you want to spend the rest of your life?"

She laughed. "I can think of worse places."

Cody's smile faded and he lifted his hand, fingering a tendril of her hair. "We need to tell him in person. Together."

She nodded. "I know."

"Maybe with Ryan, Shane and Nate around though," he added.

She smiled at that. "Maybe Emma could set up a game night."

"That would be…maybe not the best way to handle it."

"I don't know. It has some important ingredients—liquor,

fun, our friends and family." She ran her hand up and down his chest

"We should tell him alone, just us. But in public. Like dinner or something."

"Public is good." In public he wouldn't yell as much. Or throw things. Probably.

"If we take him to his favorite place, he'd be in a good mood."

"No need to spend your hard-earned money. Just tell me now."

They both swung toward the doorway, moving apart guiltily.

And clearly telling Conner everything he needed to know.

His expression hardened and he pushed his hands into his front pockets.

"Conner," Olivia started.

"Actually, Liv, I want to hear it from Cody."

Conner was staring at his best friend with a combination of hurt, anger and disbelief.

Cody moved in closer to Olivia and took her hand, slipping his fingers between hers. She held on to him tightly. This was it. No going back now.

"Olivia and I are together, Conner," Cody said evenly. "We're taken our relationship from friends to more, and…this is it."

Her heart tripped at the words. She'd assumed. But hearing him tell her brother made it even more real.

"Of course you did."

Those were not the words she'd expected from her brother.

"What?" she asked. "You're not surprised?"

"I shouldn't be," Conner said tightly. "I know Cody. I've see him in action, up close and personal. I should have known better than to think he meant anything he said to me."

"Dixon, dammit—" Cody started.

"And of course it's Olivia," Conner said with a humorless laugh. "You wouldn't go for Amanda or Iz or Emma. No, you'd go for the sweet, genuine one that trusts everyone."

"It's Olivia because it's *Olivia*," Cody said, clearly angry. "You know I care about her, dammit."

"Yes. I know you cared about Ashley too. I know you thought she was amazing. So amazing that you were planning to marry her."

Olivia felt Cody's hold on her hand tighten.

"That's right," Cody said. "But that was a long time ago."

"Because she was sweet and trusting and wanted to believe the best of you and being in love," Conner went on. "You could do no wrong. Being with her was easy, being with her meant you didn't have to be a good guy because you could be something even better—forgiven. You could go out and have all the fun you wanted and never worry about screwing anything up. She'd always be there."

"Ashley was ten years ago. I thought we'd moved on." Cody's voice barely sounded like him.

Glancing up at his face confirmed that he was, indeed, completely pissed off.

"I thought we had too." Conner gave a bark of laughter. "Your relationship with Olivia was my proof that you had matured and were capable of having a relationship with a woman you weren't sleeping with or trying to sleep with. Isn't that ironic?"

It was, actually.

Olivia flinched at the look of anger and hurt on Conner's face as he turned to Cody.

"I trusted you. With *Olivia*. You told me there was nothing to worry about."

She looked up at Cody. "You said that? When?"

"Two years ago when I saw how he was looking at you at Trudy's one night," Conner said.

Cody wouldn't look at her. His gaze was locked on Conner.

"He said 'nothing to worry about, man'," Conner said, practically spitting the words. "And I decided that he deserved a second chance. A chance to show me that he could respect a woman and *deserve* her trust."

"Fuck, Conner, this isn't about Ashley," Cody said. "This is nothing like that. I resisted with Olivia. I fought it. I tried to do it right."

"You resisted," Conner scoffed. "Sure you did. You spend every waking moment with her."

"Leaving Olivia alone, keeping my hands to myself while being close to her has been the hardest thing I've ever done," Cody said.

Her heart flipped at his words, but then squeezed in pain again when she looked at her brother. Her stomach was in knots. The two men she loved and trusted and respected more than anyone were glaring at each other unforgivingly.

"Yeah, really torturous," Conner said. "You poor thing. Fucking your way around Omaha and then going to her house the next day to bake bread and have her tell you how great you are." He pulled his hands from his pockets and made two fists. "Now that I know this, it all makes a lot more sense. I was actually *relieved* that you were looking out for her. I never had to worry about other assholes treating her badly because you were always there before I could warn them off."

Olivia looked up at Cody again. "What's he talking about?"

Cody was clearly gritting his teeth.

"Tell her," Conner said. "Tell her how you continually told guys to back off and leave her alone. Tell her that while you were out fucking everything that would let you close, she was sitting at home alone because you told all the guys they'd have to answer to both of us if anything happened."

"You did that?" she asked Cody.

Finally he looked at her. "I was watching out for you. None of them were good enough."

"But..." She was so confused. It sounded almost sweet that he had been keeping guys away from her who weren't good enough. It sounded almost like he'd been jealous. So why did it make her stomach hurt at the same time?

"None of them were *good enough*?" Conner repeated. "Or were most of them a hell of a lot better than *you* and you were afraid she'd realize it?"

Well, *that* stung. And she wasn't even entirely sure why.

"What are you talking about?" she demanded of her brother.

"You're always there. He tucked you away safely in this little 'friend' corner, where he could still see you all the time, where you're always available if he needs to feel better about himself or have a real conversation with a woman. He doesn't have to have a real relationship with anyone else because he has you, but he doesn't have to commit to you because you're only friends. He has *all* his needs met—including the one where he needs to not have any complicated expectations from anyone." Conner looked at her now, his eyes full of regret. "I can't believe I didn't see it, that I trusted it was real, Liv."

"I've resisted those 'complicated expectations' with Olivia because of *you*, you ass," Cody said through gritted teeth. "I couldn't be more than her friend because of *you*."

"I'm a very easy excuse," Conner said with a nod. "Glad I could be there for you, buddy." The sarcasm was thick. "Hate to see you actually make a commitment to a woman. That'd be terrible."

"If I was willing to make a commitment to Olivia, you would have been fine?" Cody demanded. "Really? You would have given us your blessing?"

"No," Conner shot back. "Because you've never worked for anything in your life. My *sister* and her love and trust are things you should have to work for."

Olivia was almost unable to look at her brother without crying. He was so upset. She remembered seeing him angry about Shane and Isabelle fighting, but even that had been nothing compared to this.

Of course, she knew she was different in Conner's eyes. She

was his youngest sister, the one who had needed the most from him after their dad died, the one who was—as he said—sweet and trusting. She was also the one who had needed saving from her own decisions and mistakes. To think that he'd failed to protect her from the man he was closest to would make him completely irrational. At least.

Conner didn't see her as strong or tough or worldly or any of the things she knew he saw in their sisters. Amanda was confident and in charge, Isabelle was strong and smart and capable, Emma was tough and experienced and didn't take crap from anyone.

Part of that was Conner's fault because he *wanted* to see her as sweet and optimistic. He loved that side of her. She could make him smile and bring him out of a bad mood faster than anyone.

But part of it was on her. She didn't show her tough side. She didn't need to. She had Conner and their mom and her sisters and their guys and, yes, Cody. She didn't need to be tough.

But she could be.

Maybe.

A long silence had stretched between the two men. Finally Cody said quietly, "I've always loved her, Conner."

Conner scoffed, but the words hit Olivia directly in the chest.

She turned to Cody, her heart pounding. "You've *always* loved me?"

He met her eyes. "Yes."

"What does that mean?"

He swallowed hard. "Always."

Cody had *loved* her always? She'd known he loved her as a friend, would do anything for her, wanted her. But he'd *loved* her?

"But I thought..." She trailed off, words failing her.

They'd been resisting their physical attraction. It had been about sex. And that had made sense. Sleeping with Conner's sister, having a fling, a hookup, would have been terrible. Plus,

Cody was a good guy and would never sleep with her and potentially encourage her to think there was more to his feelings if it weren't true. As much as she'd wanted him, she'd always appreciated that. Her feelings had been strong, and she wouldn't have survived making love with him only to hear *I still want to be only friends* the next morning.

He had avoided sex with her because he *didn't* love her. At least, that's what she'd been telling herself. It was also why, now that they *had* slept together, she knew that things were serious. Like maybe he was falling in love with her *now*.

But...

"How long?" she asked, her throat tight.

"Always. I fell fast after we started hanging out."

"So you've been in love with me for, what, two months?" she asked, praying he'd say yes. She could handle two months.

"Longer than that, Liv," he said gruffly.

"How long?" she demanded, her voice rising on the last word.

"As long as we've been baking together."

She felt her eyes widen. "We've been baking for like seventeen months."

"At least that long," he said with a nod.

She swallowed against the tears that suddenly threatened. "Why didn't you *tell* me?" she asked. "That's something you *tell* someone. How could you let me think you *didn't* feel that way? How could you let me feel this way and not let me know that you felt this way too?"

He frowned and stepped forward. "Feel what way?"

She stared at him. He was going to make her say it? Now? Like this? In front of her brother? "You *know* how I feel."

He reached for her and gripped her upper arm firmly but gently. "Tell me," he said. "Now. How do you feel about me?"

"You know I've been in love with you for months!" she burst out.

His eyebrows slammed together. "*What?*"

"You knew. You had to know."

"How would I know that?" he demanded, sounding almost angry. "You've been putting up barriers between us from the beginning."

"When it was just about the sex!" She worked to take a deep breath. "And you never tried to knock any of those barriers down."

"Didn't I?" he asked, pulling her closer. "I think the fucking barriers definitely came crashing down the other night, don't you?"

She flashed to the night in the bar, the kiss on her front step, the day in her kitchen, and then, of course, the night in the hotel when they were *finally* together.

"But then…we were matched up. You didn't do anything until that happened. Until the computer put us together. Until *I* said that it was destiny."

"The computer?" Conner cut in. "Seriously?"

"It matched us up," Olivia told him. "The dating site put us together."

"Are you fucking kidding me?" was Conner's response.

Cody dropped his hold on her and moved back.

"There is no way that you really believe that destiny brought you together through a dating site," Conner said.

He didn't act surprised about the site. One of the other girls must have told him. And he'd probably been fine with it, Olivia assumed, because Cody was always there looking out for her.

She crossed her arms and pressed them against the stomachache that kept getting worse.

"I don't know what to tell you," she said. "We signed up, thinking we would find other people since—" She glanced at Cody. "Since we couldn't be together." She licked her dry lips. "Then when we were matched, it felt like maybe it was a sign. But we still fought it, Conner. The first time."

Conner rolled his eyes. "There was more than once?"

She nodded. "Twice. We were set up together twice."

Conner looked at Cody. "Really." The sarcasm was almost palpable. "That's amazing. The odds of that have to be four billion to one."

Cody shifted his weight from one foot to another, suddenly looking uncomfortable.

Olivia felt ice trickle through her bloodstream. "Cody? We were matched up, right?"

Had he set it up? To keep her from other men? To finally have her to himself? How did she feel about that?

"Go ahead," Conner said to his friend. "Look her in the eye and tell her it was legit. If it was, who am I to argue? I mean, if you're really her destiny, I can't get in the way of that. Tell her it's true."

Please look me in the eye and tell me it's true. Please.

"No, we weren't matched up that first night," Cody said.

Olivia's heart dropped like a rock to the pit of her stomach, increasing the ache.

"I didn't know it at the time. I thought we had been and I was thrilled," he rushed to say. "But I got an e-mail—the day Conner was in the fire—from my date for that night, apologizing."

"I never got an e-mail about a mix-up or anything," she said.

"I don't know what happened with yours," Cody said. "But I know that my date had a flat and didn't have a phone number for me. That's why she wasn't there."

The ice in her bloodstream grew even colder—if that was possible.

"What about the next time? Were we matched up the night we..." The night of the hotel. The night they finally made love. The night that had truly changed everything.

"I don't know for sure," he said again. "I didn't get any e-mails saying otherwise. But I didn't set it up or anything either," he was quick to add.

"But?"

She could tell there was another but.

"I saw a guy and a girl outside the restaurant. It was clear they were each waiting for someone. They saw one another and started talking. They decided that they must have been there to meet each other."

"That could be true," she said, clinging to that idea.

"Yes. It could. But it could be true that they were there for us."

She pressed her hand to her stomach.

The chances of her and Cody being set up were astronomical. She knew that. But she *wanted* it to be true so badly that she'd easily gone along with it. She'd *needed* it to be true. She'd needed the reassurance that she was making the decision about being with Cody based on something other than her own emotions, something that was concrete and real and objective, something that had nothing to do with his charming smile or his chocolate butterscotch muffins or something equally ridiculous.

"So…none of it's true," she finally choked out. Everything in her felt tight and cold.

"No," Cody said firmly. "Everything about how I feel is true."

That didn't make her feel better. "Why didn't you tell me we weren't really matched up?"

"I…"

"It's easier that way," Conner said. "Cody loves doing things the easy way. It's a hell of a lot easier to feed your romantic notions to ensure that you're all his than it is to actually *earn* the assurance that you won't leave or find someone else."

"Shut the fuck up, Conner." Cody turned on him. "You've had your say. We know how you feel. Got it. Won't forget it. Now shut up and let Olivia decide how she feels and what she trusts."

But that was the problem. She had no idea what to trust—not Cody, not fate, not even the stupid computer. She also had no idea how she felt—beyond disappointed, hurt and maybe a little angry. At both of these men.

"I…need to think. Or something."

"Liv—" Cody started.

"No." She wasn't sure what exactly she was saying no to, but it was her instinctual answer.

"I'll give you a ride," Conner said.

"No." She also knew she couldn't be with him right now.

Cody reached for her. "Babe—"

But she stepped back, then turned and bolted from her office, then from the fire house, needing space from Cody. For the first time ever.

It wasn't like the pounding headache and general hatred of the sunlight pouring in his windows shocked him. Getting rip-roaring drunk three nights in a row had a way of causing both of those things. And Cody had most definitely gotten rip-roaring drunk the past three nights.

But the incessant ringing of his front doorbell was enough to make him want to cut his head off—right after he cut the head off of whoever was ringing his fucking doorbell.

He swung the door open, fully expecting to see one of his friends there to haul him back into the real world. "I swear to God—"

Olivia stood on his front porch.

"Oh." Damn. He didn't want to see her. He'd been avoiding seeing her for a week.

Because seeing her reminded him of how much he wanted to see her and how much he wanted her to want to see him.

She wanted to be with him. Or *had* wanted to be with him. He'd had her. She'd been his. No more resisting touching her, kissing her, telling her she was amazing and beautiful, making love to her.

He didn't want to step out the door into a world where that was no longer true.

Damn Conner.

And damn Conner for having a point.

Cody had never purposefully, consciously put Olivia away for later. He'd never thought of her as his backup plan.

He'd been trying so hard not to be an asshole, not to have feelings for a woman who didn't want him to have those feelings for her, feeling like a jerk because he wanted his friend's little sister in spite of the friend warning him off.

But he had scared the other guys off. He'd told himself it was to protect her, but Conner was right—he'd been *sure* she was going to find someone better than him and he was going to lose her.

So he'd kept her for himself. Maybe as only a friend, but all his nonetheless.

It wasn't the same situation as Ashley. He'd grown up a little bit since then. He hadn't strung Olivia along, knowing that she was in love with him and intending to marry her after he'd had his fun. Conner was an asshole for thinking that.

But yes, Cody had messed with Olivia's life because he didn't want to give her up. He wanted whatever he could have with her—even if it was only baking cookies.

Pathetic and selfish. Clearly he hadn't *totally* grown up. Not as much as he'd hoped, anyway.

She raised an eyebrow at his less-than-enthusiastic greeting. Then she took in his appearance.

He was wearing sweatpants. Old, ratty sweatpants. And that was all. It was three o'clock in the afternoon and he hadn't been out of bed to shower or shave yet.

"What are you doing here?" he asked as he turned and headed for the kitchen.

"Are you hungover?"

He jerked open the refrigerator and grabbed the orange juice. "Very."

"Feel like crap?"

He lifted the juice carton to his mouth and took a long swig. Then looked at her again. "Yeah."

"Good.".

Okay, so she wasn't here to make him feel better. Good to know. He finished off the juice and tossed the carton into the sink before facing her. As if that would help.

"What are you doing here?" he asked again.

"I have some things I need to say. And since you've been a coward and haven't been in to work for a week, I finally realized I needed to come here to say them."

He'd taken the week off of work to give them both some space. The working together thing was great when they wanted to see each other all day, every day. Not so much when they… didn't.

Because they were in love with one another.

This was the most confusing damned thing that had ever happened to him.

He leaned back against the counter. "Fine. I might have a few things to say too."

She moved to stand in front of him but far enough back to be out of reach. "Great. Let's do this."

He crossed his arms and waited.

She took a deep breath. "I believe that you thought we had been set up by Perfect Pick too."

He looked at her, everything in him softening with the affection she brought out in him so easily. Olivia always believed the best of him. He loved her for that.

He loved her…for that. For that. The words kept repeating in his mind.

He loved her for that.

He frowned.

Had his main attraction to Olivia been that she believed in him, forgave him, supported him no matter what? Did he want her because she made him feel like he was a great guy? Was it all about him feeling good?

If he was honest, he'd say…maybe.

Fuck.

He hadn't wanted her to find someone else. Because if she had, he would have lost his biggest cheerleader.

He'd kept her from getting serious with anyone else, but—and as far as self-awareness went, he was pretty proud of this—he hadn't been willing to stand up to Conner, say "I love your sister, deal with it". He could tell himself all day long it was because he didn't want to hurt Conner, but the truth was he'd already had so much of her—her sweetness, her humor, her optimism, the long talks and the nights in front of the TV and the family barbecues and the weekends at the lake—he hadn't *needed* to mess things up with Conner. He'd had the best of both worlds—essentially dating Olivia but maintaining his friendship with her brother.

Of course, he'd been missing the hot, sweet, amazing sex with her. But he hadn't known that. And it wasn't like he'd been celibate.

God, he was an asshole.

And he wanted to kiss her anyway. So bad it hurt.

"I also believe that part of you was truly trying to protect me by intimidating the other men."

He shifted his weight. That was also partly true, but honestly that part was quite a bit smaller than the selfish part where he didn't want to risk losing what he did have with her.

"I'd do anything to keep you safe," he said, meaning it to his bones.

"I have to know, though," she said. "What did you say to them? How did you keep them from calling me?"

He could be honest about this part too. "I told them that you were amazing and that if they were committed to making you happy then great, but if they had even the slightest doubt that they were serious about you and the relationship, then they needed to stay away because they'd have to answer to me and Conner if you were ever anything less than glowing."

She stared at him.

Yeah, it sounded over-the-top, but he'd meant every damned word. Any man who would ever have made her cry would have found Cody's fist in his face.

"That wasn't a little *much*?" she asked.

He shrugged, unapologetic. "Seemed about right to me."

She sighed. "You said you might have some things to say?"

Well, he hadn't rehearsed anything, but if she was going to insist…

"Do you have any idea how hard it's been for me to *not* tell you how I feel? How hard it's been to only be your friend?" he started. "Do you know how hard it's been to watch you lick frosting off your fingers and not spread you out on the table? How hard it's been to give you a peck on the cheek on your birthday instead of pushing you up against the wall and really kissing you? How hard it's been to dance with you at weddings and not tell you that I love you and that I want to play 'Can't Help Falling in Love' at *our* wedding?"

She was staring at him with a combination of awe and sadness. "It's been hard for me too," she said softly.

"You should have told me."

"*You* should have told *me*."

They stood, looking at each other, breathing a little harder.

He really wanted to kiss her.

"I've been thinking about this," she finally said.

He waited.

"Ryan and Shane and Nate…they didn't let Conner stop them."

Oh, no, she wasn't comparing him to the guys her sisters had fallen in love with. Was she?

"What's that supposed to mean?" he asked.

"I…" She stopped and took another deep breath. "I'm saying that maybe this isn't what you think it is. I mean, you didn't feel strongly enough to tell me. You weren't willing to tell Conner how you feel."

Un-fucking-believable.

"This is all on me? *I'm* the one who should have told him how I feel? I was trying to respect what *you* wanted." He worked on keeping his voice even.

"He's my *brother*. How could I do that to him when I thought all you wanted was sex?"

"How could you think all I wanted was sex?" he demanded. "We're best friends."

"Because that's all you ever want from women." She pressed her lips together almost as if that had slipped out.

Cody pulled in a long breath through his nose. "That's all I want from *other* women because I have *you* for everything else. With you…I want it all."

She looked truly perplexed. "But the moments when we had to pull back and slow down were *physical*," she said. "You've almost kissed me, but you've never almost said 'I love you'."

She was wrong. He'd almost said it a hundred times.

He didn't like any of this, but people didn't yell at Olivia. She simply wasn't the type of girl you yelled at without being a complete and total asshole. He'd like to think he wasn't complete and total. At least, not yet.

"I can't remember a single time that we've baked together and I *haven't* thought about telling you I love you."

Her eyes welled with tears and he hesitated. Olivia cried more often when she was happy than when she was sad. But he had no idea which this was.

"You say that," she said with a shake of her head. "I want to believe it. But it isn't even stronger than your friendship with Conner."

"That's what you wanted."

"How many romantic movies have we watched together, Cody? Seriously. How many romantic movies end with the guy saying 'Well, I love you but I don't want to upset your brother'? None. Zero. Because that's bullshit."

Olivia didn't say *bullshit*, and Cody knew her use of it now meant she was riled up. But he also thought it was damned adorable.

"You've got a point."

"Of course, I do. I want someone who's *crazy* for me," she went on. "Someone who won't let anything or anyone stop him from being with me." She took a deep breath. "You *fought* your feelings. You tried to *not* be in love with me."

Dammit. He *had* said that about waiting for a guy like Leo in *Titanic*. And he'd meant it. "I wanted to go for it. But I knew it would hurt *you* to hurt Conner, Liv," Cody said.

But she wanted the big love story, the do-anything, sacrifice-everything hero. She deserved it.

He wasn't good at that stuff. At least, he didn't know if he was good at that stuff. That took effort. Conner had been right about that too—Cody liked when things worked out and went smoothly. Who didn't? Did that make him a bad guy?

He'd spent almost all his time with his favorite person, but he didn't have to worry about ever really letting her down because they were just friends. That was *easier*. For sure. Except, of course, the wanting her so much his teeth ached at times.

"Oh, come on, Cody. All three of my sisters have done this and Conner's survived. Shane never would have—"

"Don't even finish that sentence."

Fucking Shane Kelley. Leonardo DiCaprio had set some high standards, but he had nothing on Shane. Every woman who hung out at Trudy's—and then some, since a lot of his antics had been captured on YouTube—now held him up as the ultimate romantic hero. He'd made a huge production of romancing Olivia's sister Isabelle when she was trying to end things.

He'd set the bar high. That was for sure. The women loved him. The men not so much.

Olivia was chewing on her bottom lip.

"I'm not Shane. I have a history with Conner. And you're not Isabelle. Conner feels even more protective of you," he said, proud of how calm and rational he sounded.

She nodded. "I didn't mean that you had to do what Shane did. I'm saying that I wish you *felt* like doing those things." She swallowed. "That sounds stupid. I'm sorry. I...I want..." She took another deep breath. "I want a love that is so big and bold, so strong that we don't care who doesn't like it. We've been together, kind of, for months. We knew each other, we wanted each other—but it wasn't enough to make either of us brave enough to say the words or risk upsetting Conner. So..."

"So?"

"Maybe it's not *love* love."

"Bullshit. I'll go fight Conner right now if that's what it takes," Cody said, pushing off of the counter. "I'll do whatever you want me to do."

"Really?"

Cody would happily pound on Conner. He was the one who'd put all these reservations in her mind. And in Cody's.

The fucker.

"Absolutely." Cody grabbed his car keys off the counter and started for the door.

"That's not what I want."

He turned back at her soft words. "What then?"

"I want to..." She hesitated as if she was nervous about what she was about to say. "I want to make a decision on my own, trust myself to choose the right thing. I want to learn to trust myself."

"And how are you going to do that?" He wanted those things for her. He wanted her to trust him, of course, but he understood that she needed to believe in her ability to take care of herself. He needed to know she could take care of herself too.

But he was pretty sure he wasn't going to like what she was about to say.

"I want to date. Other guys. Without relying on the computer setup. And without interference from you or Conner."

He'd been right. He didn't like it at all. He dropped the keys with a clatter on the table. "No."

"You said anything."

He really did want to punch Conner now. "Anything that doesn't involve you and other men."

"If we're meant to be, then it won't matter who else I meet and spend time with. Don't you want to know that I've been out there, and no matter who else comes along, no matter what they do, *you're* the one I want to be with?"

"No. I'm cool with believing that I'm the one you want to be with, period. I don't feel like I need to win a contest." He didn't want her to have any other options. It would take her ten seconds to find a guy who was willing to jump in, sweep her off her feet and openly love her—exactly like she wanted. He'd always known it.

But it wouldn't be *him*. It needed to be him.

"Well, first, this is your fault. If you hadn't been interfering all along, I'd already know for sure."

"I'm kind of pissed that you don't know *now* that I'm the one you want to be with," he said with a frown.

"No," she said, raising her index finger in front of him. "You don't get to be pissed or offended or whatever. You've had lots of other women, and you've only been *my* buddy, the man who'd been *resisting* me for almost two years. I don't know if I want to be with someone who was so tormented by me licking frosting off my fingers and dancing with me at weddings but never *did anything about it.*"

"Olivia, I…" Was he going to admit that yeah, okay, so he'd been pretty damned content with everything overall? That didn't seem like a good move. Because he hadn't been. Not really. He'd *really* wanted to lick frosting off of her and tell her he loved her at all five of the weddings they'd gone to together.

But no, he hadn't done anything about it.

"It's like you've been in this big buffet over the past two years, sampling a little bit of everything except for the tiramisu at the end," she said.

Ooookay. She knew he loved tiramisu.

"You've been eyeing it. You've been making sure no one *else* takes the tiramisu. But *you* haven't picked it up yet. Then suddenly someone announces that they're taking the tiramisu off the buffet for good. Now that you've tried everything else and haven't found anything better, and you might actually lose your chance to try it, you've finally chosen it. And it's damned good. Everything you ever imagined it would be. Better even. So you're happy. You're good. All is well."

He felt a smile tugging on the corner of his mouth. He was following her. She was his tiramisu. And she was right—it was everything he'd imagined and more. He supposed the dating site and her declaration that they needed to find a boyfriend and girlfriend was the threat of the discontinued tiramisu in this analogy.

"As for me," she went on. "I've been on a deserted island with only chocolate chip cookies to eat."

"You love chocolate chip cookies."

She nodded. "I do. But I've never even tried a chocolate soufflé. And there are probably at least a dozen desserts I've never even heard of that I haven't tried. And I'm on this damned island so there's not even a *chance* that I can try something else. I have these chocolate chip cookies and I love them. But of course I do—they're all I have."

He thought about that. "Hey. I'm the chocolate chip cookies?"

She nodded.

"And the deserted island is…"

"My love life."

Right. "I'm all that's been around, and even though you love me, you think it might be because I'm the only option?"

"I love you because you're you. Chocolate chip cookies are awesome even when there are a million other choices available," she said. "But chocolate chip cookies can be awesome and not be…"

"The best," he filled in bluntly.

She shrugged. "It's not a perfect comparison. But yes, maybe

I want to be with you because you've been the only option. You know, thanks to you scaring everyone off in the past year a half."

Fuck. He was getting damned tired of everyone having points but him. And that all the points seemed to be going against him.

"If you're going to try things that are new and better than chocolate chip cookies, I'm going to have to buy a lot more beer," he finally said.

She crossed her arms. "Does that mean you're going to let me off No Man Island?"

"Don't think I'm not tempted to keep you here and show you that chocolate chip cookies are delicious."

Her voice went soft when she said, "They are. It has been."

He studied the face that he'd come to know even better than his own. "Then why do you want more?

"I love the fact that you've been with so many women and still want me most," she said. "I love being your *choice.*"

"And I'm not your choice?"

"Not yet. You can't be if I've never had other options."

He sighed. "That's crazy, you know."

"Making sure that we're making the right decision is crazy?"

"Doubting how we feel about each other is crazy."

She tipped her head to the side, considering him. "How can I not doubt it? You say you're in love with me, but you've been able to keep those feelings bottled up all this time."

"Olivia…" But he didn't know what to say. She was right. He had kept those feelings bottled up all this time. "You have too."

She nodded. "And that makes me doubt too."

Well, dammit.

"When you realize you want to spend the rest of your life with somebody, you want the rest of your life to start as soon as possible," she said softly.

He groaned. Quoting *When Harry Met Sally* wasn't fair.

Well, he'd watched a lot of movies by her side. "I'm scared of walking out of this room and never feeling the rest of my whole life the way I feel when I'm with you."

She blinked at him, clearly impressed by the quote from *Dirty Dancing*. "Wow."

"Yeah, you think about that when you're on all these dates with all these new men."

She was quiet for a moment. Then she said, "Show me that you truly trust that we're meant to be. Show me that you're sure that nothing—and no one—will ever happen to make either of us feel differently."

"By saying and doing nothing while you date other men," he muttered.

"Yes. Because you said and did nothing about *your* feelings for me."

Ouch.

Cody ran a hand over his face. He couldn't keep her from going out, and continuing to scare the other guys off wasn't going to work in his favor. He couldn't force her to keep doing what they'd been doing. Things were going to change. And he had to trust that they were good changes.

But the process of getting there was going to *suck*.

Those damned romantic movies. And Leo. And Shane. And Conner.

He blamed all of them for this.

"Tell me you love me," he said.

She nodded. "I love you."

This might kill him. "Fine," he sighed. "Date. Go for it. May the hunt for Mr. Perfect commence." What kind of idiot said that to the woman he loved?

She swallowed and nodded. "Okay. I'll…okay," she said again.

After a moment when it was clear neither of them knew what else to say, she took a deep breath and stepped toward the door. "I'm going to go."

He didn't want her to leave. He wanted to grab her and hold her and beg her not to so much as smile for anyone else. "Okay."

She turned to leave the kitchen, but paused in the doorway and looked back. "By the way," she said. "While I'm dating all of these guys…"

Cody worked on not groaning with the pain that thought caused. "Yeah?"

"I don't think you should date anyone else."

He raised an eyebrow. He had no intention of dating anyone else. But she cared and wanted to keep him home. "Oh, really?"

"Well, I figure with the number of women you've already been with, if you haven't found Ms. Right by now, she's probably not out there."

Yeah, because she was here, now. Walking out his door.

And he could have sworn she wore a tiny smile as she pulled the door shut behind her.

And Cody realized he was faced with the biggest problem of all—Olivia Dixon was even more beautiful now that he knew she was in love with him.

CHAPTER
NINE

WHAT THE HELL was she doing?

Date other men. Really? Especially now that she knew Cody was in love with her?

Olivia tipped her head and studied her date. Brent was good-looking from that angle too.

She sipped her wine and wondered if it was possible to find something they *didn't* have in common. So far, they liked the same books, music and movies. He had a big family with five siblings, all of whom he got along with very well. He loved his mother. He had a great job as an accountant for a huge coffee shop chain. He was funny, polite, flirtatious—not too little, not too much. He also cooked. He braised and basted versus baking, but they clearly shared a love for the kitchen. He was a really nice guy. A good-looking, nice guy who was a ninety-four percent match with her.

And she still wanted the date to be over. Like forty minutes ago.

They'd been at the restaurant for forty-six.

Fifty-six minutes later, her date with the nicest guy she'd met in a long time—and that included Cody Madsen—finally ended. They said goodnight at the front doors of the restaurant.

"What are you doing tomorrow night?" Brent asked.

"I, um…have plans."

No, she didn't. Not a single one.

"Well, I'd love to see you again."

That was nice. Very nice. It should make her feel warm and fuzzy. Instead, it made her scramble for a way to let him down easy.

"That's very nice. But I'm…dating. Casually. Looking to meet a lot of new people. I'm not looking for anything really lasting right now."

He nodded and smiled. "Okay. Well, if you change your mind, let me know." Then he shook her hand and sauntered off toward his car.

She watched him go.

Okay? That was all she got? He'd love to see her again, but when she gave some lame, half excuse that absolutely sounded like a lame, half excuse, he said "okay"?

Frustrated and not completely able to put the reason why into words, Olivia headed for her car.

Once she was behind the wheel, she was faced with another depressing fact. It was nine o'clock on a Friday night and she had nothing to do. Her date was over, her sisters were busy and—

Cody was sitting home alone.

At least, that was where he was *supposed* to be.

But she couldn't go over there or call him to come to her place.

They would end up having sex. She was sure of it. Because *she* wanted to so badly. Something about sex with him, knowing that he was in love with her, was so damned tempting.

But it wouldn't fix anything.

And they really needed to fix some things.

She thunked her forehead against the steering wheel and admitted something startling—and very problematic.

Dating other men wasn't going to work.

Why she'd thought it would, she wasn't sure. Everything she'd said about chocolate chip cookies and other desserts was true. But she knew, deep down, that she would always love chocolate chip cookies best. Always.

She was ticked at her chocolate chip cookies at the moment, though.

She'd initially thought she was upset with Cody over the fact that he'd kept other guys from getting too close but hadn't been willing to step up and be the right guy himself. But really, even though he shouldn't have interfered in her love life, the other guys hadn't fought very damned hard to stick around either.

One of them could have told Cody to fuck off and mind his own business. *One* of them could have thought, *I don't know her very well yet but she definitely seems worth the risk of a black eye.* One of them could have not cared what Cody thought or threatened.

Clearly Cody wasn't the only one who found fighting his feelings for her not such a difficult thing.

Which was depressing as hell.

Even Brent hadn't tried very hard to persuade her to go out with him again. He'd asked, she'd kind of said no and he'd said okay.

She needed…a bar.

Mostly she needed a place that had butterscotch schnapps, and it seemed like an overreaction to go to a liquor store for a whole bottle.

A bar would also offer the opportunity for there to be a cute guy to flirt with, who would dance with her and say sexy things and then *insist* on seeing her again. Which would do as much, maybe more, for her ego and romantic heart as the schnapps.

A place like Trudy's. But not Trudy's.

For one thing, she already knew all the guys that hung out

there. Her soul mate was not at Trudy's. Unless Cody was there…

She shut that thought down and forced herself to concentrate. She couldn't go to Trudy's. She knew those guys already, her family would probably be there—including Conner, which was *not* conducive to finding romance—and Cody would very likely be there too. Not only would he interrupt anything promising between her and another guy, but *she* would be too distracted by him to really pay attention to another guy. That wasn't fair to the other guy or to her.

So, someplace else. Another bar.

But she didn't know any other bars. Trudy's was the only place she ever hung out.

Did she even know the name of another bar? She thought about it.

She'd heard her sisters talking about a club awhile back. Emma and Amanda had gone and then Amanda had taken Ryan there. That would work. A *club* might be even nicer than a typical bar.

She pulled up her Web browser on her phone and typed in the name so she could get directions.

Frigid.

She'd started looking for her soul mate there.

Twenty minutes later, she realized that her sisters hadn't told her *everything* about Frigid.

It was a sex club.

There was a bar and there was a dance floor. But there were also couches around the dance floor where people were making out without inhibition, couches farther back in the darker corners where people were making out without inhibitions and without most of their clothing, and an upper level that Olivia was pretty sure she didn't need to see.

Frankly, some of the stuff happening on the dance floor was enough.

She took another shot of the butterscotch schnapps, Irish

cream and Southern Comfort mixture the bartender had talked her into when she'd first ordered a shot of schnapps. She was glad he had. They were called cowboy cocksuckers. Hell, yeah.

"This your first time here?" he asked, swiping a rag over the bar near her elbow.

She swallowed and nodded. "That obvious?"

"The fact that you haven't blinked since you walked in was my first hint," he told her with a grin.

"This place is amazing." It was sexy and raw and thrilling, if she was honest. It wasn't the amount of skin she was seeing—and there was a lot of that—or the touching and kissing—though there was a lot of that too—it was how much *fun* everyone seemed to be having. There were all shapes and sizes and ages represented, and it seemed that the theme was *if it feels good, do it.*

"You can get a little of whatever you want here. Or a lot," the bartender told her.

"It all makes me want to jump into the middle of it and see what happens." Olivia blinked at him. She couldn't believe she'd said that. She couldn't believe she *felt* that.

She was a romantic. She'd always believed in connecting with someone, in being swept away, in feeling magic when someone kissed her. When she didn't feel that, she ended things before they got more physical. And she'd never *really* felt them. There had been sparks here and there. There had been guys she liked enough that she'd *hoped* for some magic. She'd been *almost* swept away.

But it had never clicked with anyone but Cody.

The last time she'd almost had sex with someone other than Cody had been in college. And she'd never been totally naked with anyone but Cody. She'd never had anyone's mouth where Cody's had been. She'd never put her mouth where hers had been on Cody. She had always been waiting to feel that mystical spark that told her it was right, that the guy was *the one.*

Every look and touch and kiss had been like a test in the past.

Like in chemistry class. She was always waiting for someone to cause the perfect reaction in her.

She glanced at the dance floor. And look what she'd been missing.

"I want to just go with it," she said, almost to herself.

"You can do that too," the bartender told her. But he pulled the third shot glass away from her as she reached for it. The special had been three shots for twenty bucks. "But you're here alone?"

She nodded.

"You know anyone here?"

She shook her head. There were a few people she wouldn't mind meeting out on that dance floor though. She'd been a virgin until a few days ago. She'd *heard* about a lot of stuff from her sisters and her brother and his buddies, but she hadn't *done* much. Maybe that was her whole problem. She was too hung up on the fireworks, too hung up on the idea of that one perfect person being the best and only, too hung up on the idea that there was only one person out there for her anyway.

Looking around tonight, feeling her skin prickle with the sheer decadence of the place, watching these people pleasuring each other—and more than one other in many cases—she had to admit that she might have been naive. There were some people in here who could maybe give her fireworks. And not one or two. She could point to six without even getting off her barstool.

That was it. It had to be. She'd put way too much pressure on the whole perfect person thing, the one and only thing, the chemistry and heat. Yeah, Cody made her feel good. But he wasn't the only one.

And she was going to prove it.

"I intend to make some new friends tonight, though," she told the bartender.

He gave her a smile. "Honey, you step out on that dance floor and they realize you're not just a voyeur, and you're going to have so many friends you won't know what to do."

"A voyeur?" she asked.

"The people who like to watch stay up here with me. And a lot of the people down there like being watched."

"Ah." Well, she liked watching. It was a turn-on too. "But I want to be in the middle of it." She wanted hands on her, mouths on her, people who didn't care who her brother was or if she was a forever kind of girl or who baked brownies with her to *keep* from getting physical with her.

"Being in the middle can be fun," the bartender said with a wink.

Hmm…he was cute. She wondered if he ever fraternized with the clientele.

"I'm going to do it," she decided out loud. "I'm going to go out there."

"You'll be very welcome, I'm sure," he told her with a smile.

She would be. That was one nice thing she'd already noticed about the club. Everyone seemed equal. Everyone was getting all the attention they wanted. Dress or pant size, hair color, ethnicity and experience didn't seem to matter. So what was stopping her? That was obviously what Frigid was all about—letting go, feeling good.

But she was a smart girl too. She'd seen Emma and Isabelle throwing their inhibitions to the wind…and the trouble it could cause.

She was going to call in some backup before she left her barstool. She didn't intend to go anywhere but the dance floor, but she'd never let herself really go before. Who knew what might happen?

She pulled out her phone and started to automatically dial Cody's number. In fact, it rang once before she realized what she'd done and hit the End button. Dammit. She couldn't call Cody. Fuck. She sighed and thought. Who could she call? Cody was her best friend. He was her go-to for…everything. She hadn't had this issue before. Her sisters were the only other people she really spent time with. She couldn't call Amanda.

Amanda would not think Olivia throwing all caution to the wind in a place like Frigid was a good idea.

Though Amanda had been here before.

Olivia filed that interesting thought away for later—her responsible, sometimes judgmental, I'm-always-right oldest sister had been to Frigid.

She could call Emma. Emma would love a place like Frigid. But Emma was pregnant. She could not ask her pregnant sister to come sit at a bar and wait for her to get done making out with strangers on the dance floor at a sex club.

She couldn't call Isabelle. Because of her fibromyalgia, Iz tried to be in bed by ten o'clock most nights and definitely tried to avoid places like Frigid with its loud music and crowd of people.

So…there was only one person she could call. He'd come and take care of her. This would raise his eyebrows, for sure, but he was the most laid-back, least judgmental person she knew.

She dialed. "Ryan?" she asked a moment later.

"Liv?" her almost-brother-in-law asked. "You okay?"

It was hard to hear him clearly, and she wasn't sure if that was because of noise on his end of the line or the noise of Frigid. "Want to come hang out with me for a little while?"

"Where are you?"

"Frigid."

There was a long pause and she wondered if she'd lost him.

"Ryan?"

"Yeah. I'm here. You're…*where*?"

"At Frigid. The club."

"With who?" he asked, clearly shocked.

"By myself."

"You're there *by yourself*?"

She rolled her eyes. "Yes. That's why I was hoping you'd come down here."

"Why are you there?"

"Long story."

"Does Cody know where you are?"

"No. Cody doesn't need to know where I am every second of the day."

"Have you told *him* that?" Ryan asked. Then he said, "Never mind. Yes, of course I'll come. Stay put. And…"

She waited, but he didn't say anything more. "And what?"

"Keep your clothes on."

She grinned. "Well, hurry."

She disconnected, grabbed the third shot from the bartender and tipped it back. Then she saluted him with the glass and said, "Into the middle of it. My friend Ryan's on his way."

The bartender gave her another wink. "Have a good time."

She slid off the stool, smoothed her skirt and headed for the dance floor. She'd been watching for a while. If there were rules beyond *show up and move*, she hadn't noticed.

The moment, literally, that her foot hit the dance floor, a guy slid up in front of her. He didn't say anything, which was a relief. She didn't need any more small talk. She didn't need to know his life ambitions. She didn't even need to know his name.

He settled his hands on her hips and pulled her close. Olivia wrapped her arms around his neck. And they began to move.

He was big and solid, good-looking, smelled nice. Those were all the qualifications she needed at the moment.

She closed her eyes and absorbed the feel of it all—the heat in the air, his hands on her hips, his body pressing against hers.

He was aroused. She noticed that right away. It would be difficult not to—they were practically glued together and he had plenty to show off in that area.

His hand spread over her ass and he began rubbing the material of her skirt over her hip in tantalizing circles. Tingles of awareness danced through her. Oh, good. She had to know that she could be turned on even without knowing that he loved dogs or that he had Sunday dinner with his grandmother every week. This wasn't about liking him or connecting with him on any level other than physical.

They continued to move and he ran his hand up and down her back. That felt good too. He had big hands and he was clearly confident. She liked that.

Olivia pulled back and looked at his lips. She suddenly wanted to kiss him. Just to kiss him. She didn't love him, she didn't have any expectations of him, he didn't know a thing about her. It was about dancing and kissing. But it needed to be good kissing.

She went up on tiptoe and put her lips against his.

He welcomed it. His hand cupped the back of her head and he pressed into the kiss, his tongue licking along her bottom lip.

And it was…hot. She gripped his neck harder and arched closer. This was what she wanted, what she needed. She needed to know that her body could react like this to someone without knowing if they had a single thing in common or that there was any future beyond this moment. There was no future here. It was all about how he could make her feel right now.

And it was working. Really, really well.

His fingers curled into her butt and she opened her mouth to him. His tongue stroked in along hers. He tasted of liquor and tobacco. So he was a smoker. She didn't care. She really didn't. She wasn't the girlfriend who would be asked to run to the store for more cigarettes, and she wouldn't be around to worry about him developing COPD.

"Let's go upstairs," he said against her mouth, his hands stroking over her body, making her hot and tingly.

She didn't know what exactly was upstairs, but she had an inkling. And she wasn't totally opposed to the idea.

"I've gotta have you," he said, then kissed her again.

That was good. There was a definite thrill that went along with driving a man crazy.

"Want you bad."

But…he didn't even know her name.

Olivia groaned mentally even as she tried to drown in the

kiss. She wanted his lips and hands to overshadow everything else. She didn't want to *think*.

But she still did. Even as his lips moved down her neck and elicited goose bumps that made her nipples hard, she was thinking.

Dammit.

She knew exactly what was about to happen.

She was about to change her mind about all of this.

She sighed.

She didn't want to make out with or sleep with or date other guys. She thought she should. Maybe. But she didn't *want* to.

Dammit.

"I'm not going upstairs with you," she told the man fondling her.

He looked confused as she stepped back, and his hand fell to his side. "You want to go to the couches?"

She glanced at the couches. It was true that there was *a lot* going on there. "No. I, um…need to go home."

Or something.

Hell if she knew.

Ryan should be here soon. Maybe they'd go get a milkshake. That seemed like the proper, goody-goody kind of thing she would do.

"I'll take you home," her dance partner said, though the way he emphasized "home" made it clear he didn't mean her condo.

If only she could melt at that. He was good-looking. He had good hands. His kisses had turned her on.

Seriously, dammit.

"I've got this covered."

She looked up, over the top of her partner's head.

Mac Gordon, one of the paramedics from St. Anthony's, frowned down at the man she was dancing with.

Whoa.

Mac was a big guy. He was a good five inches taller than her new friend, looked hard as a brick wall, and had a deep voice that was impossible to ignore. Beside him was Dooley Miller. He didn't look as serious as Mac did—though Dooley very rarely looked serious at all from what she knew of him from Trudy's. Still, the two stood with their arms crossed, staring at her dance partner, and the man, understandably, stepped aside.

"Whatever," was his only parting comment.

She stared after him. *Whatever*? They'd had a moment. They'd *kissed*. And all he said was *whatever*? Wow. Talk about humbling. It seemed the only man insisting on being involved in her life for any length of time was her bossy, stubborn brother.

Awesome.

Mac and Dooley moved in on either side of her.

"You okay?" Dooley asked.

She felt her eyes widen. "Yeah."

She was fine. She was mixed-up and frustrated, but these guys couldn't help her with any of that. She was, pretty much, as far as they were concerned, okay.

"You want to keep dancing?" Mac asked.

She couldn't help a tiny grin at his look of discomfort. Mac was built like a WWE wrestler, not a dancer. She could tell he really hoped her answer was no.

She headed back for the bar, choosing to stand at the far end where they could talk.

"What are you doing here?" It occurred to her to be embarrassed about where they'd found her. Neither of them seemed particularly fazed by the establishment or what was going on all around them though.

"We were with Ryan when you called," Dooley said. "Team meeting."

"Team?" she asked, puzzled. Mac and Dooley didn't play for the Hawks.

"Paramedic meeting," Mac clarified.

He and Dooley were on one of St. Anthony's best crews. They knew her brother and Ryan, the other best crew, really well.

And everyone knew that all of St. Anthony's paramedics

loved to see one of their own squirm. They'd probably heard her name, Frigid, and seen Conner's face and realized they simply couldn't miss this.

"You all left the meeting to come here?" she asked, glancing around, trying to locate Ryan.

Mac lifted a shoulder. "Yeah. The meeting was at Trudy's."

She rolled her eyes. Of course it was. In spite of their informal "meetings" and the constant competition and ribbing between the crews, the paramedics at St. Anthony's were the best in the city and respected by everyone who worked with them, including the firefighters at Fire House Three.

"Besides," Dooley grinned. "I've never been inside Frigid."

Mac nodded. "Sara can hardly be upset if I came inside to help a friend, right?"

Olivia smiled. She knew Sara, Mac's wife, and Morgan, Dooley's wife, from Hawks games and Trudy's. She was pretty sure both women were very on to their husbands, no matter what their stories were.

"Sure, right," she agreed dryly. Though she knew Sara and Morgan had nothing to worry about. She'd seen Mac and Dooley with their wives. They were very devoted, protective, clearly smitten. She loved that word—*smitten*. She wanted someone to be smitten.

Someone. Anyone. Hell, she'd be happy if someone would bring her a cup of coffee just because he was thinking of her. In spite of Cody and Conner's warnings.

"Did Ryan have too much to drink or something?" she asked. She knew the "paramedic meetings" always involved beer. At least.

"No, he's good." Mac looked over at the door. "We came along because his hands were kind of full."

"Full?" Olivia asked. "Please tell me my sister isn't here." She really didn't want Amanda to lecture her about going to a sex club alone.

"Worse," Dooley said.

"Worse?"

"Your brother is a paramedic, if you recall," Mac said.

Oh…right. Dammit. Olivia's gaze flew to the club's front entrance as well.

"Ryan said that he'd let Conner talk to you, but that he needed to wait for you to come out."

"He didn't want Conner to see something bad," she concluded.

"The shock of hearing that *you* were at Frigid was enough to keep him pretty quiet on the ride over," Mac said. "Ryan was afraid that the shock of what he might see you doing would make him insane."

"I wasn't really doing anything," she said, still a little depressed about that.

"But that's unusual at Frigid," Mac said with a grin.

"You couldn't have stayed outside with Conner?" she asked. She'd been kind of hoping for some advice from Ryan. He knew Cody. He could tell her if she was stupid to still hope that Cody was the guy she was meant to be with.

"I have a tendency to antagonize your brother," Mac said with a grin that clearly said he didn't feel bad about it. "And he was already pretty antagonized."

His statement was very true. Mac loved to rile Conner. Mostly because Conner loved to rile Mac. Conner had been flirting with Mac's wife for well over a year now. For instance.

"Okay, let's go rescue Ryan," she said with a sigh.

"Well," Dooley said as they started for the door, one on each side of her. "It's *Gabby's* hands that are full of Conner."

Olivia tripped and looked at Dooley. "*What?*"

He grinned. "Not like that. But she was at the meeting, obviously."

Gabby Evans was one of two female paramedics on the entire EMT staff at St. A's. Both women were on Conner and Ryan's crew.

"She came along to help Ryan when someone else decided to tag along."

Olivia felt her stomach tighten. "Who?" But she knew who.

"Cody."

Of course he'd been at Trudy's tonight. Did any of these guys do anything without the others, she wondered crossly.

"So Ryan's dealing with Cody and Gabby's dealing with Conner?" she asked.

"Sam and Kevin and Sierra are all here too," Mac confirmed. "They're backup in case Ryan and Gabby can't keep Cody and Conner from going at each other."

Sam and Kevin were on Mac and Dooley's crew. Sierra was the other female paramedic on Conner's crew.

"Well, gee, that's great. You all can have your meeting here," she said, feeling irritated.

She didn't need a damned army to show up just because she was in a place a little out of character for her. And failing to actually *do* anything out of character.

"Look at it this way," Dooley said, pushing the door open. "There are lots of paramedics here in case anyone needs to be patched up."

"They better have their bandages nearby," Olivia muttered. She was mad at both Conner and Cody. Which surprised her a little bit. She didn't get mad very often.

She was sure it was going to surprise them as well.

Her brother was here because he didn't think she could make a good decision without his input. Cody was here because he was afraid she was going to meet a decadent cheesecake that was going to kick the crap out of the chocolate chip cookies she was used to.

She had major doubts about that happening, but he was worried.

Well, good.

She stomped through the door and out onto the sidewalk. She saw both men immediately. Conner stood near the cars parked at the curb. He was facing the building, but Gabby was right in front of him, Sierra at her side. Cody was leaning against the outside wall of Frigid. Ryan was in front of him. Sam and Kevin were only a few feet away.

She could practically see the waves of tension around the lot of them.

She went to her brother first, planting her hands on her hips. "I don't need your permission, Conner. I don't need you to approve of what I do."

"What the hell were you *thinking*?" was his response to that. "Jesus, Olivia."

"I was thinking that I don't know what's out there, what my options are."

"And you thought *this* might be an option?"

"Of course it's an option. So are lesbianism and the convent, for that matter."

She heard Cody cough behind her. She stoically kept her attention on Conner. Okay, becoming a lesbian or a nun wasn't likely going to happen. Still they were *options* open to her. She could do whatever she wanted.

Conner sighed heavily, as if he'd never been put under such a burden in his life, then stepped forward and took her upper arm in hand, turning her toward the building.

What the hell?

He walked her to where Cody stood. She could tell by Cody's stance that he was faking the nonchalance he was trying to pull off.

"Here." Conner nudged her forward to Cody. "Date him. If that's what will keep you from freaking out and running to places like Frigid—." He rolled his eyes.

She assumed he was fine with her ending up at the convent.

"—then do it. At least I know him. I can find him and kick his ass if he messes up."

"What?" She glanced up at Cody, who was watching them— and not saying a damned word.

Well, that was typical, wasn't it? Heaven forbid he open his mouth and tell anyone anything about how he was feeling or what he was thinking.

That might be a little harsh. That was still maybe the liquor. But she would have done anything to have heard *I love you* from him months ago.

She turned back to her brother. "You think I'm here tonight because I'm trying to manipulate you into *letting* me date Cody?"

Conner was scowling at her. "Why else would you be *here*?"

Frigid was a huge stretch to her boundaries, she could admit. But this wasn't about *him*, and he was definitely making it sound like everything she'd done tonight had been a calculated effort to frustrate and infuriate *him*.

"Because I wanted to do something new." Olivia realized she was in the midst of a defining moment. She and Conner had always functioned a certain way according to simple rules—he gave her advice and she followed it. Because no one had her best interests at heart more than Conner did.

Except…

There was actually one person who cared even more about her happiness than Conner did.

Her.

It was time for her to take some control. She'd never done it before because they'd never disagreed about anything that mattered this much. But while she believed her brother loved her and meant well, he needed to know that she could and would say no to him.

She needed to know that she could, and would, say no to him.

"Conner, you're overreacting," she said calmly. "What I do, where I do it and who I do it with aren't your business unless *I* choose to tell you."

He gave her a you've-got-to-be-fucking-kidding-me look, then looked at Cody.

"You want her?" he asked, throwing up his hands. "She's all yours. Better you than anyone else, I guess."

"Easy, Dixon," Gabby said quietly. "You're not as good-looking when you're being an ass to your little sister."

Olivia knew that "little sister" were the only words that really sunk in, but they did make him take a deep breath.

She wasn't sure what shocked her more—that he was saying Cody was the best guy for her after all, even if it was by default, or that Conner thought he could *give* her to Cody.

"Dix—" Cody started.

"Are you seriously saying that given all of *your* options, *you* think Cody is the best choice for me?" Olivia asked.

Conner nodded. "Cody's definitely on top of the list of guys inside Frigid."

Oh, he was hilarious.

No one who knew him would ever have accused Conner Dixon of being humble. But this was arrogant even for him.

"I'm not *yours* to *give* to Cody," she said, stepping close so he wouldn't miss how offended she was.

"So you don't want to be with him?" Conner asked, unaffected by her ire.

She looked over at Cody. He lifted an eyebrow.

Cody was as arrogant as Conner a lot of the time. Especially when it came to her.

"Whether or not I'm with him isn't about *you*, Conner," she told her brother. "Cody and I will figure this out."

"Do something," Conner said to Cody. "Maybe her 'soul mate' can handle her."

She felt her mouth drop open. The idea that anyone needed to *handle* her was incredibly offensive, as was the sarcasm with which he'd said "soul mate". Not to mention the air quotes. Offensive enough that she pulled her arm back, made a fist and then threw it forward—exactly the way Conner had taught her.

She caught Conner on the chin only, and his head barely even moved, but he stared at her in shock, his hand against his face.

She heard Gabby snort. Sierra gasped. Then she felt Cody's arms wrap around her from behind, pinning her arms to her sides.

He picked her up like that, turned and deposited her on the sidewalk with the building to her back, then caged her in with a hand on the wall on either side of her.

"Okay, my turn," he said.

She pushed him back. Or tried to. He wasn't moving.

"You're not going to *handle* me," she told him, meeting his gaze directly.

"Damned right I am."

"No. Stop it." She tried to push him again.

"You're at Frigid. You punched your brother. Someone needs to handle you and, honey—no one's gonna handle you better than I will."

He knew he could make her melt with words like that. Jerk.

"How would I know that?" she asked, with more bravado than she felt. "You were the first. I don't have anything to compare it to."

Cody's gaze darkened and he leaned in. "You're not auditioning all these Mr. Rights in your bedroom, Liv. No fucking way."

"It's none of your business one way or another." She ducked under his arm and started to step past him.

"Like hell," he growled and grabbed her upper arm.

She tried to pull away. She wanted him. She did. And yes, fighting him now seemed like the opposite of what she should be doing if she was in love with him. But dammit, she was hurt. He'd managed to resist her for almost two years. He'd spent nearly every day with her during that time and *resisted* her.

That wasn't the I-can't-live-without-you love she'd always imagined.

She wanted to make him want it. She wanted to know that it was hard to stay away from her now. She wanted him to want her so much that he'd do anything—not *say* that he'd do anything, but actually do it.

She didn't need Shane Kelley's level of wooing, but a little more effort than walking through her front door, plopping down on the couch with her and just being there would be nice.

Of course, just *being* with him made up some of the best times they'd had. She loved how comfortable they were, how he fit into her life so seamlessly, how it seemed so natural for them to be together, sharing meals, watching TV, discussing something from the newspaper, laughing over something stupid on social media. They fit. It was nice.

But an over-the-top romantic gesture here and there wouldn't be out of line, would it?

That wasn't the accommodating oh-whatever-you-want-is-fine-with-me Olivia everyone was used to, she knew. She wasn't necessarily proud of it, but there it was.

"Stop this, Olivia," he said firmly.

"I'm getting very tired of guys telling me what I can and can't do."

"I'm taking you home."

"You know what, Cody? Fuck you. You didn't want me before, you don't get to get all possessive now."

His jaw dropped. Olivia never said "fuck" and never like that and certainly never to Cody.

She knew it was the schnapps talking for the most part, but it felt strangely liberating to shock him, to strike him speechless when he thought all he needed to get her to do what he wanted her to do was talk sexy and go all alpha on her.

She pushed against his chest again.

"Liv—"

"Okay, let her go, man." Ryan was next to Cody, his hand on his friend's shoulder.

"No, stay out of it." Cody tried to shrug Ryan's hold off.

"Cody," Ryan said, warning in his voice, his hand moving to grip Cody's upper arm.

Cody pivoted toward Ryan, then pulled hard on his arm, causing Ryan to lose his grip and Cody's hand to swing back and hit the brick wall.

"Fuck!"

"Madsen, let's go." Ryan's tone was harder now, leaving no room for doubt that he was serious.

Mac, Dooley and Sam Bradford moved in behind Ryan.

Olivia's eyes widened. Cody didn't stand a chance if those guys all got involved.

"Oh, for God's sake," Cody said, obviously exasperated. "I know none of *you* can mind your own fucking business."

He stepped back.

As flashing lights made everyone turn.

A police car pulled up at the curb.

"Seriously?" Shane Kelley asked as he got out and stepped up on the sidewalk with them. "*You're* the ones disturbing the peace? You've got to be kidding me."

"Someone said we were disturbing the peace?" Gabby asked.

"Someone called and said there were a bunch of people gathered outside, yelling and punching each other." Shane eyed Conner's face, where there was a red bump swelling on his chin.

"Well, it's us," Ryan said. "Now what?"

"You disperse and go home or I start handing out tickets," Shane said with a sigh.

"Sounds good to me." Ryan grabbed Olivia's hand and started down the sidewalk.

She followed for a few steps, then paused, trying to look back.

"Don't," Ryan said, continuing to walk.

"But—"

Ryan pulled her around the corner of the building, laughing. "Seriously? You punched Conner and told Cody to fuck off and now you're worried about them?"

"Well…" She thought about that. "Yeah."

"They'll be okay." He unlocked his car and opened the door for her.

He shut her inside, then jogged around the front of the car.

Olivia put a hand to her head. Oh, God. Had she really said all of those things? Had she really hit her brother?

Ryan got in behind the wheel and started the car, then glanced at her. "Hey."

She met his gaze.

"For the record, they both deserved it."

She took a deep breath.

Yeah, they did.

"Thanks."

Ryan shifted into drive and pulled the car into traffic. "You okay?"

"A little shocked at myself, I guess. And feeling a little… sore." It was emotional pain versus physical, of course, but she ached.

She wanted to be with Cody. She really thought she was meant to be with Cody. But she loved romance and wanted all the sweet, crazy, remember-the-rest-of-my-life gestures, too. Was it really so wrong to want him to *show* her how he felt? He'd said it, but he'd also spent months purposely *not* showing her.

"Hey," Ryan said, giving her a smile. "Falling off of such a high pedestal is bound to smart a little."

"A pedestal?"

Ryan nodded. "The pedestal that Conner and Cody put you on a long time ago."

That didn't sound as strange as it maybe should have. "And I fell off tonight?"

"You were at a sex club, you punched your brother and you told Cody off. Yeah, I'd say so."

"Oh." She thought about that. "Is that a good thing or a bad thing?" Being up on a pedestal meant they thought a lot of her. But it was also unrealistic. Like she was untouchable or something.

"Yes, it's a very good thing," Ryan assured her. "Now you're even better than perfect…now you're someone they have to deal with."

She smiled and settled back into the seat. Then she thought about his words. "Wait, is *that* a good thing or a bad thing?"

Ryan laughed. "From my perspective? A very good thing. Anyone who keeps Cody Madsen and Conner Dixon on their toes, who makes their lives a little less easy, is someone I really like."

Olivia thought about that. Keeping them on their toes? Yeah, that sounded like a good thing to her too.

And even better than Cody knowing she wasn't so easy after all was *her* knowing that she deserved some effort.

Yes, that was a very good thing.

CHAPTER
TEN

CODY KNOCKED SOFTLY AT FIRST. Then harder and louder when there was no answer. Then he rang the doorbell. Repeatedly. But Olivia wasn't answering.

So he used his key.

He'd initially tried to give her the chance to open the door to him. It was after midnight and she was pissed at him. Maybe more at Conner, but at him too.

If she'd thought about it for three seconds, she would have expected him to show up at Frigid once he found out she was there. But she had been riled up and a little tipsy, so her thinking wasn't going to be deep and rational.

He'd hoped by the time Ryan drove her home, she would have calmed down a little. But he had to be honest—seeing her riled up had been hot…and a huge relief.

Olivia had stood up to him. She'd shown that she wasn't going to let him call the shots and walk over her feelings. If he pissed her off or hurt her, he could trust her to tell him. And maybe even smack him upside the head if needed.

Her refusal to answer the door, however, said that he might get an earful, or the smack, sooner rather than later.

Well, he wasn't going home.

"Liv?" he called as he stepped into the house.

The light next to her couch glowed softly, as did the light over the sink in the kitchen. Otherwise the house was dark. Had she gone to bed?

That would work fine for his purposes here. He headed in that direction.

He flipped on the light in the hallway leading to her bedroom as the bathroom door swung open and Olivia stepped out.

With a towel wrapped around her hair—and nothing else on —she started to scream, then realized who he was.

The sense of déjà vu nearly knocked him on his ass.

Unlike the first day, when his brain and mouth disconnected and he'd stood staring, now his brain, heart and cock definitely connected.

He stepped close, looking down at her without a word. She lifted her chin so she could meet his gaze. She didn't try to cover herself this time. She didn't act shocked that he was there. The heat and hunger in her eyes matched everything that was swirling through him.

He lifted a hand and pulled on the towel, releasing her hair, the wet mass falling to her shoulders. He combed his fingers through the strands, looking into her eyes.

"I wanted you," he said, softly but firmly. "I wanted you so damned bad, I didn't know what to do. The other women, every single one, were about trying to find someone who could help me forget you. It never worked." Her hair wrapped around his fingers as he slid his hand up the nape of her neck and against her skull, cupping the back of her head. He applied only the slightest pressure, but she stepped forward, up against him. "Because *you're* mine. And I'll be fucking possessive of you whether you like it or not."

Before she could speak, he coaxed her onto tiptoe and covered her mouth with his. He didn't need any words from her right now. Right now he needed to claim her. Needed to make sure that he truly did possess her. Make sure she knew that *she* possessed *him*.

The kiss was hungry, as always when he got his mouth on her. He stroked deep and firm with his tongue, tasting her thoroughly, before walking her backward into the bathroom. The bedroom was only a few feet away, but he should have done exactly this in her bathroom the first time he'd found her naked. He wanted a do-over.

Olivia didn't protest. In fact, she threw her arms around him and plastered herself against him. He reached between them, popped the button on his jeans and unzipped, then cupped her ass and lifted her against the wall.

She wrapped her legs around his waist and he reached between them.

"Gotta make you ready," he muttered against her lips as he slid over her clit and into her.

"So ready," she panted, squirming against his hand.

"You're going to come hard," he promised. God he wanted that. He wanted her screaming his name. *His* name.

"Yes. I'm already close."

She was hot and wet moving against his hand, and he wanted, no, *needed* to feel her muscles clamping onto him as if she'd never let him go.

"You were at Frigid," he said. "Somebody there get you worked up?" Dammit. He'd still take her, still make her come hard, calling his name, but...dammit.

"No," she said, shaking her head.

"You didn't meet anyone?" Bullshit. He knew all about Frigid. No way had Olivia gone unnoticed.

"I danced."

"And?" He curled his fingers in her, flicking his thumb over her clit.

She gasped and clutched at his shoulders. "Nothing."

"Tell me, Liv. What else?"

Her head fell back against the wall behind her. "A kiss."

Cody felt the possessiveness that absolutely, no question about it, ran clear to his soul, rear up ferociously. "And?" he growled, lifting her and dipping his head to take her nipple into his mouth.

She cried out, then panted, "Nothing. It felt good. I wanted it to feel good. But I could only think about you."

The wave of jealousy abated only slightly. "What about me?"

"How I wanted it all to be you. How I've always wanted it all to be you. How I want to get naked with you all the time but how it's so much more than that. How I want you absolutely fucking crazy about me, Cody." Her thighs tightened around him as she gripped his shoulders harder. "I want to make you beg, I want to be the only one you ever touch, I want to be the one you can't live without."

"Liv, you're—" *All of that. Everything.*

But he didn't have a chance to tell her because she wiggled against him again and he could tell she was trying to get her feet on the floor.

He let her slide down the length of his body, but if she thought there was going to be even an inch of space between them…

She dropped to her knees.

Well, maybe an inch or two wouldn't be so bad for a little while.

She wrapped both hands around his length, squeezing and stroking before leaning in and dragging her tongue from his balls to his tip. Three times.

He tangled his fingers in her hair again. The wet heat from her mouth, the sight of her kneeling before him, the fact that she'd been thinking about him while she'd been at Frigid, presumably trying out a plethora of other desserts, all combined, and he knew he wasn't going to last.

Then she sucked on him.

His entire body went tight. *"Fuck,"* he hissed. He withstood the exquisite suction for about twenty seconds. Then he tugged on her hair, tipping her head back. "You're mine," he said, looking directly into her eyes. "All mine."

She licked her lips slowly. "Show me."

He stared at her, the two words vibrating through him.

Oh, he'd show her. He'd show her all night.

He pulled her to her feet, slipped on a condom, lifted her against the wall again and thrust deep.

"Cody!"

Yes, that's what he wanted. All day. Every time.

He pulled out and thrust again, watching her face, memorizing every detail of being buried deep in her body, connected with her far beyond anything he'd ever experienced.

"Mine," he said fiercely. "You belong with me."

She was panting, trying to move her hips against his but lacking leverage in her position against the wall.

"This body, your heart, everything—I want it all," he told her.

He felt her muscles tightening around him.

"And I'm yours. All yours," he promised. "Whatever you want of me."

Her muscles tightened again and she made a sweet noise, a cross between a sob and a gasp.

"Everything we've always had," he promised her. "And everything we've always wanted."

Her muscles clamped down and she cried out loudly, his name bouncing off the tile in the bathroom.

He pumped into her as her orgasm ripped through her, watching and feeling it go on and on. Then his body had to answer, and his climax seemed to start in the soles of his feet and streak through to the top of his head. He pulsed into her, emptying himself completely, giving her everything he had—physically and in every other way he knew how to give.

"I'm so *easy* for him." Olivia covered her eyes with her hands so she couldn't see her sisters' faces around the table at Trudy's. "Even after Frigid, when I was so mad at him, I still let him in and gave him a blow job and let him stay the night."

She didn't hear any response from the women in the booth with her. She was safely tucked into the corner, and while the noise in Trudy's was typically loud for a Saturday night, she knew that she'd be able to hear them clearly. If they were talking.

She spread her fingers and peered out at them. Amanda looked concerned, Isabelle looked thoughtful and Emma looked amused.

Olivia dropped her hands and sat up straighter. "Really? You've got nothing?"

"How's the orgasm thing going?" Emma asked.

Emma was across the table, next to Isabelle.

"Really good," Olivia told her. "Really, really good."

"That's why you're letting him in even when you're pissed," Emma said. "You liked him before he was even getting naked with you, and you liked him when he wasn't able to get you off every time. Now that he can, of course you're letting him in." She sucked on the straw in her ginger ale.

Olivia groaned. "See? Easy. I shouldn't forgive him just because I like the sex."

Isabelle elbowed Emma. "It's not just that. This is *Cody*. You've never said no to him. You've always forgiven him."

Olivia pointed at her. "There! See? I've always been easy for him."

"What do you mean by easy?" Amanda asked.

"Easy to get along with. Easy to leave at home to date other women. Easy to resist."

Amanda shook her head. "You want to be difficult?"

"It's..." Olivia sighed. "What I was going to say was going to sound like the most selfish, spoiled thing ever."

Amanda laughed. "Honey, you haven't been selfish or spoiled a day in your life. I'd say you're due."

Olivia looked at her oldest sister. Fine. If there was anyone she could say this to, it would be her sisters. "He doesn't have to work at it in bed anymore."

"Because the orgasms are easier now?" Isabelle asked. At Olivia's nod, she asked, "How is that not a good thing?"

"Because..." Olivia swallowed, feeling her cheeks get warm. "At least there, he had to put in some effort. At first I felt bad that it was hard, but then I realized that it said a lot that he was so willing to work at it."

Isabelle nodded. "I get that. And now he doesn't have to?"

"Right. He doesn't have to work at anything. And maybe Conner's right."

"Conner isn't always right, Liv," Emma said. "If you're easy for anyone, it's *Conner*. You've always thought that he could do no wrong."

"And for *years* of my life, he didn't do anything wrong," Olivia told her. "But I want to be more difficult for him too."

Isabelle chuckled. "You want to be more work for both of them?"

"Yes. Because it's nice when someone's willing to put in the time and effort. Everyone loves me because I'm easy. I don't make a fuss about stuff. I'm not bossy like Amanda and I'm not stubborn like you," she said to Isabelle. "And I'm not unpredictable like Emma. I'm even keel and an open book, right?"

"Everyone loves you because you're amazing," Amanda said.

"Amazingly easy to get along with."

"How is that possibly a bad thing?"

She wanted to put this into words but afraid she'd sound immature or whiny. She was loved. She knew that. And she was grateful for every person in her life who made her feel special. But... "Shane loves Isabelle even when she's *not* easy to be with. In fact, he loved and fought for her through the least easy time in her life."

Isabelle's expression went soft and goofy. "That's true."

Olivia looked at Emma. "And Nate loves Emma. Exactly as she is. And we all know that Emma is the epitome of difficult."

Emma shrugged. No one could argue with that.

"And Ryan loves you," she said, turning to Amanda. "Even when you're bossy and always thinking you're right. And *you* loved him when *he* was the one being difficult."

Amanda reached out and took Olivia's hand. "What are you worried about?"

She bit her bottom lip, studying her napkin. Finally, she said quietly, "That Conner's right. That Cody like things easy. And that's the main reason he wants to be with me—because I am easy. Especially for him."

"This is crazy," Emma said, setting her glass down hard. "Cody's been there for two years while you were *amazingly* difficult, putting up all those rules and constantly saying nothing could happen because of Conner. But he stuck around. He scared those other guys off so he wouldn't lose you. He never knew that he could have anything other than your friendship, but he didn't want to lose even that. Then when you finally put out, he had to really work to make it good…and he *did*."

Olivia stared at her. "He put those rules up too."

"Who initiated them?" Emma shot back.

Olivia opened her mouth. Then closed it. "I did."

"Exactly. He wanted to tell you how he felt, but he didn't because he didn't want to lose what he did have with you."

"How do you know that?"

"Those nights after the big blowup with Conner in your office when he got crazy drunk, the guys took turns taking care of him, making sure he didn't do anything stupider than killing brain cells," Emma said. "He told Nate that it killed him not to tell you how he felt, but he knew that would make it harder on *you*. And that he was happy being your friend. He said that if all he ever got to do with you was laugh and eat brownies, then he'd take it. And if you had a boyfriend, he wouldn't have had even that."

Olivia tried to process that. "So I was going to be alone—and fat—while he found Miss Perfect and settled into a happy life?

Emma grinned. "Honey, he was never serious with any other woman. Why do you think that is?"

"What do you mean? He didn't find the right one. Of course, he slept with them anyway." Olivia sucked up the remnants of her strawberry daiquiri. She probably needed to start drinking something stronger.

"Come here." Emma slid out of the booth and stood, holding her hand out for Olivia. Amanda scooted out of the way.

"Where?" Olivia asked.

"There are some people you need to talk to. Trust me." Emma tugged her out of the booth.

Neither Amanda nor Isabelle protested. In fact, Amanda signaled the waitress for another drink.

Olivia tugged the hem of her shirt down. Fine. Whatever.

Emma led her toward the stage, where a couple of the doctors from St. Anthony's were doing karaoke.

"Hey, girls," Emma greeted the small cluster of women standing to one side, watching the show.

"I was wondering if you would help us settle an argument."

One of the women, a built redhead who looked amazing in her tight black jeans and boots, eyed Olivia. "What's it about?"

Olivia wondered at the look of contempt in the woman's eyes.

Emma looked like she was trying not to smile. "Olivia doesn't know the reason that Cody has never gotten serious with anyone."

The redhead propped a hand on one hip. "You're Olivia?"

Olivia looked at her sister. For some reason it seemed like a bad idea to admit it.

"Yes, this is my sister Olivia."

"You're the one he's always talking about?

Olivia felt her eyebrows rise. "Who?"

The redhead rolled her eyes. "Cody Madsen."

"Cody's always talking about me?"

"It's annoying."

"This is *Olivia*?" the blond standing with Red asked.

Emma smiled. "Yep."

The blond looked her up and down. "No kidding."

"Right?" Red asked. "I expected more."

Hey. Olivia frowned. Emma snorted.

"I've heard that from other girls too," Em said. "That he talks about her a lot."

"He's clearly in love with her," the blond said, with some disgust in her voice. "But whatever. It's not like I wanted to marry him, but it would have been nice to have him find *me* as interesting for one night."

Emma turned to Olivia. "See? He's been in love with you for a long time. You don't think that it's been hard on him to not be able to have you? But he's stuck around anyway."

Red looked surprised. "You didn't know he was in love with you?"

Olivia didn't know what to say. She shook her head.

Red laughed. "Oh, boy. Well, honey, let me tell you, all the girls in this bar hate you. Because he's head over heels and won't ever get serious with anyone else. And the fact that you've been stringing him along all this time has made more than one of us want to smack you."

Olivia felt her mouth drop open. *She'd* been stringing *him* along? Conner had been so adamant about Cody being the one doing that to her. He'd said that Cody had tucked her away in the "friend" corner where he could have her, but didn't have to worry about the complications of a relationship.

She felt her face get hot and she suddenly couldn't take a deep breath.

She *had* done that to him. Exactly that. A complicated relationship would have involved telling Conner and dealing with his anger. She would have had to stand up to her brother a long time ago. She would have had to risk disappointing him. So she'd tucked Cody into a friend corner too—where she could have him but not worry about Conner being upset. Conner had said Cody had the best of both worlds—hot sex and a home-cooked meal. Well, so had she—Cody *and* Conner both thinking she was amazing.

Emma turned Olivia to her. "You okay?"

"I don't know."

"You finally gonna do something about that boy?" Red asked.

Olivia wet her lips. Then nodded.

"Good," Red said. "Any guy who's waited around that long without getting any lovin' deserves to finally get what he wants."

He had. He'd done that. He'd stuck around, watched romantic comedies, baked bread, escorted her to parties and events, and he'd kept his hands to himself. Mostly.

Wow. A guy didn't do that if he didn't have deeper feelings.

How had she never seen that before?

She just needed to ask one more question. She headed for her almost-brother-in-laws. Who were sitting, as usual, with her brother. Cody was notably absent.

"I have a question."

Ryan, Conner, Shane and Nate looked up at her.

"If Isabelle wanted to only do art projects with you," she said to Shane—her sister was into everything from knitting to decoupage, "would you stick around?"

Shane swallowed the drink of beer he'd taken. "What?" he asked.

"If you had gone on the road trip and in the end all she wanted was to do crafts together, would you have stuck around?"

He glanced to where Isabelle was sitting, then back to Olivia. "You mean for almost two years? Without knowing how she *really* felt about me and without any indication she'd ever change things?"

Okay, so he knew what she was talking about. Olivia nodded.

He blew out a breath. "I don't know, Liv. That would've been really hard."

Olivia felt her eyes stinging with tears. "How about you?" she asked Nate. "What if Emma only wanted to hang out and watch movies?"

Nate's gaze flickered to Emma and heated instantly. Olivia rolled her eyes. The two of them were downright combustible.

"No way could I have kept it just to that," he said. "I have no self-control where she's concerned."

Emma leaned over and planted a hot, wet kiss on him.

"What if that's what she told you she wanted?" Olivia asked, her throat tight.

Nate didn't move his hand from Emma's ass. "It would've been too hard for me to be only her friend and not have more. I'm not that good of a guy."

"You would have left her alone then?"

"Knowing how Cody feels about you, I think he's a damned saint," Nate said. "I don't know how he did it."

"How did you know I was talking about me?"

Ryan laughed. "You've kept Cody at arm's length all this time," he said. "And you're wondering why he stayed."

"Would *you* have stayed?" she asked him.

"For Amanda?" His gaze found his fiancé across the room. "I would have tried. We did try the friend thing, if you remember." He looked at Conner. "But no. I'm not that good of a guy either."

"Well, Cody's kept me at arm's length too," she said crossly.

"No," Ryan said. "He's stayed at arm's length, but no…"

"Well, if he didn't like it, he should have stopped coming over to bake," she said.

"But he did like it," Shane said. "Not as much as he would have liked more. But he liked baking with you more than he liked going out—and stuff—with other women."

"And stuff?" Olivia asked. Then she realized what he was talking about and held up a hand. "Never mind."

She thought about that. It was…surprising, for sure. But sweet. And romantic. Huh. And here she'd been thinking Cody wasn't doing the romantic thing for her.

"Did he think we would eventually be more than friends?" she asked Shane. "Really?"

"For a while." Shane nodded. "But eventually I think he resigned himself to not having more than that with you."

"Then why did he stick around and not find someone else?"

"Like I said, he liked being with you more than anyone else."

"But in almost *two years* there was never another girl?" Olivia asked. She distinctly remembered a few nights at Trudy's watching Cody get flirty with another girl. Girls whom he seemed to actually like.

"There was Tracie," Ryan said. "He liked her. But she didn't like how much time he spent with you. When she told him it was her or you, he picked you."

"And Kari," Shane said. "He liked her a lot."

Olivia remembered both Tracie and Kari. She hadn't liked either of them. Tracie was too bubbly and smiled too big. Kari had been too…perfect for him.

She couldn't deny that she felt fine about him choosing her in Tracie's ultimatum. "What happened with Kari?"

"You happened," Shane said with a chuckle. "It seemed like they went on a few dates, but then every time they were together, you called. Once you needed help unclogging your drain, and another time you needed a date to some high school reunion party thing, and another time you had a flat tire."

She blushed. She remembered those times. The flat tire hadn't been intentional, of course, but the other things…yeah, she'd known he was on a date with Kari.

Conner was watching her with narrowed eyes. "You intentionally sabotaged his dates?" he asked.

"Hey, I had a flat tire."

"That you could have call any of *us* about," he said, indicating the entire tableful of guys.

"I needed a date to my reunion."

Conner shook his head.

"What?" Olivia asked.

"That's not very…sweet."

Emma laughed. "Surprise. Baby sister Olivia is devious." She patted Conner on the top of the head. "We'll let all of that sink in."

She took Olivia's hand and tugged her back toward the booth. She nudged her into the seat next to Amanda.

"There," Emma said. "Now you know."

"That I've been stringing him along too?" Olivia asked. She rubbed her forehead. "I didn't mean to."

"The clogged drain while he was dating Kari?" Emma asked.

"Okay, I didn't mean to *all along*," she said. She lifted her head. "I never meant to keep him from being happy."

"He was never not happy," Amanda said with an affectionate smile. "As long as he's had you, he's been happy."

Olivia thought about that. It was true. She knew it. He'd been sexually frustrated maybe, but he'd been happy.

"So now what?"

Before any of the girls could answer, someone set a plate covered in plastic wrap in front of her. She looked from it up into Cody's eyes.

Her heart slammed against her ribs. He was watching her with a combination of affection and heat that made everything in her strain toward him.

"Chocolate soufflé," he said, gesturing toward the plate.

Oh. Wow.

"And this is the best damned chocolate chip cookie in the entire universe." He set another plate in front of her. This one had a bow on it.

She swallowed, suddenly on the verge of tears.

She studied his face. He looked…determined. And he'd made her a chocolate soufflé. Holy crap.

"Cody, I—"

"No."

She stopped and bit the inside of her cheek.

"Not yet," he said simply.

She couldn't think of anything to say, and before anything came to her, he pivoted on his heel and headed out the door.

"Chocolate soufflé?" Emma demanded.

"He's…" Olivia swallowed. "He's giving me the chance to try other desserts."

Emma raised an eyebrow. "I don't know what that means. But is this *real* chocolate soufflé?"

Isabelle lifted the corner of the plastic wrap. "It's real."

"Gimme." Emma pulled the plate toward herself. "We're gonna need some forks here. Stat."

💋

"But you *hit* him?"

Olivia grinned at the sound of amazement in Amanda's voice. "Yep."

Ryan had finally spilled apparently. Olivia couldn't believe that the guys had kept her punching Conner a secret for two weeks. She'd known it would eventually come out, but she gave them points for not telling her sisters for so long.

She glanced around her office and noted that none of the firefighters, especially Cody, were around. She held the phone between her shoulder and chin as she typed the Perfect Pick website address into her Web browser.

She shouldn't do this at work, she knew, but she'd just take a minute.

She'd gotten out of the Love Is Blind program after she'd told Cody she was going to make her own decisions and learn to trust herself. But she'd stayed with Perfect Pick. Having access to the whole site, full profiles, photos, and the ability to be in contact with the men before meeting them in person put her in control. She wasn't relying on the computer to set her up—it was simply the medium she was using to *control* who she met and dated.

Of course, that had been before she realized that she wasn't available.

She'd intended to delete her entire account the night Cody had brought her the chocolate soufflé. She'd logged in two weeks ago specifically for that purpose.

But before she could, she'd seen the little icon indicating she had a private message—it was hard to miss the cartoon head with its mouth wide open and a heart coming out of it. It was the first private message she'd gotten. Curious, she'd clicked on it.

The message had been from user CAM609. She'd looked him up but he hadn't added a profile picture yet. He'd only been a member for two weeks, joining right about the time she'd planned to leave the site. Still, they were a ninety-three percent match.

But she wasn't up for meeting anyone. Which she told him.

He'd responded with *Then let's talk. Maybe you can help me out.*

With what? she'd asked. It was probably a line, but what the heck.

Romance.

Uh-huh. Totally a line. *Romance, huh?*

I'm not so good at it. Wouldn't hurt for me to have a mentor as I try to romance someone special.

She'd almost shut it off. But then she'd typed, *You're on a dating site but you think you need help with romance?*

How can I get better at it if I don't practice?

Okay, he had a point. She was nothing if not pro-romance. *You really just want my advice?*

If that's all I can have right now.

That *right now* was a bit of a red flag as well. Was he thinking this was the best way to get close to *her*? But what did it matter?

It was online. He didn't know her. He'd never meet her unless she agreed to meet him.

She was in control here.

Okay. How can I help?

They'd been talking for two weeks now.

She hadn't told anyone about CAM609. Because it was nothing, really. He made her smile. He asked her questions about women, ran his romantic ideas past her, and she gave him answers and advice. It was fun. No one knew romance like she did. She actually had niggles of jealousy for the woman—or women—who were on the receiving end of the ideas she and CAM609 came up with.

But she was keeping him her little secret. Her little secret that she was chatting with almost hourly.

"Liv, are you paying attention?" Amanda asked across the phone line.

No. She had two new messages. Were they both from him?

"Yes, of course."

"Is dinner going to be okay?"

Amanda had to be asking about dinner at her place with the family. And if Conner and Olivia would be okay.

"Yes." As far as she was concerned, things had been taken care of the other night. She'd put her foot down, told him to mind his own business, and if he did, things would be fine.

It was up to him.

She wasn't going to bend over backward to make up, and she wasn't going to worry about if he was mad.

She felt so different. Free. This must be how Emma felt all the time. Emma had never let anyone tell her what to do. Conner had, of course, tried, but Emma simply figured out how to hide things from him. She'd never actually listened to him.

"Can I ask you something?" Amanda asked.

"Of course."

Olivia clicked on the message icon.

Only one of the messages was from him. Simply CAM609.

She didn't know his name or how old he was or anything other than the fact she was having a great time chatting with him and felt like she was bringing a little more romance into the world.

She wanted to tell Cody about it.

Because she wanted to tell Cody about everything. She *had* told him about everything.

Their entire relationship had been built around talking because they couldn't do anything else.

And now they weren't talking.

Well, not really. They talked, of course. She was his administrative assistant. But they didn't *talk*.

She saw him every day at work, and they weren't exactly avoiding each other. He gave her long, heated looks. She tried to walk by his office as often as she could—in the skirts that she now felt free to wear. They stood stupidly close when they both ended up at the coffeepot. And there were the desserts—he brought her a new one every day.

But they didn't talk—not like they used to. And they didn't hang out. And they hadn't had sex again.

It was strange. But she knew he was giving her space. Or was trying to.

She would have thought he was easily resisting her again, if it weren't for the way he looked at her.

There was heat and longing and…love in his eyes.

He wanted her and she wanted him and they weren't together.

Stupid.

But she planned to change all of this soon. It was her move. She knew that and she appreciated it. But she wanted it to be right, to be perfect. This time the heroine was going to give the hero the big, memorable movie moment. She just had to come up with the right way to do it.

"Was the look on Conner's face as funny as I'm imagining?" Amanda asked.

Olivia laughed. "Yes. It was pretty priceless."

She should have punched Conner a long time ago.

Of course, he'd never been so insulting before the other night. He hadn't called her since then, and she knew he was waiting for her to call him. She was the one who forgave people.

And she would forgive him. But she was going to make him sweat first.

Yeah, she'd definitely lost some of her sweetness.

"What happened all of a sudden? I can't imagine you hitting anyone."

"He was being so…controlling."

"Well, yeah. It's Conner."

"But he was so *rude* about it."

"I'm glad you did it."

"Really?" That was not something she would ever have expected Amanda to condone.

"Yeah. He seemed to come around with Shane and Iz, and he's fine about Emma and Nate. But he's never actually said that he's happy for me and Ryan."

"Really?" Olivia hadn't known that. "That's shitty. I know he loves you and Ryan together."

"You think so?" Amanda asked.

"Well…" She'd *assumed* so. Ryan and Amanda were perfect together. "Who cares? Are you happy?"

"Of course. Ryan is amazing. I think we're amazing together."

And there in her sister's soft tone, Olivia knew that it didn't matter one bit what Conner thought. Ryan was Amanda's soul mate.

"Then I think we both have to come to terms with something serious," Olivia said.

"What's that?"

"I do believe that our brother is full of shit."

Amanda snorted this time. "I think you might have something there. Should we tell him?"

"You know, I think he knows." Olivia thought more about that.

Conner had inherited the job of patriarch of the Dixon clan at the ripe old age of seventeen. Olivia had only been eleven. What did he know about being a father? What did he know about *anything* at that age? But they hadn't had anyone else to look up to. Their mother told them to listen to Conner, so they had.

He'd been guessing all along.

And she was sure he knew it and had been simply praying that his sisters wouldn't figure it out.

"Then dinner will be fine," Amanda said.

Yes, dinner would be fine. Everything would be fine. She might even let Conner in on the fact that she knew about him being full of it. Maybe it would be a relief to him to know they knew.

The chime on the Perfect Pick site sounded, indicating she had another new message.

She couldn't resist the urge to click on the icon.

It was from him.

The older of the messages simply said, *I'm thinking of you.*

The new one said, *I want you to imagine the biggest, brightest, most expensive bouquet of your favorite flowers sitting on your desk right now.*

She smiled. He must have had a good date the night before.

She liked the treasure hunt?

The idea was to plant notes and hints leading his date to the final destination for their night out.

You're amazing was all he said in reply.

Well, hearing that never got old.

"Olivia?"

Her sister was still on the phone. "Yeah, sorry. Yeah?"

"What's funny about mashed potatoes?"

Olivia thought about that. "I'm pretty sure nothing."

"Then why did you laugh?"

Because this guy with the cute personality was online. "Uh…"

"You're at work—I should let you go."

"Yeah, okay, probably. I'll talk to you later."

"Bye."

She hung up, eagerly putting both hands on the keyboard.

So what's next? she typed.

I'm hoping to meet a woman I've been chatting with for a while.

She smiled. He was really getting out there. She was happy for him.

It was weird, but she felt like they were friends. In addition to the whole romantic-advice thing, they'd talked about why they liked the movie *Alice In Wonderland* with Johnny Depp and which books should never be turned into movies. They'd debated over whether Skittles or M&M's were better; why if he could only have one kind of pizza and one kind of beer for the rest of his life, he would want good pizza and bad beer instead of the other way around; why she preferred to think portals for time travel existed but that life on other planets did not. They'd talked about so many things that seemed like nothing, but were actually better than knowing what he did for a living.

What's the plan? she asked.

I'm going to invite her to meet me at a restaurant.

After all these lessons and advice, you're just going to show up at a restaurant. Booorrrringg.

There was a pause. Then he typed, *I guess I'm hoping I'll be enough with this one. Without all the pomp and circumstance.*

Oh. That made her feel bad for teasing him. *I was kidding. Of course you're enough.*

There was no response for almost three minutes. Then he said, *I have to tell you something.*

Uh-oh. *Okay, what?*

I haven't been on a date yet.

Oh, boy. *You've been faking it with me?*

Ha. Ha. I haven't gotten up my nerve yet to ask out the one I want.

You're going to be fine. Be yourself. Talk about Skittles.

There was another long pause.

You should come too. Cliff's. Six o'clock tomorrow night.

Olivia blinked at the screen. She should go too? *Table for three?*

She got a smiley face in return. Then, *Not* with *us. Just be there. In case she doesn't show up or in case she hates me.*

He was sweet and funny. No way would this woman hate him.

She hoped.

But yeah, getting stood up would suck. Of course, in *her* case it had worked out great because Cody had been there. Still, getting stood up or having a bad date sucked. No matter who you were.

And she would hate if this guy got discouraged by a bad date. He was trying to be romantic. He wanted to find someone special. She could at least buy him a drink and boost his ego if things turned out badly.

Tomorrow at six. Got it.

The door to the office area of the fire house swung open and she looked up. It was Cody. She hit the button to minimize her screen quickly. And guiltily.

"Hey."

"Hi."

Her heart thumped. He looked so good.

His eyes were bloodshot, he hadn't shaved today—or maybe for a couple of days—and he clearly hadn't ironed his shirt.

She wanted to hug him. And do his laundry.

"This is a pumpkin flan." He set a small ceramic plate covered in plastic wrap in front of her. "And this is—"

"Another cookie," she filled in with a smile. Besides a new dessert every day, he'd also brought her a chocolate chip cookie.

He nodded and set another plate down. This one had a huge bow on it. The thing was, he didn't have to try to influence her opinion toward the cookie. They were amazing. They were chocolate chip, but Cody had somehow found and perfected *the* best chocolate chip cookie recipe in the entire universe.

Or maybe it was that he had listened to her rant about finding the right dessert instead of settling for chocolate chip cookies—and that yes, he was the cookie in the analogy—and he was using the whole thing to romance her.

He was *romancing* her. The entire thing made her truly understand the word giddy. And it made her panties wet.

It might be because she was in love with him, but the cookies were truly amazing.

Better than the chocolate soufflé he'd brought to Trudy's and better than the crème brulée, the caramel apple crisp, the white chocolate raspberry cheesecake, the caramelized banana pudding, the mocha lava cake, the lemon supreme bars, the blackberry cobbler, the strawberry pie, the crunchy pecan bites, the Snickers pie, the red velvet brownies, the almond-amaretto pound cake and the buttered rum cake with the bananas Foster sauce. Fourteen desserts in fourteen days. He was unrelenting.

They were all incredible. And, holy cow, that buttered rum cake was nearly orgasmic. And for her that was really saying something.

She grinned up at Cody. He'd think that was funny.

But he was watching her with a thoughtful and affectionate expression. Her smile faded and her heart swelled. She loved him. And he was showing her how he felt about her. Blatantly. No one brought sweets into Fire House Three without *everyone* knowing about it. And the reason why they were suddenly inundated with desserts was the first thing everyone wanted to know.

"I'm trying to help Olivia realize that chocolate chip cookies are, and always will be, king," was how he'd first explained it.

King. She rolled her eyes even thinking about it.

"By bringing all these fancy-schmancy holy-shit desserts in?" one of the guys had asked.

"Yep." He'd met her eyes across the room. "I'm not worried,

though. I know where her heart truly lies."

The look between them had been noticed, and commented on, by more than one of the firefighters.

"Are we gonna have to get the hose out for you two?" one of them had called out.

"Nothing can put these flames out, boys," Cody had said.

Her *cheeks* had certainly been burning as the house broke out in whistles and *whoo-hoos*.

"Olivia's way too smart to fall for a guy like you, Chief," someone hollered.

Cody had winked at her. "Yep, but don't tell *her* that. I kind of like kissing her."

He'd done it. He'd publicly declared his feelings. At work. With men he would see every day and who would rib him about it every day if she continued to keep him at arm's length.

She loved it. So much.

Yes, the chocolate chip cookies were still the best.

"This looks amazing," she said of the flan.

He nodded. "It's awesome."

"But I'm pretty sure this cookie is still at the top of the list."

He gave her a long, intense look. "Even without trying the other?"

She nodded.

Her heart thudded at the heat and, yes, definitely love she saw in his eyes. "Whenever you're ready for the ride back to One Man Island, you let me know."

She had to swallow hard at his emphasis on *ride*. "It was No Man Island."

"Not anymore." Then he gave her a wink and sauntered into his office.

He was so damned cocky. So sure of her. So sure of himself.

She took a bite of the flan. And moaned. Yeah, he was king all right. Then she unwrapped her cookie.

Holy crap. He'd put the chocolate chips in the shape of a heart.

CHAPTER
ELEVEN

THE CRACKLING of the flames was still audible, but for the moment, it was far enough away that Cody could relax.

Well, as much as he was able to relax with his entire fucking leg throbbing like a son of a bitch. Of course, plunging down nine steps and catching an exposed piece of metal on the way when the staircase collapsed could be expected to smart a little.

"Jesus, Madsen." Conner ran toward him and knelt at his side. "You couldn't wait for your guys to go in?"

"There was a dog."

The dog that had gone running out of the building the moment Cody had hit the floor.

"There was a dog," Conner repeated as he examined Cody's head and shined a flashlight into his eyes. "Idiot."

"My head's fine."

"I disagree. But I don't think *this* incident is the problem."

"Thanks," Cody said dryly.

"But I assume you're still sitting here because something isn't fine?"

"My leg."

Conner glanced at the outstretched limb with the huge rip and the oozing blood. "What else?"

"My wrist hurts a little, but I'm not worried about it."

"Got it." He pulled Cody's boot off, checking for his pulse, assessing his circulation and sensation. "So, I guess you do things the hard way when you need to—running into this fucking building was the hard thing to do. You're chief. You should have sent someone else in."

Cody hissed out a sharp breath as Conner moved his ankle and knee.

"And you ran in right behind me."

"Because my sister will kill me if I let you die and don't at least get hurt trying to save you."

"Nice."

"And I was…wrong."

Conner's eyes were on Cody's leg, so Cody couldn't read his expression. Cody frowned. Maybe he had lost more blood than he thought. "Did you just say you were wrong about something?"

There was a long pause. A really long pause. Then Conner sighed. "Yeah. I was wrong about you stringing Olivia along."

Cody looked up at his friend, the surprise as sharp as the pain in his leg when Conner rubbed gauze over the edges, soaking up some of the blood so he could see what he was doing. "What?"

"I was wrong. Sounds like you were both…hanging on tight. To whatever you could have because of your feelings. I didn't…I didn't see that. I saw my little sister happy though."

"Olivia's a naturally happy person," Cody said. Then he gritted his teeth as Conner cut up along the seam of his pants to get to his wound. One of them anyway. The worst at the moment.

"She is," Conner agreed. "But she won't be…if you're not around."

Cody's voice was tight when he spoke, his leg feeling like it was on fire. "I'll always be around. But she's not...breakable, Conner," he said, referring back to Conner's own words the last time they'd been in a burning building together.

Conner nodded but didn't look up. "I'm starting to see that I'm pretty good at this being wrong stuff."

Again a jolt of surprise went through Cody. Conner Dixon didn't admit shortcomings easily. Mostly because he didn't have many. But when he did, he *really* did.

It was nice that he realized it.

Conner got to the point on his leg where the pain was most intense. "Fuck," he muttered.

The wound was gory. The skin was pulled back, bloody and raw. And it was deep.

"You got muscle, man," Conner said. "And a big vessel. Fuck." Conner applied more pressure as he pulled a tourniquet from his bag.

Cody tried to distract himself from the pain. Besides, he wanted to have this conversation.

"Listen," Cody said. "I know that it's hard for you to believe that I'll be there for Olivia. I understand. I've fucked up in the past. I haven't appreciated what I had. I've definitely taken the easy road. But—"

"Knock it off."

Cody stopped and looked at his friend. "What?"

"You're a great guy, Cody. You were an ass when you were twenty, but who wasn't?" Conner looked up. "Ashley would never have told you to fuck off. She should have. But she never would have."

Cody didn't know what to say. If Conner were the one lying here with a bloody, gory leg, he'd blame his friend's words on shock. Maybe Conner was still suffering from knocking his head when he'd fallen into that basement.

"You okay, Conner?" he finally asked.

"Yeah. I'm good. I was thinking back to what I told you when I was stuck under the totem pole."

Cody couldn't help but grin at that condensed description of the events. "Yeah?"

"I told you that I felt good knowing that all the girls would be taken care of. And that I knew you would take care of Olivia. And you'd find her the right guy."

Cody nodded.

"I was right on that one," Conner said. "You found her the right guy. You."

Cody was having a hard time swallowing. He would be with Olivia no matter what anyone else thought, but knowing that Conner was okay, that he actually thought Cody was the right guy—that meant more than he had even realized it would.

"And Olivia *will* tell me to fuck off. As you witnessed," he said, his tone light.

Conner grinned. "I did love that."

Cody grinned back.

"But seriously, that helped," Conner said. "I've never seen Olivia feisty like that. Knowing that she can do it, and that she will do it with you, also makes it easier for me to trust that she'll be okay."

"She's stronger than we both gave her credit for," Cody admitted. "She's still sweet and forgiving and thinks I'm awesome, but…" He shrugged and gave Conner a sheepish look. "I can assure you that, over time, as she has to put up with me, she'll likely think I'm less awesome."

Conner shook his head. "I hope not."

"What?"

"I know I've been hard on you," Conner said. "And I'm sorry."

Cody felt his leg throb as his body tensed in surprise again. "For what?"

"For not telling you that I'm not just happy about you and Olivia because I think you'll take good care of her. I'm happy because she thinks you're amazing. You deserve to be with a woman who knows that."

Cody opened his mouth to reply, but had no idea what he was going to reply with.

He felt a little dizzy—pain and blood loss, surprise, relief—and he closed his eyes and breathed deep through his nose. He couldn't wait to tell Olivia about all of this at dinner tonight…

Son of a bitch.

He had a date tonight. With Olivia. She didn't know that, but he had to be there. If he wasn't, she'd think she'd gotten stood up again. And it would ruin the great big romantic moment he'd planned.

"This is a problem," Conner said evenly, attempting to clean the wound further.

"Yeah, no shit."

Conner radioed to his crew, asking for a stretcher.

"Can't you just bandage it?"

Conner looked at him like he was nuts. "Thought your head was fine."

"Head's dizzy. But not crazy."

"So, no, I can't just bandage it. You're going to the ER. And you're gonna be there for a while."

A wave of pain and nausea hit, and Cody worked to breathe through it and not puke.

When it passed, he said, "I've gotta be somewhere tonight."

"Too bad." Conner was examining the rest of his leg. It was already turning black and blue.

"No, it's really important."

Conner looked up at him. "Too fucking bad. You're going to the hospital. Don't be a dumb ass."

"It's Olivia."

"What is?"

"I'm supposed to see Olivia tonight."

Conner sighed. "So call and tell her what happened. She'll want to be with you anyway."

"I love her, Conner."

"I know."

"This is it. She's the one I want. For good."

"I know."

"She's meeting me tonight, but she doesn't know it's me. I convinced her to meet a fourth guy from the dating site. Tonight. But it's me. I'm going to show her that it doesn't matter what that site says or what y—anyone—says. We belong together. I have this whole big…thing planned."

He'd been chatting with her as CAM609. At first he hadn't believed that she didn't know it was him. But as they'd chatted, she'd told him about things the man she was in love with did to make her feel special, things she loved about him, and about their love story.

She was telling him about *him*. And she really didn't know.

The whole thing was awesome. It was like reading her mind. He was walking around cockier and more confident than ever.

But now he knew for sure that she was in love with him, that she wanted to be with him, that they were meant to be. He'd been romancing her for two weeks.

Two weeks and twenty months.

Surely that was enough.

Conner was looking at him, a myriad of emotions in his eyes. "You're going to propose?"

He wasn't going to be able to duck if Conner took a swing, and he wasn't going to be able to pull himself out of this building if Conner got pissed and left him. Still, Cody nodded. "Yeah."

Instead of swinging or stomping out, though, Conner nodded thoughtfully. "She'd love that. The surprise. A whole big production."

"Yeah."

Conner studied him and Cody worked on not squirming.

"Okay, here's what's going to happen," Conner said as the sounds of the gurney rolling over cement came to them.

Cody was pretty sure he was ready to hear this. "Okay."

"You're going to St. Anthony's. And I'm going…" He frowned. "Where am I going?"

"You mean where I'm meeting Liv?"

Conner nodded.

"Cliff's."

"All right, I'm going to Cliff's at…what time?"

Cody actually felt himself smile. "Six."

"Where's the ring?"

"Conner," Cody began as Gabby and Ryan showed up with the gurney. "Are you telling me that you're going to propose to your sister for me?"

Ryan and Gabby looked at Conner with wide eyes.

"Well, you want it to be memorable and unique, right?" Conner asked.

He got to his feet as Gabby and Ryan helped Cody onto the gurney.

Cody leaned to meet his friend's eyes. "You sure?"

Conner sighed. "Strangely, I am."

Olivia approached the door to Cliff's with butterflies in her stomach.

This wasn't her date, but she was excited. She hoped that her online friend found what he was looking for. She hoped that she was about to witness the first date that this couple would be telling their grandkids about.

She stepped through the door and looked around. She didn't want to interrupt, but if there was a guy sitting by himself, she might go and say hello. And wish him luck.

There were a few occupied tables, but only one with a guy alone.

But there was something very familiar about that guy.

She pulled her purse up higher on her shoulder and headed for the table.

"Conner?

He shoved his chair back and stood. He didn't look surprised to see her. "Hi, Liv."

He did, however, look really nice. He was dressed in a suit and tie. "Wow. You look great."

"Thanks." He fussed with the knot of the tie.

"What are you doing here?" Then it occurred to her. "Wait, you're here on a *date*?"

"Um." He cleared his throat and loosened the tie slightly. "Kind of."

Her brother didn't date. He flirted and hooked up from time to time—something she chose not to spend a lot of time thinking about—but he didn't *date*. That would imply that he was interested in a relationship, which he was not. He was quite adamant on that point, actually. He always said that he'd had plenty of women in his life and he was looking forward to a time when he didn't have any females to take care of.

"Well, that's…great," she said.

Conner tugged on the cuffs of his shirt and cleared his throat again. "I, um…"

"You okay?"

He finally looked her directly in the eye. "Yeah. I'm okay. I'm good."

"You're nervous about your date?" That was sweet. And unexpected.

"I, um…"

Conner was cocky. Always. Especially with women.

She reached for his arm. "Conner, what's going on?"

"My date is…with you."

She snatched her hand back. "What? Gross!" She frowned. "*We* were set up by Perfect Pick?"

His eyes widened. Then he laughed. Glancing around, he nudged her toward the chair opposite him. "No. God. We weren't set up."

She took the seat. "What's going on?"

"I'm here—"

The waiter approached with two glasses of water and the wine list. They paused for him to go through the evening's specials.

When he'd moved off, Conner tried to explain again. "I came down here because—"

"Oh, my God! Conner Dixon?" A beautiful brunette, who had been sitting at a table with two other women, stopped beside Conner's chair, a hand on her hip.

"Uh, hi, Lisa."

"What are you doing here?" The woman turned to Olivia. "Is this the new girlfriend? I see you put a tie on for her."

"This is my sister," Conner said quickly. "And it's her birthday. And she's been dumped. So yes, I thought I would dress up and take her out."

Lisa's face softened. "Oh, I'm sorry."

"I've been dumped?" Olivia asked.

Conner glanced at her, then back to Lisa with a smile. "I'm trying to cheer her up."

"I understand. I'm sorry I interrupted." She started to turn away, then turned back, leaned over to kiss Conner's cheek. "You're so sweet." Then she moved off.

Olivia leaned in on her forearms. "You're incorrigible."

"I'm *talented*. I got rid of her and she still thinks I'm the sweetest guy she knows."

"Am I being dumped?" she asked. "If you're here to tell me to stay away from Cody again, we're going to have—"

"That's not why I'm here."

"Well, if you're here to tell me that you talked to Cody—"

"That's not why I'm here either."

"Then why are you here?"

He started, then stopped. He started again, then stopped again.

Olivia grew concerned. "Conner, is everything okay?"

He didn't reply.

She reached out and grabbed his hand. What was he trying to tell her? Had he gotten one of his flings pregnant? Was he leaving Omaha? Was he dying? "Conner, are you sick?"

"Sick?" He shook his head. "No. I'm here about Cody."

She narrowed her eyes. "You *are* here about Cody?"

"Yes."

"I'm in love with him, Conner. There's nothing you can—"

"I'm not trying to break you up."

A horrible thought hit her. Oh God. What if *Cody* had gotten one of his flings pregnant? What if he was leaving Omaha? What if *he* was dying? She gripped her brother's hand harder. "Conner," she said, trying not to grit her teeth. "Is Cody okay?"

"Um."

She squeezed his hand. "*Conner.*"

"He's at St. Anthony's, actually."

"*What*?" She sprang from her seat.

"There was an incident on a call." Conner got to his feet too. "But he's okay. Well, he'll *be* okay."

Her heart in her throat, Olivia took a step closer to him. "What. Happened?"

"Burning building, staircase fell in, big gash on his leg. But," Conner said quickly. "I was the one that went in after him."

She stared at him. Then she pivoted and started for the door.

"Olivia, wait!" Conner grabbed for her and hooked her purse strap, bringing her around to face him.

"Conner, I have to go!"

"No, wait. Not until I tell you why I came down here."

"You came down here to tell me that the man I love is in the hospital!"

The other patrons were turning to look at the drama unfolding in the middle of the restaurant, but Olivia didn't care. She tried to jerk her purse from Conner's grip.

"I wouldn't have come clear down here in a *tie* to tell you that," Conner said. "I would have called you."

"But you… But I…" She fumbled for words. "So you *didn't* come down here to tell me about Cody's accident?"

"No. This is much bigger."

Even the wait staff had gathered around at this point.

She faced him. "Bigger than Cody being in the hospital?"

"Yes."

"Tell me. Now."

He took both of her hands in his. Which freaked her out. "Of all the girls, I always felt like maybe you needed me the most," he said. "And I have to say that I'm so damned proud of you, Liv. I love you so much."

There was emotion in Conner's voice that made her go back to the thought about him maybe dying.

"Conner…"

"And I want you to know that what I'm about to say to you is from my heart."

This was…so weird. "Conner—"

"I'm actually a little bit glad that this is how this worked out."

"Conner, seriously. If you're dying and you got all dressed up to tell me I'm never going to—"

"Dying? I'm trying to propose!"

There was total silence in the restaurant for five seconds. Then a fork clattered against a plate and the place erupted into applause.

"I don't understand," Olivia tried to say, but their waiter swept over to them, urging them back into their seats and gushing about a special dessert for the big occasion.

The maître d' came by with a rose. The piano player at the baby grand launched into "The Wedding Song". And people at the tables around them leaned over to congratulate them.

Finally, Olivia and Conner looked at one another. And burst out laughing.

The waiter appeared again, popping the top on a bottle of

champagne, and when their glasses were full, Conner raised his up.

"To my beautiful little sister and the most romantic moment of her life."

"Glad you could be here," she said as she clinked her glass against his.

They sipped. Then Conner said, "Cody was on his way here tonight. He said he was meeting you but you didn't know it was him."

"But I was coming here to meet…" She trailed off as she realized what had happened. "He's CAM609."

Conner looked puzzled. "What?"

"That was the username of the guy I thought I was meeting here tonight."

"Yeah, Cody."

"But I didn't know it was him."

"How?" Conner asked, digging into the salad the waiter had set in front of him. "C.A.M. are his initials and his birthday is June ninth."

Olivia felt her eyes widen. "Oh, wow." It hadn't even occurred to her. And she felt stupid—and kind of guilty—about that. "We've been chatting online for two weeks. I was coming down here tonight to be sure his date went well with the girl he was supposed to be meeting."

"He was supposed to be meeting you."

"But I thought there was another girl."

"How could you be sure? Just because he told you that?"

Well…yeah.

"You came down here to meet some guy who *said* he had a date with another girl?" Conner asked.

She shrugged.

"What if he'd said that to get you down here?"

"He *did* say that to get me down here," she pointed out. "It was Cody."

"But if it had been another guy. You obviously would have come."

"Yes. But I thought…"

"Jesus, I'm glad you're marrying Cody. I can't handle you out there on a dating site." He swallowed the rest of his champagne.

Olivia watched him, then started grinning. "I'm not engaged to Cody."

"Yes, you are."

"No one's asked me and I haven't given an answer."

"But you *will* say yes," Conner said. He pointed at her. "I mean it, Liv."

"And now you're telling me that I *have to* marry Cody?"

"Yes. Dammit, Olivia."

Her grin grew. "Well, okay."

It took Conner a second to realize that she'd stopped arguing.

She took a bite of salad, then looked up quickly. "Is there a ring?"

"A…ring." Conner groaned. "Shit. He didn't give it to me."

"That's okay. I'm actually kind of in the mood to see him soon." Then she shoved her chair back and jumped to her feet again. "Oh, my God, Conner! Cody's in the hospital."

The waiter arrived with their entrees.

"Can't we stay and eat—"

Olivia was already on her way to the door and didn't hear the rest. She glanced back. Conner was looking longingly at the food and talking with the waiter.

Well, they'd arrived separately. He could get the food to go—and pay the bill.

She was on her way to get engaged for real.

"Okay, Amanda's got the car outside the ER entrance and Emma is going to distract Nate when he comes down the hall. We have about three minutes to get you out of here without being seen,"

Isabelle said as she steered the wheelchair into the exam room where Cody had been stitched up and given blood and antibiotics.

He'd called the Dixon Divas the moment he'd been alone.

"Great." He eased himself off the bed and into the chair, of course banging his sore leg hard against the bed, then the footrest of the chair. "Fuck!"

"Be careful," Isabelle hissed. "You're going to get us in trouble."

Cody lifted his injured leg onto the footrest with both hands. "You and Emma used to get into trouble every other minute."

"Not with Olivia," she said, pushing the chair to the doorway.

They both peered out and looked in both directions. The hallway was clear of people they knew. For now.

She pushed him through the doorway and hung a right.

"You're all worried about Olivia being mad?" Cody asked.

"Yes," Iz answered without hesitation.

He chuckled.

"Hey, we've never seen her get really riled up. It could be worse than any of us imagine," Isabelle said. "And she's never cared about anything the way she cares about you."

Cody loved hearing that. He hadn't heard from Conner or Olivia and it was well past the time they should have met at the restaurant. And *he* still had the ring in his pocket. He'd forgotten to give it to Conner as proof of how serious he was.

Isabelle took the next corner a little tight and Cody felt the chair tip.

"Hey." He put his hand out on the wall to brace himself.

"Shit."

"Just nice and easy," he coached, feeling damned helpless and anxious.

They rounded one more corner, the sliding ER doors in sight, when they heard, "This seems like a bad idea."

Busted.

Isabelle leaned down. "I can try to shove you hard enough that you'll make it to the doors, and I'll run interference if you want."

"You're the best almost-sister-in-law I've ever had," he told her, his hands going to the wheels and stopping the chair. "But no."

They both turned to find Nate, Ryan and Conner standing behind them, arms crossed.

"Where's Olivia?" he asked when he saw Conner.

"On her way to find you in the exam room that I told you to *stay* in," Nate answered.

"I needed to see her."

"And you would have two minutes ago if you'd stayed put," Nate said, coming around to the back of the chair and pushing Cody back in the direction he'd come.

He tried to defend himself. "I didn't know she was coming here."

He held his breath as Nate got his sore leg really close to the wall.

"You really didn't think she'd come straight over here?" Conner asked.

Cody craned his neck, trying to see his friend and soon-to-be brother-in-law. "You had a chance to tell her about the proposal though?"

Conner chuckled. "Yeah. Thanks for the champagne by the way."

"Champagne?"

"I think it was on the house," Conner said. "Once they found out we were engaged, they were pretty excited. But I didn't look at the bill before I plunked down your credit card. Maybe they charged us for that. And the roses. And the dessert."

"Dessert?" Cody repeated. "You stayed for dessert? While I was bleeding in the hospital?"

"You weren't bleeding by dessert time," Nate said. "Where do you think you are?"

"Yeah, yeah." Cody still couldn't really see Conner behind him. "What took you so long to get here?"

"I had to convince her that I wasn't dying and give her my little speech and…"

"*You* had a little speech?" Cody asked. "This was supposed to be about *me*."

"She's my little sister," Conner said. "Of course I had a little speech. It was awesome by the way. I almost made her cry. Of course," he added, in a near mutter, "that was when she thought I might be dying."

"Did you propose to your sister or not?" Cody demanded as they rolled into the trauma area.

The family of four gathered in one corner of the waiting area looked appalled.

Cody huffed out a frustrated breath.

"Yes, he proposed to me."

Cody looked up at the sound of the soft, sweet voice. "Olivia."

Nate rolled him the rest of the way into the exam room he'd exited only a few minutes ago. "We'll leave you two alone for a bit," Nate said, pulling the door shut behind him.

"Hey, Doc," Olivia said.

"Yeah?"

"Is he okay?"

"He's going to be fine. Now that you're here, I doubt he even remembers he has a leg."

"Is he okay to…"

Cody grinned. He was more than okay to… She'd just have to be on top for a while. "I'll give it my best."

"…get on one knee and propose properly?" she finished.

Nate laughed. "Sorry. No. And if you rip my stitches out, you have to put them back in."

She wrinkled her nose. "We'll make do."

Nate closed the door behind him, and Olivia turned to Cody.

"I can't believe you're CAM609."

"I can't believe you didn't figure it out."

She gave him a sheepish look. "Yeah. Sorry."

He laughed and grabbed her hand, tugging her into his lap. "I forgive you. I think it was sweet that you were going down to Cliff's to be sure my date went well."

"I will admit I wondered what I was going to do if your date didn't show."

Since it had been *him*, he hadn't given a lot of thought to her reactions. The friendship they'd struck up online had simply confirmed that much of what drew them together was far more than their physical chemistry.

"Hey, you got kind of cozy with this guy you didn't know."

She leaned back slightly. "But it was *you*."

"But you didn't know that. You told him some pretty personal stuff."

"About how I felt about *you*."

"But you thought he was a stranger." She'd been *very* friendly. Warm. Sweet. The guy—had it not been Cody—would have absolutely fallen for her.

"But he wasn't a stranger. He was *you*."

"You were pretty quick to make new friends."

"There was something about him—you—that felt right," she said with a shrug. "Now that I know it was you, it makes complete sense."

"But you were willing to go along with it before you knew it was me," Cody said, feeling very conflicted and not completely sure why.

"We clicked. *Because it was you*," she said. "That wouldn't have happened with anyone else."

"But you didn't know that. You thought he was some stranger. And you were going to the restaurant to meet him." He suddenly didn't like that.

"To help him with his date. With someone else. I mean, to help *you*." She shook her head. "This is really confusing."

"What if the whole needing help with his date thing was a ploy to get you to go out with him?" Cody asked.

"Conner said something like that," she said. "But if that had happened—and it wasn't you, which it *was*—then I would have broken it off with him."

"With me?"

She huffed out a breath. "I would have been breaking up with him—*you*—for…*you*."

"But we really connected online. We were talking and joking and…"

"Oh, my God, *you* kiss me. Now." She took his face in her hands and shut him up with her mouth.

She tasted like everything he'd ever wanted, everything he'd ever need.

He cupped the back of her head and deepened the kiss, needing her and her sweetness and love surrounding him, filling him up. Forever.

She leaned back, panting, a few minutes later. "There. That was *you* and *me*. That's all we need."

"I can't believe you were going to break up with me."

"For *you*," she said with a laugh.

"But we were a ninety-three-percent match online."

She raised an eyebrow. "Online? What about in person?"

Cody reached into his pocket and withdrew the ring he'd picked out with Ryan's help three days before. He slipped it onto Olivia's finger, then lifted her hand for a kiss.

"My ring looks good on you."

Her eyes were filled with tears as she nodded. "It sure does."

"Marry me, Olivia."

"Yes."

"It's official. You can't take it back now."

She laughed. "There's no way I'm going to take it back."

"Okay, then I can tell you—I might have lied a little on the Perfect Pick thing when I signed up as CAM609."

"What do you mean?"

"Well, we're a ninety-three percent match when I'm CAM609. But when I looked at my percent as me, the profile you first helped me put in…"

"Yeah?"

"It's lower."

"Lower? Like what? Ninety percent?" she asked.

"Lower."

"Eighty-five?"

"Lower."

Her eyes got big. "No way. We get along great. We have a ton in common."

"Not according to Perfect Pick."

She wrapped her arms around his neck and kissed him, then snuggled close. "Who cares? It's a dumb website. I don't need them to tell me that we're perfectly matched."

"Okay, good." He stroked his hand up and down her back. Waiting.

Less than a minute passed before she asked, "But out of curiosity…"

He laughed. "Seventy-one."

She pulled back to stare at him. "No."

"Yep. A measly seventy-one percent."

She took his face in her hands, studying his eyes, then said sincerely, "Well, I'd take seventy-one percent of you over one hundred percent of anyone else."

He grinned. Then frowned. "Hey. You're gonna have one hundred percent of me, girl," he growled playfully, pushing her off his lap and starting to stand.

But the pain in his leg grabbed him, and he slumped back into his chair with a groan.

She stood watching him, shaking her head. "What were you saying about one hundred percent?"

He looked her up and down. Then he grabbed her hand and hauled himself to his feet. With as much sincerity as he could manage while gritting his teeth in pain, he said, "I *am* one hundred percent your match."

She put her hand against his cheek and gave him a smile full of love and promise. "No, you're not, sweetie."

"But—"

But he wasn't.

"Okay, fine. But I am perfect for you."

"*That* you are." She smiled up at him. Then she blinked. "Oh! I almost forgot to tell you about the tiramisu."

"Tiramisu?"

"I thought it could be the first dessert we make together as an engaged couple. It goes with your romantic theme, and since I got my favorite, I figured it was only fair for you to have yours."

He grinned. "Tiramisu is always a good idea."

"Okay." She started walking backward toward the door. "So, I got the custard and the rum."

He started after her, but his leg protested. He gave in and grabbed the crutches they'd propped at the end of his bed when he'd said "fuck no" to learning how to use them. Now he hobbled toward the door.

"And we have the coffee and whipped cream at home," she said, stepping out into the hall.

He followed. "And ladyfingers?"

"Ladyfingers?"

"You didn't get ladyfingers? They're kind of a big part of the recipe."

She kept backing down the hall. "Darn, I didn't get any. Gee, I wonder what we could put all this stuff on instead of ladyfingers."

Cody paused and her mischievous grin confirmed that she was thinking exactly what he was thinking. He started hobbling faster.

"Hey." Nate tried to stop him, but Cody kept going. "How are you feeling?"

"One hundred percent, Doc," Cody said, flashing Nate a grin as he headed for the exit. "Absolutely one hundred percent."

Thank you for reading Cody and Olivia's story! I hope you loved Why You Should Never Kiss Your Best Friend!

Now it's time for Conner Dixon to fall in love!

Grab *Why You Should Never Kiss Your Roommate*, Conner and Gabby's story!

Conner Dixon has sworn to never live with another woman after raising his four younger sisters. He's retiring—from worrying, fixing problems, and cleaning up messes. But when a fellow paramedic's apartment burns down and she needs a place to stay, he can't say no.

Gabby's penchant for poker and her ability to overhaul a transmission definitely make her different from his usual women—not to mention her total lack of interest in getting involved with him. With her sights set on medical school, his crazy mix of family and friends is the last thing she needs right now.

But within forty-eight hours of moving in, she's up to her eyeballs in a family crisis and he's in uncharted territory with a girl he wants to rescue…who doesn't need him at all.

Grab *Why You Should Never Kiss Your Roommate* now! Or read on for an excerpt!

Find all of my books (including a printable book list) at ErinNicholas.com

ო

And join in on all the FAN FUN!

Join my **email list!**
bit.ly/Keep-In-Touch-Erin
(be sure you get those dashes and capital letters in there!)

And be the first to hear about my news, sales, freebies, behind-the-scenes, and more!

Or for even more fun, join my **Super Fan page** on Facebook and chat with me and other super fans every day! Just search Facebook for Erin Nicholas Super Fans!

ო

Enjoy this excerpt from Why You Should Never Kiss Your Roommate!

"You gonna be okay?" he finally asked.

She nodded.

He nodded back. If Gabby said she was okay, she was. She was smart. If she wasn't okay, if she needed something, she'd tell them. She was brave, but she asked for help, which helped Conner, and the rest of the crew, trust her.

Right now, though, he was having a hard time not hugging her.

She looked very different from the Gabby he was used to. Her hair hung free, for one thing. It was no wonder no one on Mac's crew had recognized her at first. Gabby always, *always*, wore her hair up at work. Ponytail or bun. Always.

Now it was free, spilling down her back and over her shoulders. It was long, way longer than he would have guessed—had he ever spent more than two seconds thinking about it—and it was a deep-mahogany color, the lights inside the ambulance catching red highlights throughout.

He definitely wanted to hug her. He had a soft spot for the damsel in distress, there was no denying it. It had always been that way and had only gotten stronger raising his four younger sisters. There wasn't a damned thing he could do about it. A woman in need would always flare up his protective instincts.

But, he couldn't hug her. This was *Gabby*. There was something about her that held him back from the good-hearted teasing and flirting he did with Sierra, from the winks and smiles he gave the other women on staff at the hospital, from the hug he would have given any of them if they'd just watched their home burn down.

Gabby gave off this I've-got-it, I'm-good vibe.

But right now he couldn't look away from her mouth.

He took a deep breath. "Let's get Sierra over here." Before he did something stupid. Like hugging her anyway and getting decked. "Katz!" he shouted to Sierra, his eyes on Gabby.

She pulled the oxygen mask off and stood from the back end of the ambulance. The plain-white cotton blanket they'd wrapped around her slipped off and she turned to toss it into the rig.

Conner froze.

She had, obviously, been in bed when the smoke alarms went off and she'd done the smart thing and had *not* taken time to change clothes or grab personal possessions.

The thin pink tank top with the spaghetti straps clung to her, curving over two small but firm breasts and hugging her flat stomach. The short-shorts were gray and also thin and ended only two inches below the curve of her tight ass. Her legs were long and smooth and Conner suddenly couldn't swallow.

Holy shit.

She might not need or want him, but his body suddenly thought it needed and wanted *her*.

He'd only ever seen her in uniform, or in jeans and T-shirts at Trudy's. And they weren't the fitted T-shirts with sequined logos calling attention to her breasts like a lot of women wore. They were plain old T-shirts.

"Oh my God, Gabby, there you are!" Sierra enfolded Gabby in her arms, hugging her tight. "Are you okay?"

"You knew this was her apartment building?" Conner asked, stepping forward with a frown. Of course Sierra would have known that. He knew the girls were friends outside of work.

"Yes, of course."

"Why didn't you say anything?" Conner demanded.

Sierra scowled at him. "Because I went to intubate a three-year-old when we got here and I've been busy since."

"You should have said something."

Sierra kept her arm around Gabby's waist, but she turned to face him. "To you? Why? I told Cody."

Conner felt his frown deepen. Cody had known? And he hadn't said anything to Conner?

"And then I saw her working on a couple of vics, so I knew she was okay," Sierra said.

"Fine." Sierra was here now. He could leave her alone. "So, um, Gabby…if you need anything, all you have to do is ask, okay?" he said. "I'm sorry about…all of this."

She gave him a small sad smile. "Thanks. I'm glad no one was hurt. And like they say, it's just stuff. But it was *my* stuff. So, yeah, this pretty much sucks."

He nodded. He could imagine. "Well, I'm serious—anything you need."

Her smile brightened and he felt stupidly pleased that he'd cheered her up somehow.

"Thanks, Conner."

"Okay."

He stood looking at her. Her hair was really long. And it

looked thick. It was really shiny too and had a slight wave to it. She looked good with her hair down.

Sierra cleared her throat and Conner glanced at her. She gave him a what-are-you-doing look.

Right. What was he doing? Nothing. Leaving. He was done here.

But he didn't feel like he was done.

He had no idea what else he thought he might need to do, but he didn't feel done.

"You okay, Conner?" Sierra asked.

He nodded. "Yeah. I'm…glad you're safe, G."

"Thanks."

Her smile, even bigger than before, called his attention to her mouth again.

That along with the skimpy sleepwear and the surprising curves and the tousled hair…

One thing was clear—Gabrielle Evans was *not* just one of the guys.

She was a woman. And she did need something.

So, Conner did the typical Conner thing. "Okay, let's go." He stepped forward, grabbed the blanket and wrapped it around Gabby's shoulders again.

"Let's go?"

She looked up at him with her big brown eyes—he'd never noticed what color her eyes were before—and he caught his toe on the grass.

"Where are we going?" she asked.

"To my apartment."

Gabby stumbled this time. "What?"

"I have a guest room. You need a place to stay tonight."

"But, I—" She glanced at Sierra.

Sierra shrugged. "I have a couch. You know it's all yours if you need it."

"Yeah, Conner I'll just—"

"Stay with me," he said firmly, taking her elbow and starting for his truck.

"But Sierra—" Gabby glanced over her shoulder at her friend.

"Has a couch. I have a full guest room with a guest bath."

"But—"

He sighed. This was his instinct—to take care of the women around him—and this was the right thing to do. Gabby needed a place to stay and he had a place for her.

Plus, she was a safe woman to take care of. She didn't *really* need him. She needed four walls and a roof. He could meet that need. But she didn't need comforting, she didn't need a hug, she didn't need him to make her feel better.

"This isn't a negotiation," he told her, putting her in the truck on the passenger side.

"I don't have any clothes," she said weakly as he started to slam the door.

Conner paused. Right. No clothes. He knew she meant that was a problem, but it took him a bit longer to come to that conclusion.

Grab *Why You Should Never Kiss Your Roommate* now!

CODY'S ULTIMATE CHOCOLATE CHIP COOKIES

Special thanks to Joann Berggren, Donna Neels Harris, Laura Gamble and Stephanie Staton for contributions to this recipe

- 1 cup butter, softened
- ½ cup butter flavored shortening
- ¾ cup sugar
- 1 ¾ cups packed brown sugar
- 1 ½ tsp instant coffee granules
- 3 large eggs
- 1 tsp vanilla
- 3 2/3 cups flour
- 2 tsp baking soda
- 1 tsp salt
- 1 (12 ounce) package semisweet chocolate chips
- ½ (6 ounce) package milk chocolate chips
- 1 (8 ounce) package toffee bits

Preheat oven to 375 degrees.

Mix butter and shortening until creamy. Add sugars and beat until fluffy. Add eggs one at a time, beating well after each addition. Add coffee granules and vanilla and continue to mix.

In a small bowl, combine flour, baking soda and salt.

Gradually add flour mixture to creamed mixture, beating until well blended. Stir in the chocolate chips and toffee bits.

Scoop ¼ cup amounts onto a cookie sheet about 3 inches apart.

Bake for 7-10 minutes or until lightly browned.

Let cool for 2 minutes before removing to a cooling rack.

WHY YOU SHOULD NEVER... THE SERIES

Why You Should Never...

Kiss Your Boss (Ben & Jessica)

Kiss Your Blind Date (Sam & Dani)

Kiss A Grump (Mac & Sara)

Kiss Your Fake Boyfriend (Dooley & Morgan)

Kiss Your Ex-Husband (Kevin & Eve)

Kiss Your Brother's Best Friend (Ryan & Amanda)

Kiss Your Ex (Shane & Isabelle)

Kiss Your Enemy (Nate & Emma)

Kiss Your Best Friend (Cody & Olivia)

Kiss Your Roommate (Conner & Gabby)

MORE FROM ERIN

Want more hot protective guys who wear badges? Try my Badges of the Bayou series!

Badges of the Bayou
Gotta Be Bayou (Spencer & Max)
Bayou With Benefits (Michael & Ami)
Rocked Bayou (Colin & Hayden)

*

If you love steamy romance with big groups of family and friends, check out my Boys of the Bayou series!

Boys of the Bayou
My Best Friend's Mardi Gras Wedding (Josh & Tori)
Sweet Home Louisiana (Owen & Maddie)
Beauty and the Bayou (Sawyer & Juliet)
Crazy Rich Cajuns (Bennett & Kennedy)
Must Love Alligators (Chase & Bailey)
Four Weddings and a Swamp Boat Tour (Mitch & Paige)

*

ABOUT ERIN NICHOLAS

Erin Nicholas is the New York Times and USA Today bestselling author of over thirty sexy contemporary romances. Her stories have been described as toe-curling, enchanting, steamy and fun. She loves to write about reluctant heroes, imperfect heroines and happily ever afters. She lives in the Midwest with her husband who only wants to read the sex scenes in her books, her kids who will never read the sex scenes in her books, and family and friends who say they're shocked by the sex scenes in her books (yeah, right!).
Find her here:

facebook.com/ErinNicholasBooks
bookbub.com/authors/erin-nicholas
goodreads.com/author/show/3155383.Erin_Nicholas
tiktok.com/@erinnicholasbooks